*Sean is trapped by a pain͟
moon nights, she mig͟h͟t͟ h͟o͟l͟d͟ h͟i͟s͟ f͟u͟t͟u͟r͟e͟ i͟n͟ h͟e͟r͟ h͟a͟n͟d͟s͟.*

DUST BORN

Sean Quinn returned to Cambio Springs to help his shifter clan find their way out of trouble, but before he can hit the road again, a new threat emerges on the border of his hometown. A threat that could leave Sean stuck in Cambio Springs when he's most desperate to escape.

And one unsuspecting human might be stuck right there with him.

Ever since Juniper Hawkins came to Cambio Springs to visit her big brother, strange things keep happening. Not the least is running into the man who almost made her change her wandering ways. Juni isn't the kind of woman to settle down even when the object of her affection is a tall, dark, and handsome photographer who kissed her senseless, then abandoned her in Southeast Asia.

Not that she's still irritated about that.

DUST BORN is a brand new novel in the Cambio Springs Mysteries, a paranormal romance series by eleven-time *USA Today* bestselling author Elizabeth Hunter.

"I fell in love with the residents of Cambio Springs when I first read the previous books a few years ago... *Dust Born* was everything I had hoped for and more!"

What Manda Reads

praise for dust born

This story truly had it all, secrets, adventure, romance, action, history and inspiring friendships.

This Literary Life

I loved *every* minute of this read! The characters were layered and colorful. There's intrigue, romance, action, family, and wonderful dialogue and characters. The story truly grabbed my attention immediately and took me on an amazing journey.

TXBRITGAL, Goodreads review

If you're also hesitant about shifters, do NOT be hesitant about this book. It's a wonderful read and a page turner, plus you can jump in here and not feel like you missed anything.

Jessica, Goodreads review

As always with Elizabeth Hunter, there are super-developed characters and world-building, exciting fight scenes, and hot sexy times.

Kate, Goodreads review

I have to say, it was worth the wait! I absolutely loved this series... Sean's book was exciting, sexy, and very captivating.

I fell in love with the residents of Cambio Springs when I first read the previous books a few years ago... *Dust Born* was everything I had hoped for and more!

dust born

cambio springs
book four

Elizabeth Hunter

*This is for every reader who
just couldn't let Sean and Juni go*

Book Cover: Elizabeth Hunter
Illustrations: Natalia Gaikova and Kathryn Bentley
Editor: Amy Cissell
Line editor: Anne Victory
Proofreader: Linda, Victory Editing

First edition 2023

chapter
one

SEAN QUINN STARED at the shot of whiskey the bartender poured into his glass. It was shot number three. If he drank it, he'd definitely be looking for a ride home. Two he could handle, especially as long as he'd been hiding out at the Cave, but three? Nope. He'd have to call someone, and calling someone in Cambio Springs meant calling family.

It wasn't as if the sleepy desert town had more than one taxi driver, though with the new resort opening, more cabs or rideshares might not be a bad idea. He'd have to talk to some of the younger members of the clan—well, those who'd kept their noses clean—and suggest it.

"Ugh." He groaned and banged his forehead on the bar.

Tracey, the bartender who was watching the Cave that night, patted his shoulder. "Family stuff?"

"Isn't it always?" His voice was rough, no doubt from the second shot of whiskey. He reached for the third. To hell with it. He'd call one of the kids to come pick him up. It wasn't as if younger Quinns weren't used to scraping their elders off the floor of drinking establishments.

Nice family you got there, Quinn.

Yep. It was great. He should have never come back.

Never ever...

Sean Quinn had never fit into the isolated town of shapeshifters in the middle of the Mojave Desert, and it was impossible to blend in when you lived in Cambio Springs. Everyone knew everyone. Half the town was related to each other, and people who married or moved in knew the score. Everyone had their place.

The wolf and cat clans battled for political and financial dominance. They were the most visible citizens. Doctors, lawyers, business leaders, and teachers. They were proud and fiercely protective of their weird, eccentric little community. The small bird clan kept to themselves, the most likely members of the Springs to roam around the world, though they always returned. The bear clan, who owned the Cave, were the guardians of Cambio Springs, quiet, conservative, and rock steady.

And then there were the Quinns. Cold-blooded reptile shifters; Sean's clan was smart but conniving. Charming troublemakers who were loyal only to themselves, the snake clan consisted of a strange mélange of reptile shifters spread over Cambio Springs and the outskirts. A few were reliable, but most fell victim to the family inclination to get what they wanted or needed by any means necessary, which included lying, cheating, gambling, and bullying.

And then there was Sean, who desperately wanted to just go along and blend in.

He was an observer by nature. He loved watching people. Watching nature. He spoke through his camera lens, hoping to connect with those who found beauty in unexpected places. And prior to the year before, he'd managed to do that pretty well, keeping in touch with his closest childhood friends while forging his own path and traveling the world.

And then... it had all turned to shit.

The one reliable Quinn cousin left in town had moved back to take the reins of his unruly family and had promptly been murdered by an ignorant human. That meant the only semireliable one left was Sean. So when the family called, he came.

That was the rule in Cambio Springs whether you wanted to or not: if family called, you came. The clans might squabble among each other, but within each clan, loyalty was sacrosanct.

Fuck. His. Life.

A heavy hand fell on his shoulder, and Sean turned to see Oliver Campbell, one of his oldest friends and the new leader of the bear clan.

"Hey, Ollie. What's up?"

"I heard you were here."

"Yep." Sean blinked to clear his gaze. "Do you know you sound like a tractor engine?"

Ollie hardly ever cracked a smile, so a slight curve of his mouth meant he thought Sean was hilarious. "A tractor engine?"

"Yeah. All rumbly and shit." He rubbed his eyes. "Is Allie here?"

"Home with the kids." Ollie slid onto a barstool. "Tracey called me. Said you looked like you needed someone to talk to."

"Fuck." Sean sighed. "Yeah, probably. I've got three kids in the clan suspended from school right now because they thought shifting into rattlesnakes to scare the new kid in class was a hilarious rite of passage. And now my sister is giving me shit, saying that the boy the kids shifted on was provoking the Quinn kids, calling them white trash. Stuff like that. So I don't know how the hell to deal with any of that. Do you?"

"Huh." Ollie grunted. "There are three rattlesnake shifters in the same class? That seems like a lot."

It would be. Usually the more lethal shifters were spread out unless there was some threat to the community.

"Not three in one class. Rattler wasn't their natural form."

A shifter's natural form was whatever they first shifted into when they hit puberty. It was what they transformed into on full moon nights. It would always be their most comfortable and easiest shift.

For most shifters, variations on their natural form were possible but difficult. His friend Jena could shift into any number of raptors from her natural hawk form, but it took skill and a lot of energy. Their friend Alex could be a natural wolf or a coyote if he tried.

But among the snake clan, multiple forms were the norm. Sean's natural form was a diamondback rattler, but he could shift into nearly any reptile he wanted. He'd tried lizards and every slithery thing imaginable. Constrictors and pythons, horned toads and water dragons. He was notorious and famous in his clan for his abilities.

Only his sister Maggie came close, but nearly every teenager in the Quinn clan learned how to shift to a rattlesnake. They were mean and they scared other shifters.

And that was gold for a Quinn kid.

Ollie asked, "So is Maggie right? Were the kids provoked?"

"Man, I don't know. Half the time with that crew, I feel like I'm bailing water out of a sinking boat." Sean motioned for Tracey to pour another shot in his glass. "The old man did what he could to raise us, but most all of our parents were shit. It started turning around with the younger kids, but most anyone from about twenty-five to forty is just a mess. And this shit at school isn't help-ing. The principal—"

"Cat," Ollie muttered.

"Exactly. She has no patience for the little shits, and I can't blame her." He downed the shot and heard himself start slurring. "And here I am, trying to hold everything together and be a parent to a bunch of teenagers when I don't even have my own fucking life figured out."

Sean could never tell what was going on with Ollie. Marrying the love of his life had done nothing to soften him. He was still about as understanding as a brick wall.

"Maybe I should call Alex," Ollie said.

"No." Sean put his head in his hand. "I'm just... venting. I'll be fine." *I think.* "And... I should go home. I have a meeting at the high school in the morning because apparently that is a thing I do now."

Because fuck his life.

"Need a ride?"

At least there was that. If Ollie drove him, Sean wouldn't need to call any of the teenagers he was supposed to be setting a good example for.

"Dude," Sean said. "If you could give me a ride, that would be—"

"Oh perfect." Ollie hit his shoulder. "Check out who just came in. Destiny is on your side, Quinn."

Sean turned and blinked.

She wasn't destiny; she was disaster.

Juniper Hawkins was standing at the bar, holding a couple of bags of what looked like takeout. She'd had blue streaks yesterday, but today they'd changed to gold and red. She walked toward the bar, her steps light and her smile wide. Colorful tattoos decorated her tan arms, and her hair was pulled up into a messy bun.

She was so fucking cute he wanted to bite her.

"Sean Quinn, you still can't hold your liquor." Juni cocked her head at him, her smile never wavering. "Ollie, do I need to pour this one into bed?"

"If you could drop him at his place, you'd be doing me a favor."

"No." Sean pointed at her food. "You're heading home. To eat."

"It's fine," Juni said. "Jena and Caleb are gone, so I'm being the lazy auntie. I can drop you off. After all" —her smile turned from bright to mischievous— "we are neighbors now."

"YOU CAN TALK TO ME, you know." Juni glanced across the truck cab. "I don't bite."

But I do.

"I'm just trying to figure out why you're still here," Sean said. "The feature for the magazine was done months ago."

"And was very well-received. Rani suggested we work together more. Want to go to Costa Rica?"

God yes. "I can't right now." He rubbed his eyes. "And seriously, if you're getting job offers in Costa Rica, why are you here?"

"Maybe I like this place."

Sean snorted. "Why on earth would you like this town?"

"My brother is happy here. He wasn't happy for a long time, you know? Our mom wasn't the nicest to him."

I know how that is. He leaned against the cool window of the pickup, pressing his forehead to the glass and closing his eyes to the oncoming headlights.

"I've got time right now," Juni said. "I'm between jobs, and I've got a nice amount of cash tucked away. There's really nothing else I'd rather do than hang with my brother and his new family, you know?"

"You never mentioned him before." Sean swung his head around to look at her. "Like... *before* before."

Juni's smile was impish. "So by *before* before, do you mean—?"

"You know what I mean."

"But do you mean India?" She batted her eyelashes innocently. "Or Thailand? Or did you mean Kenya, when we were staying at that lodge and there was only one tent so we—"

"I'm not talking about... I mean, yes, *that* before, but we're not talking about Kenya. Or Thailand."

"Or all the times when you completely avoided any and all personal questions and told me" —she dropped her voice— "'Listen, Juni, this isn't happening. We work together.' Only it happened anyway, and you just felt really guilty about it."

His mouth was gaping. He knew it; he just couldn't control his mouth enough to close it.

Screw you, whiskey. This was Ollie's fault. Somehow.

"I didn't sleep with you," he blurted out. Probably because of the not-controlling-his-own-mouth thing.

Her eyes flashed. "No, you did not. Didn't you want to?"

"Of course I fucking did."

"We were both adults, Sean. So why—?"

His laughter cut her off. "You were twenty-two, hippie girl. I was nine years older than you and we worked together."

"And now I'm twenty-five and you're thirty-four and we don't work together, so what's your baggage, Quinn?"

He closed his eyes and shook his head. "You have no idea."

"Fine, be secretive. Just don't give me shit about not spilling everything about my family, okay? You sit over there being the King of Avoidance and we both know it."

"Fine." Sean crossed his arms. "We both have our secrets." He had so many secrets they threatened to break his back.

"That's right, we both do. And don't patronize me again. I may be young, but I've been on my own since I was eighteen."

It was another thing they had in common, but Sean kept his mouth shut. His desire for Juni wasn't something he could indulge in. It wouldn't be fair to either of them. He'd once thought that maybe one day they would be able to make something work, but...

Not anymore. Not with Sean being tied to Cambio Springs. Juni might have been parked in his hometown for a few months, but she was not the type to settle down.

She turned off Main Street, then took another right after the Black Bird Café, Jena's diner. She went south, out to the edge of town where Caleb and Jena's house sat. They had a few acres stretching from the main road to a winding creek where cottonwood trees lined the banks.

Juni—in her apparent quest to drive Sean crazy—had taken the nice, fixed-up Airstream trailer behind Jena and Caleb's house as her own while she was back in the States and figuring out what to do.

Sean was living in the other trailer on the far edge of Jena and Caleb's property near the creek. He was working on fixing it up in exchange for rent. He owned the title to two houses in town, one of which was massive, but his sister was living in that one with some of the other single Quinn girls, and Marcus's widow and kids were living in the other. Since it was just him, Sean was camping out at Jena's.

It had nothing to do with being near Juni. At all.

Of course it doesn't, you masochist.

Sean would have to be blind not to miss the laser-like eyes of Caleb Gilbert, chief of Cambio Springs Police Department, new father, and Juniper Hawkins's older half brother. It was probably only Jena's intervention that had kept Caleb from murdering Sean already.

"So you know my baby sister, huh?"

Sean watched her from the corner of his eye.

Did he know Juni? Not as much as he wanted to.

Not nearly as much.

chapter
two

JUNI HAWKINS HAD JUST SLIPPED into her most comfortable pj's when her computer buzzed with an incoming call. She glanced at the old-fashioned clock on the table and smiled.

Miller time.

That was, Lauren Miller time.

When Juni had decided to stay in Cambio Springs for a few months instead of heading back to her home base in Los Angeles, her best friend Lauren had demanded a weekly video chat. Since she owed basically her entire adult life to Lauren and her family, Juni did not refuse.

She slid in her stocking feet over to the small kitchenette in the Airstream and sat on the bench. "Hey!"

"Hey yourself." Lauren was looking tired and more than a little... old. "Just got back from rehearsal."

"Oh right." That explained the exhaustion and the aging.

As Juni watched, Lauren smeared cold cream over her skin and let it sit. She was working in a minor role in a revival of *My Fair Lady* that was due to start performances in June. It wasn't "the big break," but it was steady work and Lauren was having a blast.

"How's the play?"

"Good." Lauren grinned. "I'm a complete nobody compared to all these people, but they're nice to me anyway."

"Any word on that toilet paper commercial?" Juni reached for her open beer on the counter. Luckily it was only an arm's length away.

It was an Airstream trailer. Everything was only an arm's length away.

"Not yet." Lauren started wiping off her cold cream, and her natural, pale pink complexion was revealed. "Hopefully by the end of next week."

Lauren had been Juni's best friend since middle school. It was Lauren's family Juni lived with when she left her mother's house at eighteen, refusing to spend one more night in the toxic environment her parents refused to quit. It was Lauren whose father taught her how to use a digital camera. Then a DSLR. Then—when he realized she had a knack for photography—he got her a job as a photographer's assistant where she worked every weekend and played backup at hundreds of weddings in the greater Albuquerque area.

When Lauren had decided she wanted to pursue acting in LA, Juni went with her, immediately landing a job with another wedding photographer. Wedding photography in LA allowed Juni to meet some pretty cool people, including the editor for a travel magazine whom she pestered until she got an assistant's job.

The job paid almost nothing except airfare, but Juni jumped on it, put a rush on her very first passport, and joined an international photo shoot in India. Working for peanuts made her hirable. Her hard work and talent made her memorable.

She learned a ton, worked her ass off, and met Sean Quinn.

"So I saw him again tonight," Juni said.

Lauren rolled her eyes. "This guy. I'd say he must have been the best sex ever or something, but you haven't even slept with him."

"I know, but when I do, it'll be epic."

"Says who?"

"Says my instincts. Some things you just know."

"Instincts, schminstincts." Lauren leaned back on their couch and sighed. "Come home. Everyone misses you. Or go to Costa Rica. Take that job. You said they offered to put you in first class for the flight."

"I know!" Juni's eyes lit up. "Awesome, right?"

Juni had managed to accumulate enough freelance work that she could pay her bills without doing weddings if she lived *very* frugally. Which was fine. She knew how to stretch a dollar. And she didn't look down on a job. *Any* job. If she needed a new lens or a plane ticket, she could pick up taking pictures for a few events from her friends in LA. She'd driven for rideshares. She'd walked dogs. She'd even worked as a personal assistant—which meant a photographer—to a social media influencer, which had to be the worst job *ever*.

Lauren said, "I know you're having fun with your brother and his kids, but seriously Juni, why—?"

"I don't know." She took a gulp of beer. It was getting warm quickly, just like everything in this town. The spring heat was quickly turning brutal. Though the nights were still cool, the days were getting hotter and hotter. "There's something about this place that draws me."

"You mean draws you to an emotionally unavailable man?"

"Lauren—"

"I'm not going to lie. That resort looked amazing, but the golf course and the spa and the holistic yoga at daybreak is just... It's really not your scene."

"My scene?" Juni rested her chin in the palm of her hand and stared at her best friend. She could see their cozy house in Venice Beach in the background. "No, I guess not."

"So... why?"

Juni loved the beach. She loved cool ocean breezes and weird neighbors and concerts and graffiti. She loved walking down the sidewalk and catching the scent of tacos or Korean barbecue in the air.

In Cambio Springs, the streets smelled like dust and creosote after the rain. The scent of asphalt rose with the temperature, and the red rock formations that marked the boundary of the small town offered the only shade once the sun passed its zenith.

There were few trees and no ocean breezes, but something about the place felt familiar to Juni, and it wasn't just because her brother had settled there.

"You know Caleb and I barely knew each other growing up, right?"

"Different dads. He's a lot older." Lauren nodded. "Yeah. I get it."

"I guess I want to know if I can have anything that looks like a normal family. Does that make sense?" That wasn't the only reason. Sean Quinn was a big part of the fascination, but she didn't want Lauren's opinion on that. Not again.

"What's normal anyway?" Lauren pouted. "You're part of my family."

"I know I am." But not really. "I'll think about the Costa Rica job. For real. I just got the email yesterday. They know I don't always answer messages right away."

"Go to Costa Rica." Lauren leaned toward the screen. "Go. To. Costa. Rica. Leave the desert. You worked your whole life to get out of there, remember?"

"I remember." She remembered lots of things. "Your eyes are droopy. You should go to sleep."

"You too."

"I will." She finished her beer. "See? I'm even having a wild night out on the town."

"With me, one hundred fifty miles away."

"Didn't I come back weekend before last?"

"Yes. And then you went back. When you should just be

coming home. It's not like your brother is three states away now. He can visit you here."

Juni thought of her tiny niece and her two hilarious new nephews. She thought about movie nights with Caleb and Jena, family dinners, and barbecues with their weird and wonderful collection of friends.

She squeezed her eyes shut. "I know what you're saying, Lauren. I'm just not ready to leave yet."

"Because of Sean?"

"No." *Yes.* "Not because of Sean." *Partly because of him.* "There's just something here I can't put my finger on yet. There's some... weird wonderfulness I haven't figured out. When I do, I'll head home."

"Promise?"

"Promise."

THE NEXT MORNING dawned with a rosy sunrise over the hills in the distance. Light poured over the spring landscape, casting shadows from the towering Joshua trees as birdsong filled the air.

Spring in the desert meant that the few flowers that bloomed burst into riotous color for precious weeks before they drew into themselves for the long hot stretch of summer. The paloverde tree by Juni's bedroom window was covered in bright yellow blooms, and a black-and-white speckled lizard sunned itself on the edge of her aluminum-clad trailer.

She rolled up to sitting and pressed her finger against the glass. It was cold, and the lizard darted away.

For the first week she'd stayed at Jena and Caleb's house, Juni had stayed on the couch, refusing to displace anyone in this new family she barely knew. Then one morning, Sean had asked Jena if he could switch to the trailer on the edge of their property and fix it up in exchange for rent.

And suddenly the trailer near the house was empty. Conveniently.

So Juni moved into it. For a while.

She knew Sean didn't need the money. He had a house in Laguna Beach, and he could name his price with most magazines. He could probably buy a house in Cambio Springs for cash.

Instead, he spent his time fixing and fiddling with a broken-down Airstream Jena and Caleb had bought online and gutted.

Why?

Juni peeked out the window toward the silver-sided sphere where he was probably still sleeping after his bender the night before. The trailer sat near the creek that ran behind the house, a good acre away from Juni's place. Instead of the silver Audi she'd seen him drive in LA, there was a slightly beat-up blue pickup truck parked behind the trailer.

What was Juni doing in Cambio Springs? A better question was: What was *Sean* doing here?

She rose and pulled on a pair of sweatpants before wandering down the tiny hall to heat water for tea.

Sean had never spoken fondly of his childhood home. Large international photo shoots could be a little like summer camp. After a long day at work, the crew would sit around and shoot the shit, tell stories, and drink too much. Had Sean ever bullshitted about his childhood or where he grew up? Not once.

He was silent, a man of mystery in their loose circle of wandering work colleagues. More than once, he seemed to just disappear, dissolve into nothing, particularly when people were talking about their past.

She pulled down the box of green tea and ripped open a packet. Then she reached for the mug she'd used the day before and rinsed it out in the tiny sink.

Juni hated that she was so fascinated with him. She had little patience for men who tried too hard to be intriguing. The problem with Sean was that he didn't try. He just *was*. The chemistry when they first met in India had been immediate and elemental, but for months Juni was convinced Sean actively disliked her.

The first time they'd kissed had been in the middle of Songkran, the Thai New Year's festival, which was celebrated in the spring by the entire country going absolutely nuts and spraying each other with water. Buckets of water were thrown at cars, water balloons were plentiful. Squirt guns were national currency. Sean and Juni had been assigned to cover the festival in the northern city of Chiang Mai.

They were shooting footage of the parades from the upper-story balcony of their hotel when Juni felt a stream of water hit her back. She turned, completely shocked to see the always-serious Sean Quinn holding a giant water gun and wearing a smile.

"Enough work."

They'd left their cameras in his hotel room and run through the streets, each getting progressively more soaked as they explored the festival, shooting their water guns. Sean held her hand as they made their way through the churning crowd so they didn't become separated. By the time they reached the square in front of the university, they were both laughing, soaked, and covered in flower petals. The simmering chemistry between them had reached a rolling boil.

He turned in the middle of the crowd and kissed her. She could still feel the warmth of his hands on her cheeks as he held her face to his and took her breath in a single instant. When he pulled away, his eyes were locked on hers. His lips were flushed and swollen.

"That was stupid."

"Probably."

He kissed her again. And again. They spent the day wandering the city, eating sweets and spicy noodles, and making out in hidden corners. Juni felt like she was part of something for once, instead of always behind, separated by a camera lens.

It was the single most romantic day of her life. And when night fell and they made it back to their hotel, Sean left her in her room alone.

"We really shouldn't do this."

Irritating, know-it-all man. She stared at the tea steeping in the mug, counting seconds until it was dark enough to wake her and get her moving. Her feet were cold on the wooden floor of the trailer. She could hear Caleb yelling something out the door, but she was pretty sure it was directed at the boys.

She worked with Sean again in Morocco. And again in Kenya. Then again in Kerala. It was always the same pattern. Days of connection and nights in solitude. Juni got tantalizing glimpses of who Sean was when he let his guard down, experienced hints of the passion he kept a tight rein on, only to wake up some random morning to a note left at the front desk telling her he'd moved on to a new assignment.

Wanker! She'd get a text or a message a week later sometimes. And sometimes not.

Juni burned her fingers on the tea bag as she dumped it in the trash before walking to the kitchen table to open her computer and check her email. Her finger hovered over the email from the hotel in Costa Rica.

It was looking pretty good right now.

Sean had always refused to sleep with her, as if crossing that one boundary of intimacy would be the single step too far. Maybe he was right. They did work together regularly, and unlike some of her colleagues, Juni didn't want to take part in the somewhat incestuous cycle of hookups and breakups so many of them fell into.

When Juni dated, she found interesting men in Los Angeles—mostly in some creative field—and she didn't tell anyone except Lauren. Most of those relationships only lasted until her next overseas assignment. Men didn't like women who had an aversion to staying in one place for more than a few months at a time.

Except Sean.

Maybe someday...

Or maybe not.

She clicked on the email from Costa Rica and began to type out a reply.

After all, she and Sean had been living in the same place for months, and he was doing everything he could to avoid her. Maybe she didn't know him at all. Maybe the man who'd held her hand and kissed her during Songkran was no more than some kind of desert mirage.

When you got too close, you realized nothing was there.

chapter
three

SEAN DROVE up the dusty driveway of the Quinn ancestral home on the outskirts of Cambio Springs. Old Quinn lived in it now, lording over a kingdom of cacti, but before him, Donald Quinn and his family had occupied the house.

"Dirty Quinn" was Don's nickname, and he lived up to it. Don Quinn was a liar, a manipulator, and a cheat. According to the old man, Don had no loyalty to anyone not in his immediate family. He played on everyone's fears, turning people against each other until there was so much tension in the Quinn clan the other families actually took the unprecedented step of allying with a young Joe Quinn to roust Don from power and run him out of town.

Dirty Quinn was gone, but his legacy remained. Sean's parents were both drunks who trusted no one. They'd moved out of the Springs before he was grown, leaving him with Old Quinn because they couldn't be bothered.

Other families were similar. One parent took off. Another fell into alcohol or drugs. Hell, half of his parents' generation was in jails or prisons scattered around the United States—until they escaped from the yard—while their children stayed at home, raised by morally questionable grandparents, aunts, or uncles.

Two teenage boys and a girl were lounging on Old Quinn's front porch when Sean pulled up. He waited for the dust to settle before he left the truck, grabbing the bag of beer and groceries he'd bought from Norman at the Quick Stop. His head was still pounding from the night before at the Cave and the ride home with Juni. It hadn't been helped by the contentious meeting he'd had at the school that morning with the high school principal, the Osterall kid's parents, and his sister Maggie.

Yes, much to his surprise, Maggie had shown up at the parent conference. He'd allowed his sister back into town six weeks before, and she'd been surprisingly low-key on her return. She'd moved into a house with two younger women and gotten a job at the resort in the landscaping department. She applied, Alex had offered, and she'd accepted.

Maybe it was because she was prickly herself, or maybe she'd just been living in the desert her whole life, but his sister was a master of dry landscaping and had a real gift for working with native plants like the cacti and succulents the resort used in their landscaping. She was thriving in her work, and Alex told Sean she was even up for a promotion.

Still, she wasn't any of the kids' parent or legal guardian. It was only because Sean and Maggie were snake shifters that the meeting had gone ahead at all. None of the kids' parents had shown up. It was down to Sean and his sister to be their advocates, which wasn't an unusual situation at Cambio Springs High School.

Sean stood tall in front of the three kids. "Do you know how many uppity wolves and cats I had to deal with this morning because of you little shits?"

The kids had the grace to look a little ashamed. The girl—Fiona—leaned forward. "Uncle Sean, that kid—"

"Yeah, the Osterall kid is also a little shit. Luckily, his parents had the good sense to show up with a written apology for bad language and 'inappropriate behavior'" —yes, he used finger quotes, he was ancient now— "even though their kid is the one who got cornered."

The tallest boy was named Aiden. "So he admitted he was calling us white trash?"

Fiona said, "Because he was."

"He didn't admit that, but I think Ms. Vasquez doesn't have any illusions this kid is a saint. Know who else she knows is a likely cause of trouble? You three."

The second boy, Job, looked down. He was a year younger than his cousins, and he was the one kid in the group that Sean was genuinely surprised to see in trouble.

Job Davis was normally a good kid. He was quiet and earned excellent grades even though he spent most of his time helping his younger siblings. Job's father had skipped out around the time Job had his first full moon shift at eleven. His mom, Olivia, just barely managed, and Job was her pride and joy.

"It's my fault," Job said. "He was saying stuff to me and... I shouldn't have said anything."

"Yeah, you should have." Sean sat across from Job. "You definitely should have said something. Even shifting on your own is understandable." Shifting was nearly impossible to control if a shifter was threatened, especially among the reptiles, who were almost always the smallest animals in the room. "What you shouldn't have done" —he directed this to Fiona and Aiden— "was take the matter into your own hands and terrorize a wolf kid. Now, instead of being a victim of bullying, Job's the instigator."

Job's eyes flared, and his mouth set into a firm line. "I'm not a victim."

Sean understood the impulse. Damn, he understood it. When he'd been young, the last thing he wanted was anyone's sympathy. "Is not being a victim worth a week of in-school suspension?"

In-school suspension—all day locked away in a little room at the school with no access to outdoor activities and no socialization —was about as strict a punishment as young shifters could receive.

Job's chin went up. "I'll do it."

"Yeah, you will." He glanced at Fiona and Aiden. "So will both of you. And because Fuzzybottom Osterall came with an apology instead of with sketchy details like me and Maggie—"

"Maggie was there?" Job perked up. So did the other kids. *Interesting*.

"Yeah, Maggie was there. She's the reason you guys got one week instead of two. But Osterall got a day. One single day. So in the future, when you're having issues with someone, you guys gotta tell me. I can't act like a clan leader and protect you all if I don't know what's going on."

Aiden shrugged and mumbled, "It's not like you're gonna be around much longer anyway."

Sean sat up straight. "You know about some exotic travel plans that I don't? You guys think you know shit about my life? I dropped everything to come back here for you." It was irritating, but a good reminder. Because in a sense, these three kids—all the kids of the clan—*were* the reason he'd come back. "I'm here for as long as you need me. And if I ever leave town again, I'm gonna make sure that everyone has my info, okay? Take out your phones."

The three teenagers all found interesting things to look at on the ground while they grabbed their mobile phones.

"Sean Patrick Quinn," he said, then recited his phone number. His email. His LinkedIn handle, for fuck's sake. "Now don't tell me you can't give me the details when shit happens."

"Thanks, Uncle Sean." Fiona's voice was small. "Do you have Instagram?"

He was an international photographer. Of course he had Instagram. "Same as my LinkedIn profile, but do *not* tag me—it's a work account."

"Okay."

"Yeah, sure."

"Got it."

Sean stood and pointed his chin at the door. "The old man inside?"

"He's been listening at the door for like the entire time you've been here," Fiona said.

"Call the school and find out what your assignments are. You're back tomorrow in the ISS room."

Dejected faces all around.

Good. They should feel dejected. They shouldn't have done what they did to the wolf kid. Even if it was completely something he would have done at their age if one of his cousins had been harassed.

But Sean wouldn't have gotten caught.

He opened the door of the old house and walked straight to the kitchen, not even looking at the old man in the corner of the dining area. "Sorted things out at the school."

"I heard. Lena give you much trouble?"

Sean shrugged as he opened the ancient refrigerator and stored four of the beers. "She did what she had to do. The school has rules." He cracked open two cans and walked back to the kitchen table, setting one in front of Old Quinn. "They got off easy."

"A week locked in a little room all day?" Joe Quinn lifted the cold beer to his mouth. "Don't think I don't know you would have done the same as them at your age."

Sean leaned in and lowered his voice because even if they were in human form, Quinn kids had good hearing. "Yeah, but I wouldn't have gotten caught. And that's the difference."

"So you're not punishing them for doing it, you're punishing them for getting caught?" The old man chuckled. "You really are a Quinn."

"I'm not punishing them at all. The school is doing it. The difference is, I'm not going to bad-mouth the principal like you would have. I'm not going to claim what they did was justified and shit on everyone outside the clan and rail at all those dirty wolves and cats never respecting our family."

Old Quinn's eyes narrowed. "You been spending too much time with those friends of yours."

"That's what you always said. But you know what? Every one of my cousins who spent their lives blaming everyone else for their problems is where now? Pissing away their talents or in jail or roaming around working shit jobs because they can't build anything real. I'm not gonna have another generation fall into that trap."

"This town doesn't give a damn about snake—"

"This town gave our ancestor a place when he got caught stealing from them." Sean slammed down his beer. "Imagine *that*. Rory Quinn was trying to steal their supplies, and they let him tag along. I'm not gonna kiss wolf or cat ass for anything, but I'm not going to spit on them either. I'm done with that. And if I'm gonna be back and I'm gonna take the reins like you want, the clan is done with that too."

Old Quinn sat back and sniffed. "Shoulda picked your sister."

"I mean, if you never want to retire, I guess so." Sean finished his beer fast, which reminded him he hadn't eaten any breakfast. He stood and walked to the kitchen. "I'm gonna cook you some eggs."

"Don't have eggs."

"What the...?" Sean opened the fridge and really looked. "Your fridge looks like a college kid's. You got three kinds of hot sauce, yellow mustard, and half a loaf of old bread. What do you eat, old man?"

"There's soup in the pantry."

Sean closed the fridge. "You got kids hanging around here all the time, half of them with parents who barely give a damn. You need food."

"I'm not feeding everyone! I'm not made of money. If they're hungry, they can shift and hunt."

Sean cursed under his breath and walked to the door. "I'm going to the grocery store. Clean the old shit out of your fridge so I can fill it when I get back." He opened the door and put his sunglasses on. "And stop making the kids hunt rats instead of giving them a sandwich!"

HE PUSHED a loaded cart through the Save-a-Bunch grocery store. He usually never bought this much food, but what he'd seen in Old Quinn's kitchen was ridiculous. The man needed to eat properly. Just because he didn't mind shifting to hunt rodents, birds, and small lizards in his animal form didn't mean the kids had to eat like animals all the time too.

Not like you didn't do the same.

He couldn't remember a time when he was growing up that he wasn't hungry unless he'd been eating at one of his friends' houses. And even then, he didn't eat too much. While Alex or Jena would clean their plates and ask for seconds, Sean always left a little behind. He didn't want anyone to call him hungry even when he was. He didn't want anyone to think he was asking for something he didn't earn.

He stopped and added two flats of beef ramen to the bottom of his cart.

When he'd first been living on his own, he kept only a small amount of food in his fridge. He mostly ate out anyway because he didn't know how to cook. Slowly he learned one thing. Spaghetti with meat sauce. Then he learned how to make meat loaf because he'd had it at Allie's house and loved it. His wasn't as good as Allie's, but it was decent.

Over time, he'd learned how to work a stove. How to buy food and make meals. He already knew how to clean because that had been his job at Old Quinn's growing up.

Sean learned how to get a checking account and balance his books. He'd learned how to pay bills and sign a lease. How to get a credit card. How to buy a car.

He'd taught himself how to live like a normal person even though he wasn't. As he pushed the loaded grocery cart through the store, he reminded himself that's what he was here for.

He was here for the kids.

He was here for their future.

He was here because—just like him—they mostly had no one who gave a shit. Because they were poor and kind of dirty and they lived on the ragged edges.

Sean gave a shit about them because he'd been them.

"Look at you."

He looked up to see Juni smiling at the end of a grocery aisle.

Her dimples were out. Fuck, he loved her dimples.

She walked over and leaned on the edge of his cart. "You having a party and didn't invite me?"

If I invited you to a party, you'd be the only guest and we wouldn't leave the trailer for three days.

Sean cleared his throat. "It's for my uncle's house. All my cousins hang out there, and he's on a fixed income, so I'm pitching in so they don't eat him out of house and home with their teenage appetites."

She looked down. "Beef stew. Four dozen eggs. Spaghetti and pasta sauce. Industrial pack of bologna and four loaves of bread." She nodded. "You've covered the basics." She looked up. "You sprang for the fancy mayo. You must really love these kids."

He couldn't help but smile. "Yeah, kind of. Three of them got in-school suspension today, so the love is strained."

"Ouch."

"They're going to be hungry and miserable for the next week or so. I do what I can to keep the peace."

Juni narrowed her eyes. "I have to say, the extended families in this town are something else. It's all..." She knit her fingers together. "I mean, Jena's family is small, but your friend Alex is a McCann and he's the... mayor? I can't figure that part out."

"Not the mayor, just the richest person in the Springs. He

owns the resort and the spa. And the McCanns donate a lot to the community and employ a lot of people, so they're very prominent."

"And Alex is married to Ted... Theodora?"

"She hates her name. Goes by Ted. Or Doctor Ted. She's the only doctor in town."

"Gotcha. And between the two of them, it seems like they're cousins with almost everyone. Like Jena's friend Allie is cousins with Alex, but she's married to Ollie Campbell, who is also related to a bunch of people. It sure seems like everyone knows like... *all* their relatives, you know?"

Sean shrugged. "Small town. Close-knit. Aren't all families like that?"

"I mean, *my* family was, but I always knew it wasn't the average American middle-class standard, you know?"

"You talked to your mom lately?"

Juni made a face. "Caleb has encouraged me to do so. I have been thinking about it."

Sean made no other comment. He knew Juni's relationship with her mom was difficult, but he was the king of dysfunctional families, so he shut his mouth.

She was tapping her foot and looking nervous. "I took that job in Costa Rica."

Fuck. A corner of his heart died. "Good." He cleared his throat again. "That's good. That's great."

"I know you've been wanting me to move on and leave you alone."

He didn't want that. That was, in fact, the opposite of what he wanted. "I don't want... I didn't... You know how I feel."

She laughed. "No. I don't know how you feel, Sean Quinn. Communicating has never been your greatest strength."

Anything between them was impossible, but she didn't deserve thinking she was unwanted. Sean had felt that way most of his life, and it was a shit feeling.

"I never wanted you to leave me alone," he said. "I'm just glad you're not stuck here too."

"Please don't try to make me feel better." She forced a smile. "I'll be back to visit. I'm not some despairing female, okay? I have a life."

Sean couldn't resist the urge to touch her. He reached out, enfolded her hand in his, and squeezed lightly.

Juni stopped speaking.

"It's not that I want you gone," he said softly. "It's that I want both of us gone. But I can't leave—maybe not for a long time. I have things I need to do for my family here, and I'm not happy about that. I always thought..."

"What?"

Maybe someday the girl with the wild hair and the wanderer's heart might want a travel companion like him. That she might be able to wrap her mind around his shifting. That she might agree to see the world through his lens.

Sean said, "I'm glad you're going to Costa Rica because it's a great opportunity. Plus the weather should be nice right now."

She pulled her hand away. "That's it?"

That's all I can give you.

She gave him a wry smile. "I don't know what else I was expecting." She turned and started walking away. Then she turned back halfway down the aisle. "At least this time I'm the one leaving you behind."

chapter
four

"AT LEAST THIS TIME, *I'm the one leaving you...*"

Juni replayed her words over and over in her head. Why had she said that? She'd wanted to hurt him, but in doing that, she'd only revealed how much he'd hurt her.

She chopped a cucumber on the bright green cutting board in her sister-in-law's kitchen and listened to the hubbub of family life buzzing around her. Two teenage boys created a fantastic amount of noise, combined with one toddler standing on a chair and shouting her love of fruit snacks into the void while Jena checked on a pot roast and her big brother Caleb shouted from the hallway.

"Jena, have you seen my brown belt?"

"Why would she know where your belt is?" Juni asked.

"Hanging in the closet next to your black belt. Can you come feed Becca?"

"Yeah." Caleb disappeared into the bedroom and came out a few moments later, buckling a brown leather belt. "Hey, baby bird."

Becca was leaning on the back of the bench at the kitchen table, arms raised as she sang a song about fruit snacks. "Daddy, I so hungry."

Juni glanced at Jena with half a smile. "Didn't she eat an hour ago?"

Jena rolled her eyes. "She's impossible. Probably about to hit a growth spurt. The boys did this too."

A muffled argument drifted out from down the hall. "Just because it's a moon night—"

"That's not why! You're so stupid, Bear."

"Boys!" Jena shot Caleb a wide-eyed look.

Caleb grabbed Becca with one arm and strode down the hall. "Kids, keep your voices down!"

He disappeared into the hallway just as a giant thunk echoed through the house along with something that sounded like a growl.

Juni's eyes went wide. "Are they okay?"

Becca's laughter pealed through the air. "Wuf wuf wuf!"

Juni turned from the cutting board. "Is she barking?"

Jena laughed a little. "She does love dogs."

"Settle down!" Caleb's voice rose, then got suddenly soft.

"Ignore them." Jena sidled up to Juni and checked her cutting board. "Boys. They're always a little rowdy. Your knife work is darn near professional, Juni."

"You think so?"

"Yeah." Jena put an arm around her. "Good to know if the photojournalism thing falls through, you can always be a chef."

She laughed a little. "Am I allowed to admit that I'm a little nervous about the Costa Rica job?"

"Why?"

Juni peeled another cucumber. "Because normally it'd be something I did with a partner. When I was in Asia, I'd always have at least one other person with me. Sean, more than once."

"And he's not going?"

"He wasn't even considered." Juni bit her lip. "I'm not trying to be selfish. God knows our relationship has always been... complicated."

"I know Sean's been very closemouthed about how he knows you when he talks to Caleb."

"Yeah, well, it's none of my brother's business," Juni muttered. "But beyond all that personal stuff, I'm worried about Sean's career. I know he needs to stay here for family stuff, but in our line of work, if people forget to call you for a job, you're in trouble. All of this runs on word of mouth and who makes a name for themselves. You can't do that if you're stuck in Cambio Springs." She looked up from peeling. "No offense."

"None taken." Jena shrugged. "It's a different pace of life. None of us ever wondered why he left."

"What about now?" Juni glanced at Jena from the corner of her eye. The older woman intimidated Juni even if she did nothing to provoke it. "Do you understand why he came back? Why he's determined to stay?"

Jena was in her thirties. She'd gone to culinary school, had two children, buried her first husband, owned her own successful business, gotten remarried, had another baby, and she still managed to juggle all that and come across as cool and wise.

"I know why Sean is here," Jena said. "I know what it's like to have family responsibilities. And he has way more than I do; his... family is bigger."

"Isn't there anyone else?"

"Honestly?" Jena took a deep breath. "He's one of the only ones left. One of the only responsible ones anyway."

"Why?"

"Why is he the only responsible one?"

"Yeah."

Jena blew out a breath. "So many complicated reasons, but one of them is *because* he left. He got out. Sean made his own way in the world and figured out how to live life on his own terms. There's a lot of dysfunction in the Quinn family. Sean learned how to overcome that, and he's trying to share that with his younger cousins."

"And if he ends up sacrificing everything he's built in his career to help them?"

"You have to ask Sean," Jena said. "Do you think he knows he's in trouble professionally?"

"He has to know."

"So if he knows, he's decided that the cost is worth it."

"But—"

"Whether we agree or not." Jena raised a hand. "And keep in mind, you're not the only one who disagrees with Sean's choices—but they are *his* choices."

Juni shook her head. "I don't understand a family who wants to drag down the most successful person in that family because they can't get their act together, you know?"

Jena looked like she wanted to say something, then shut her mouth.

"I'm just saying," Juni continued, "if they cared about him like he cares about them, they wouldn't hold him back so much."

"Well, there you go," Jena said quietly.

"What?" Juni paused chopping the vegetables. "You don't think they care about him as much as he cares about them?"

Jena frowned. "I think that's pretty obvious."

"So what is he thinking?" More bangs, crashes, and toddler laughter made Juni's head turn toward the hall. "What on earth is going on back there?"

Jena handed her a red onion. "Cut that too, will you? For the salad."

"Are you not worried about—?"

"You know, you asked what Sean is thinking, and I can only tell you what I think myself." Jena rattled the pots and pans on the stove. "I think Sean's a good man who wants to help his family. For them, but also for himself."

"How does helping them help *him*? As far as I can see, all they're doing is taking advantage of him and hurting a career he worked incredibly hard to build."

"It's not always about your career." Jena wiped a line of sweat off her forehead. "Do you think I planned to be back here, running my family diner? I had different dreams too. But..." A wistful expression came over Jena's face. "Life is funny. It takes you in directions you never dreamed it might. If I hadn't come back here, I would never have met your brother."

Caleb, Becca, and Lowell, Jena's oldest son, walked out from the back of the house, looking like they'd barely survived a war.

"Bear'll be out in a minute," Caleb said. "He's just... cleaning up."

Juni smiled. "Combat over?"

Caleb plastered an innocent expression on his face. "Huh?"

She glanced at Lowell, who was nearly taller than Caleb now. "What's got your feathers all ruffled?"

Low blinked. "Excuse me?"

Juni laughed. "It's an expression. You and your brother having a fight?"

Becca bared her teeth. "Rawr! Rawr!"

"Becca." Jena's tone was sharp. "Go wash your hands, baby."

"I'll take her." Low reached for his baby sister and took her from Caleb's arms. "Come on, Bibi, let's go get you washed up."

"I not Bibi. I'm a big bwown wolf!"

"Uh-huh." Low shot Juni an amused look. "Sure you are."

Juni shook her head as she watched her normally unflappable brother sit at the kitchen table, looking like he'd barely survived. "I'm telling you guys, I am never having kids. I like yours, but I am not cut out to wrangle children like you do."

Caleb barked a laugh. "Famous last words."

Jena shrugged. "It's not for everyone."

"Not for me." Juni tossed the chopped red onion in with the cucumber as Jena threw in the cherry tomatoes. "Now, are we ready to feed this menagerie or what?"

JUNI WAS in her trailer an hour after sunset when she heard the two boys fighting again.

"—not your decision to make. They said you couldn't go."

"I'm not some little kid anymore. Kevin's going."

"So you think you should go and I should what? Stay here and watch Bibi?"

The boys habitually called Becca "Bibi," which Jena told her stood for Baby Bird. Not an unlikely nickname considering how often the little girl wanted to eat.

They'd already had dinner and retired for the night. As far as Juni knew, Jena and Caleb were going to a city council meeting. Were Low and Bear actually arguing about going to that? She inched her curtains to the side to get a look.

Bear was as tall as Lowell and nearly twice as wide. "Kevin is an adult now. You're not."

"I'm not a kid."

"And I am?"

"You barely—"

"Shut up!"

The boys' voices died back. Bear grabbed Low's arm and dragged him into the house.

Why were two seemingly normal teenage boys arguing about going to a city council meeting? Were kids in Cambio Springs really that hard up for things to do? Wouldn't it be more normal to drive into the desert to some random spot, light campfires, and drink illegal beer?

What kind of respectable teenager wanted to sneak out to a... city council meeting?

Juni kicked up her feet and thought about it. She checked her email. Checked her over three hundred thousand followers on social media and mentally planned her content for the next week.

She looked back out the window, but the boys hadn't reappeared.

Why did they want to go to a stupid meeting?

She grabbed her keys and headed out the door. She wasn't going to the meeting. After all, she wasn't a resident of Cambio Springs. She just... wanted some ice cream. That was all. She'd drive to the convenience store and grab some ice cream.

Juni jumped in her car before the boys could question her. She puttered down the dirt road leading from her trailer to the main drag, turned right, and headed in the direction of the Quick Stop, which was the only store open at nine o'clock on a weekday night.

She passed the church, which sat on a low rise just off the main road, and all the lights were on. Cars and trucks flooded the parking lot.

Hmm. Must have been where the city council meeting was.

Lots of cars.

Maybe *all* the cars.

Hmm.

Juni pulled over. She tapped her fingers on the steering wheel. She looked up the road. Down the road.

I mean... it's probably farmers yelling about loose chickens, right?
Repaving the roads?
New playground equipment?

That was a lot of cars to be arguing about new playground equipment.

She flipped the truck around and drove up the rise and into the parking lot, sliding between an El Camino and an old Bronco. Juni shut off the engine and waited. Nothing moved. No one came and tapped on the window.

She was just curious. About small-town life, right? After all, she was a journalist. She was always curious about what happened in interesting places.

Is Cambio Springs interesting? Really?

The number of cars in the parking lot would indicate it wasn't interesting at all, because if the town had anything else to do, surely every single person in town wouldn't come out for a city meeting.

Because that's sure what it looked like. Every. Single. Car.

Juni opened the truck door and shut it as quietly as she could. Then she walked toward the church, listening for voices drifting out. The wind was a constant companion in Cambio Springs—it tossed the short strands of hair around her face, teased her legs, and gusted against her back. It pushed her toward the glowing yellow lights of the First Community Church of Cambio Springs.

"...before something else happens and we have to—"

"You're saying we need to act first, not wait to..."

The wind carried the snippet of voices away.

As Juni got closer, she realized she didn't want to walk in. If she walked into the meeting, everything would stop. She knew she wasn't an insider here in the town, and she knew how small towns worked. So far everyone in the Springs had been friendly but cool.

That was fine. She understood that. But she wanted to understand the real dynamics of the town her brother had moved to, and to do that, she had to stay invisible.

She walked to the left of the big double doors and leaned against the wall next to a window. She angled her ear to hear more of the conversation coming from inside the church. There was the usual shuffling and whispering, but there were louder, clearer voices too.

"All I'm saying is that Lobo has been quiet for months."

"After everything that happened last year, it's not likely he just forgot about us."

"But what if he did?" a tentative female voice asked. "What if that's exactly what happened, and by being... proactive, we just make him angry?"

"He hasn't forgotten us."

Juni's eyes went wide when she heard Sean's voice.

"I talked to the man myself. Walked right up to him and tried to get answers."

She tentatively peeked around the window frame to peer inside the church.

"I'm telling you, he hasn't forgotten us. This is personal to him." Sean looked weary. He sat at the front of the room next to an older woman; his friend Alex, who owned the resort; a silver-haired man; Jena's steely-faced father; and two older people Juni didn't recognize.

"This is personal," Sean repeated. "I don't know why—I wish I did—but it is. And as far as I'm concerned, it's a damn miracle that snake hasn't sent any other people sniffing around." He folded his hands in front of him and leaned forward, looking out over the crowd. "I know that no one in this church really wants to think about what we need to do next."

His eyes scanned the crowd, and his presence was magnetic. Sean might avoid crowds—might avoid people, period—but that didn't mean they didn't react to him. There was something powerfully compelling about his speaking voice—

"I see you." His eyes locked with hers.

Juni pulled away from the window.

Shit shit shit shit shit.

"I see you," he said again. "I've been away a long time, but I see every person in this church, and I understand the fear. You want to pretend there's no danger so we can all get back to living our lives. That things don't have to change. But that's not the way it's going to go. We can wish for impossible things, but that doesn't mean we get them."

Juni's heart was pounding. She walked away from the church, ducking behind the first car that cast a big enough shadow, and slipped away into the night.

Who was Lobo?

Why was he dangerous?

Why was the town afraid of him?

What happened last year?

And was this why Sean really couldn't leave?

She jumped into the old pickup and started the car, hoping

desperately that the wind muffled the sound of the motor, then headed down the road.

Ice cream, right?

Yessir. That's why she was on the road. That's what she was craving. Ice cream, not answers about weird little desert towns, guys named Lobo, or city council meetings that were strangely well-attended.

Juni kept her eyes locked on the pavement and headed to the Quick Stop.

chapter
five

SEAN SAT in the elder's seat abandoned by his uncle and glanced down the table at the other shifters with him.

Alex sat next to him, the unrivaled center of the town as the alpha of the McCann wolves. Lena Vasquez, Alex's mother-in-law and the head of the cat clan sat on his other side. At the end of the table were Ben Campbell and Tom Crowe, the elders of the bear and the bird clans. They were also the oldest members of the council and the ones who tended to speak the least.

That also meant that when they spoke, people listened.

Five elders, five clans, and Sean was the reluctant head of one of them now.

"I just don't understand why we have the town on *lockdown*" —a man in a plaid shirt and worn jeans was speaking— "when there hasn't been a sighting of one of these foreign shifters in months."

Alex responded to the man, who was one of the wolves. "We've already told you. Until we find out what Lobo's intentions are toward the Springs—"

"And how the hell are we supposed to find that out if no one is investigating?" The woman who spoke was dark-haired and dark-eyed, one of the lean women who made up the cat clan. "You've told all of us who work out of town to pull back, focus on keeping outsiders away, but that's not changing anything and it's not doing the resort any favors either." She glanced at the two women on either side of her. Cousins, if Sean was guessing. "Lena, you know that with the right motivation, we could find out who these animals are."

Lena raised an arched eyebrow at Alex but didn't say a word.

Alex turned to Sean. "You want to take this?"

"Sure." Sean leaned forward and spoke directly to the woman. "We do know some things. We've been looking into who Lobo is, and we've found some info."

"Like what?" she asked.

Sean glanced at Alex, who nodded.

"To the larger world, his name is Efrén Abano. He is an extremely well-connected real estate developer with interests in the US and in Latin America. He builds shopping malls, hotels, and high-rises, but his pride and joy is the Esencia hotel chain, which is huge in Mexico."

Someone said, "I think my brother-in-law stayed at one of those places in Cancun."

Fascinating. Sean didn't say it. "Abano is single. Very private. He's well-traveled. And he's incredibly wealthy. Like private jet and vacation homes around the world wealthy."

"And to us?" She crossed her arms over her chest.

"To us?" Sean sighed. "We have no idea how he's connected to Cambio Springs."

A murmur rose in the crowd as neighbors talked among themselves and exchanged whispers.

"I met with him, tried to warn him off, and he gave me nothing," Sean said.

A voice rose from the crowded pews. "I want to hear from the Campbells."

Sean leaned forward and looked at old Ben Campbell, white-haired and stooped. He was Ollie's grandfather and the leader of the bears.

"All of you know that our people have guarded the Springs for as long as we've been here," Ben Campbell said. "And all of you know that we're takin' this very seriously. After all, this man's people attacked my own family."

Lobo's first attack on the Springs had been directed at Allie McCann, who was folded into the Campbell family when she and Ollie got married.

"Sean's information matches up with what our connections have been able to find," the old man continued, "but we're running into dead ends left and right." He sighed. "It's a different world out there now. In some ways it's impossible to hide, and in other ways you can hide who and what you are better than ever with enough money. And one thing we do know is this man has a lot of money."

More murmurs from the crowd. Cambio Springs wasn't a rich place. To know that a rich man was targeting them and knew the secrets they'd spent generations hiding was more than a worry—it was a dread.

"What is he?" An angry voice rose. "Do we even know?"

"He's a shifter," Sean said. "I smelled that much when I met him. What kind specifically? We don't know. The man who was working for him, the one who attacked Allie a year ago, he was a snake. But we know they had cats working for them too. As for Lobo himself, we don't know."

Alex piped up. "Wolf seems obvious, but that could just be a nickname."

"Is this guy involved in drugs? I heard he's involved in drugs."

"I heard he worked with the mafia."

"The mafia runs drugs."

Speculation was beginning to get a bit rampant, and the crowd's energy was building.

Sean raised his hands and his voice. "Hey all, let's focus on what we do know and not toss rumors around. For now we only have rumors about the drug thing. We do know what his legitimate businesses are, so let's focus on that."

"Why don't we focus on how he knows about us?" The woman in the front row spoke again.

The church grew quiet again.

"That's what we're all wondering, right?" She turned and looked around the room. "We all know how to keep our mouths shut. Even the kids know. The few times anyone has said anything, people laugh it off or don't take it seriously."

"That's exactly right," Alex said. "But for now, we don't know how Lobo knows about us or what exactly he knows or if he has anything... concrete that could put us in danger. That's one reason we're asking people to stick close to town for now."

More muttering around the room.

"I can't afford this shit."

"I got bills to pay, Alex."

"My boss is already pissed."

Alex added, "And if anyone is hurting, there are jobs at the resort!"

More than one person cursed, and Sean cringed. There was supporting McCann projects, and then there was being beholden to the wolves.

Many families in the Springs worked in the building trade. Plumbers, builders, electricians, and painters. They were skilled tradespeople, and while the resort had brought a lot of work at first, by the time construction was finished, people had to find other jobs to keep busy.

Danger from outside meant that the town got more insular and people needed to stay close. It was financially devastating for many families.

"Hey!" Alex said. "I'm not trying to say everyone has to work for me, but if you need some extra because we're asking people to lie low and stay close, we're hiring."

The man in the plaid shirt stood up again. "I had to turn down three tile jobs in Palm Springs in the past two months. You have any idea how much I could have made with those? You think being a waiter at a juice bar is gonna make me the same level of income, Alex?"

Sean watched the frustration building in the crowd.

Something had to change.

The entire town had been waiting for a shoe to drop, and the tension was wearing on everyone. Lena said fights at the school were on the rise. People were short-tempered with each other at the Save-a-Bunch, and even Norman Quinn—the only desert tortoise in the clan and the mildest-mannered reptile Sean knew—had lost his temper with a customer at the Quick Stop the week before.

Lobo had been holding Cambio Springs hostage with fear, and Sean was done with it.

He stood, and everyone in the room quieted.

"I know people," he said. "Alex and me..." He glanced at his oldest friend. "We know people. I promise you, we'll find out who Lobo is and we'll find out what he knows. We're not waiting anymore."

From the back of the room, he saw Caleb Gilbert, sheriff of Cambio Springs and Juni's big brother, staring at him with the hint of a smile curving the corner of his mouth.

Really? That was what Caleb's expression said. *Really, Sean?*

"I'm going to find out what he wants from us, and then *together*" —he looked at his fellow elders— "together we'll deal with it. As a community. We protect this town the same way we built this town. *Together.*"

The old church was silent when Sean sat and Lena Vasquez stood.

"I want to thank everyone who came tonight." Lena was the school principal as well as the head of the cat clan. "I know there are some parents who want to meet with me after the meeting about the new extracurricular-activities policy. I'll stay an extra half hour for anyone who wants to meet, and then I think it's better that we all head home, cool off, and think about the best way to protect our kids, our town, and our future." She looked at Alex and at Sean. "Thank you both for all you do." She looked back at the crowd. "For now the meeting is dismissed."

SEAN, Alex, and Caleb sat at a back booth at the Cave while Ollie pulled four pints at the bar.

"So what's the plan?" Caleb asked.

Sean felt the weight of both men looking at him. "Alex knows criminals."

"What the fuck?" Alex spread his hands. "What are you talking about?"

"We both know your little friend Cam has mob connections, dude."

"Officially, I know nothing about that. And Cameron DiStefano is trying to go legitimate. His protection racket is the last part he needs to dismantle, and you know how hard that's going to be. You don't just end relationships like that around here. They serve a purpose."

"He's the one who told you that Lobo had a drugs connection, right?" Caleb sipped his beer. "Where are you with that?"

Ollie came back with more pint glasses and set them on the table before he pulled a chair over and sat at the end of the booth.

"Dead end." Alex shrugged. "Whenever I push him, he clams up. Says he's not in that world anymore."

"You talking about drugs?" Ollie asked. "Transportation? What?"

"Drugs."

Ollie muttered, "I'll ask the Drifters what they know, but I'll have to be careful. Razio likes to talk, but a lot of it is bullshit."

The Cave was an unofficial meetinghouse for the Red Rock

Drifters, a motorcycle club that ran through the high desert and owed Ollie some loyalty. They were small-time transporters and they kept their ears open, reporting back to Ollie when anything interesting popped up.

"Tony Razio is one of the people Cam is still connected with, so I don't know that he'll know anything Cam can't tell me," Alex said. "The problem is, on paper, Efrén Abano is clean. I don't know who his accountant is, but the man is a choirboy as far as the US government is concerned."

Caleb was slumped back in his seat. "Who is Cameron DiStefano trying to bring in to take over his protection racket?"

"He's not bringing anyone in—he has guys in his organization who want to break away."

"And he's cool with that?"

Alex frowned. "I think he's okay with it. He's been shifting his family resources to real estate and construction for about eight years now. If some of the old crew don't want in on that, better them take over the protection than someone they don't know."

"And the drugs?" Sean asked. "I don't want any of that shit touching the Springs."

Drugs had hit the Quinn clan the hardest by far. The wolves and the bears had their stable families and their rosy-cheeked children, but dysfunction and addiction ran rampant through his clan. Old Quinn had turned a blind eye as more and more of Sean's parents' generation fell into drug or alcohol abuse because the old man was too damn stubborn to ask for help, but Sean wasn't about continuing that cycle.

"It's taken over my family," Sean said. "And the rest of the town has brushed it off because it's 'just the Quinns' for as long as I can remember."

Ollie's voice was low. "We can't keep your kids from leaving town and finding that shit, Sean."

His temper spiked. "I don't expect the Campbells to police every teenager in my family, but it would be real nice if I didn't have to lecture the kids from one side of my mouth while leaders in this town promise favors to drug-adjacent motorcycle gangs so they give us information."

Caleb said, "I agree with Sean."

Alex and Ollie both turned to the sheriff.

Sean didn't say a word.

"You're not law enforcement," Caleb said. "When I was a detective, I worked with criminals, but I had something legitimate to offer them. A deal. A word with the DA. Something. You guys are talking about trading favors with a motorcycle club and a mob boss."

"Former mob boss," Alex interjected.

"Who is going to want something in return." Caleb spread his hands. "And what do you have to give them? You don't have anything they want." He glanced at Ollie. "Nothing legal anyway."

"We keep their secrets, they keep ours." Alex narrowed his eyes. "I'm not going to apologize for what we have to do to keep our families safe."

"I'm not asking you to." Caleb leaned forward. "My moral code may have gotten a little more... flexible when I realized who you all were and how this town has to operate, but what you guys are talking about is just stupid. You want to find out who Lobo really is and what he's involved in, you do it the legitimate way. You find something you can take to the cops."

"And pray a slick lawyer doesn't get him off the hook?" Alex asked. "No, thank you."

"So we make deals with drug dealers and mobsters then?" Sean slid out of the booth and stood. "And fuck the snake kids, right? I mean, if they had any backbone like us high-and-mighty wolves, they wouldn't take drugs anyway."

Alex cursed under his breath. "Sean, that's not what I'm saying."

"It may not be what you're saying." Sean glared at his oldest friend. "But it's exactly what you're doing."

chapter
six

JUNI MET her big brother in the back booth of the Blackbird Diner, the booth closest to the kitchen where her brother could sit, read an actual newspaper like an old man, and keep an eye on his wife in the kitchen.

She slid into the booth and immediately reached for his cup of coffee. "Did you put sugar in it?" She sipped the black coffee and grimaced. "How can you drink it with nothing? No milk, no sugar."

"I like coffee." The corner of his mouth inched up, and he folded the newspaper and set it down. "How was your night?"

"Boring. How was yours?"

"The same." He took his coffee back. "Get your own, brat."

"Share the wealth, cop." Juni couldn't stop the smile. It had been moments like this with her brother—nearly twenty years older than her—that had made life bearable when she was growing up. "How's life?"

"Eh." He pushed the newspaper to the side and glanced at someone behind the counter, waving them over. "Not bad."

"You had that... city council thing last night, right?" She sipped more of his coffee and set the mug down. "How did that go?"

Caleb ignored the question and called to the server. "Hey, Luis, can you get my sister her own coffee so she leaves mine alone?"

She looked over her shoulder and saw a smiling man behind the counter.

"You got it, Chief. Cream and sugar, Juni?"

"Please. Thanks, Luis." She turned back to her brother. "You love it here."

His crooked smile inched up a little more. "Do I like sitting in a comfortable booth reserved for me in a diner that smells like bacon and eggs, catching my wife's smile while she's cooking breakfast for her friends and neighbors?" He lifted his mug again. "I can't say that I hate it."

Juni folded her legs under her. She hated sitting in booths, but she hated chairs more. "In a town where everyone knows you and the crime rate is probably zero point zero."

Except for someone named Lobo that you're not telling me about.

Luis brought a steaming mug over emblazoned with the Blackbird logo. "Here you go, Juni."

"Thank you."

"No problem." He set down a small cream pitcher and a sugar bowl. "And that's that almond milk you like, not the regular creamer."

She turned a beaming smile to him. "Look at you. You're so thoughtful. Thank you, Luis."

The man's cheeks turned a little pink. "No problem."

Caleb rolled his eyes. "And bring her an omelet or something too. She doesn't eat."

"Are you Mom now? I eat." She turned to Luis. "But can I get like, half a veggie omelet? The full ones are way too big."

Jena called from the back. "I'm already making you a two-egg one, Juni."

"Thank you, best sister in the world." She winked at Luis and then turned back to Caleb. "Your wife is so much cooler than you."

"In a million ways," he said. "When are you leaving for Costa Rica?"

She'd told Caleb and Jena about her trip, expecting them to be relieved to get her out of their hair, so she'd been pleasantly surprised to see disappointment flicker across their face before their happy questions started.

It felt nice to be missed.

"You ready to get rid of me?" She smiled. "Get me away from Sean Quinn?"

He narrowed his eyes. "I'm ready for you to be happy and working again."

"It's not for another month probably. They want me to go in June when the rain starts. It's the end of the dry season right now, so it'll be greener in June but still sunny most of the time." She doctored her coffee and took a sip. "Very low tourist season too, so it'll be deserted."

"Which is better for pictures, right?"

"For what the magazine wants me to do, yes. I'm doing a big review for a luxury ecolodge in the rainforest. No permanent structures, low impact on the environment, but still has a spa and a five-star restaurant, you know?"

Caleb shook his head. "I do not know, but I'm guessing it's a little like the resort here, yeah?"

"Kind of." She drank more coffee. "There's some ecofarming stuff too. I'm going to visit an organic-coffee operation in the area."

Jena piped up. "You better bring me some coffee."

"I will."

"Omelet up." Jena reached over and hit the old metal bell on the pass. "Are you sure you don't want cheese?"

Juni was mostly a vegetarian, but she traveled too much to be vegan. "Just a little tiny bit."

"Thank God," Jena muttered.

Caleb smirked. "You know how my wife feels about cheese."

"I feel the same way, which is why I can't completely give it up."

Luis slid the omelet with the sprinkle of feta in front of her. "Eat up."

"Thank you." Juni dug in. "I love having a sister who's a chef."

"I'd say it's even better when your wife is a chef, but a lot of time the kids have to put up with ham and eggs or jar spaghetti from me because she's exhausted when she gets home."

"I can see that." But her veggie omelet? Incredible. "So how was the meeting last night?" *Don't think I didn't notice you skirting around that question earlier.* "Did someone's goats cause damage? Did the chickens get out?"

Caleb glanced out the window. "The usual stuff. It's more of a community meeting thing we do once a month. There wasn't much crime stuff. The school principal met with some parents. Talked about jobs at the resort that needed filling. Stuff like that."

"Cool." She looked at him. "You guys are pretty isolated out here, right? It's what, an hour to a big city? What happens if there's an emergency?"

Caleb's smile was more amused than happy. "I'm here. We take care of things, Juni. You don't have to worry about that stuff, okay? Cambio Springs is really safe."

Are you sure?

"And if there was something I needed to worry about, something that might harm Low or Bear or Becca, you'd tell me, right?"

Caleb narrowed his eyes. "What are you hearing that has you worried about stuff like this?"

She shrugged and looked at her food. "I don't know. I just had this... I don't know. I had this feeling the other day. It's so isolated out here—"

"No more isolated than the rez."

"I didn't grow up there, remember?" By the time Juni came

around, their mother had separated herself from most of her extended family. "I'm a city kid. I worry."

Caleb studied her. "Is this about Sean?"

Juni blinked. "How could— That doesn't even make sense, Caleb. How is my worrying about the kids about Sean?"

"You must know some of his history, and it's not pretty."

"That's not what this is about." She attacked her omelet. "And yeah, I know his family isn't very healthy, which is maybe part of the reason I worry about the kids. It's not like there's a ton of things for kids to do around here, and you're the stepfather to two teenage boys now. Don't you worry about them getting involved in dangerous stuff? That seems like a normal fear, Caleb. I don't think—"

"Our boys are fine." Caleb's voice dismissed her. "They ride dirt bikes and help their grandfather repair furniture and fix up cars when they're bored. They don't hang with Quinn kids."

Quinn kids.

Sean's family.

Juni leaned forward. "Do you hear yourself?"

Caleb crossed his arms over his chest. "I didn't mean it like that."

"I'm sure you don't think you do, but you're the sheriff here. You don't think I feel that attitude everywhere? I mean, it's pretty obvious to someone who doesn't live here. There are Cambio Springs people and then there are the Quinns."

Caleb sighed and uncrossed his arms. "All I'm going to say is that there are reasons for that. There's been a lot of bad shit over the years, and—"

"Sean considers you and Jena two of his closest friends, and if you two have that attitude about his family, can you imagine how people who *aren't* his friends feel?"

Caleb dropped his voice. "Sean got away from his family. That's the only reason he's as well-adjusted as he is. And we both know he's still got major issues, so don't tell me his family—"

"He's throwing away his career because he cares about the *kids*, Caleb. Do you know how hard it is to make it in this business? Do you know how hard he had to work? Talent only gets you so far. Sean is throwing all of it away to try to break this cycle in his family. You and me—of all people—should know about trying to break cycles."

"You told me you were done with him, but you're still his biggest defender, so what is this, huh? What's going on between you two?"

"Nothing! But I am his friend, and you say you are too, so why—?"

"Hey!" Jena plopped down next to Caleb in the booth. "What's the intense whispery conversation going on over here?" She looked between Caleb and Juni. "Are you talking about a certain mutual friend?"

Juni pressed her lips together. She was starting to understand exactly why Sean had left this dust bowl, and she didn't want to insult Jena. "I'm just worried about him."

Jena's calm brown eyes stared at Juni with a wealth of life and wisdom. "You know, he's one of the most loyal people I've ever met, but he doesn't see himself that way."

"No, he doesn't. In fact, if you ask him, he's the opposite of loyal. He feels guilty for abandoning them and leaving to make a life for himself." She looked at her brother. "We know something about that, don't we, big brother?"

Caleb remained silent, pressing his lips together in a flat line.

Jena cocked her head. "You know, sometimes outsiders see things more clearly than people who have lived here their entire life."

"Well, if I'm anything," Juni said, "I'm an outsider."

"So what's the solution?" Caleb kept his voice low. "What's the great plan?"

Juni slid her plate to the side and pressed her fingertips

together. "I just think... it would be nice if someone in this town was as loyal to Sean Quinn as he was to them."

SHE WAS MAKING A MISTAKE. This was a huge mistake.

She knocked on the door of the trailer anyway.

The curtains in the lit windows flickered, and a moment later, Sean opened the door, straightening a shirt he'd just pulled on.

Damn. Juni watched him smooth the shirt over the sliver of muscled abdomen at his waist. She muffled the sigh that wanted to escape.

"Hey." He stood at the entrance of the trailer, his arms hanging over the curved doorway. "What's up? Is your AC giving you issues again?"

"Uh..." That would have been a good excuse, but unfortunately her air conditioner was working perfectly since he'd fixed it a couple of weeks ago. "No. The AC is good. Thanks."

He looked tired, and there were shadows under his eyes. "How's... uh, trip planning going? For Costa Rica."

"Good!" She brightened her voice and pointed at his chest. "I may want to pick your brain about light settings because you've shot night safaris before and I haven't. And Rani booked me for this night jungle walk in the rainforest, so—"

"Oh yeah." His guarded expression lifted immediately. "I can help you with that. Are you on foot or in a vehicle? If it's a walk, I'm guessing on foot."

"I'm not sure how I feel about that part. Aren't there jaguars down there?"

He shrugged and walked out of the trailer. "They'll have rangers with you, and I'm sure they'll be armed. I wouldn't worry about that. The guides are going to be pros."

"Yes." She clapped her hands together. "You're right. I

shouldn't worry. They wouldn't make very good money if they got the tourists killed in the jungle, right?"

He smiled. "Exactly. You're going to need to tweak your light settings, adjust your expectations, stuff like that. It's mostly about the shutter speed and aperture, but you're so good with movement that I don't think you're going to have issues with that." He narrowed his eyes. "If you've got time—"

"I do. Rani doesn't have me going down there until June."

"Just spend some time out here at night, playing around with it. Caleb can take you out, and the light pollution here is almost nonexistent, so it'll be a good way to practice."

Juni nodded. "And being out in the desert at night around here... No worries?"

Sean blinked. "I mean, you'll want to avoid full moon nights because there will be a lot more light, but if you go with Caleb, he has a gun so..." He rubbed his neck. "The uh, animals won't bother you. I can tell you some spots that would be good."

"Cool." She rocked back on her heels. "Cool, cool. Who is Lobo?"

Sean froze. "Where did you hear that name?"

"Around." She cleared her throat. "Just around. Whispers. People... whispering about someone named Lobo and then clamming up when they see me, and it seems like there's some big secret and this person is dangerous and my brother is a cop here and I worry so—"

"Drug dealer." Sean crossed his arms. "He's... a drug dealer. We think. And Cambio Springs is on the road between the Coachella Valley and Las Vegas. Off the interstate, you know? So there are some concerns about the trafficking situation, but I know Caleb and... uh, Alex and some of the city council are on top of it. There's nothing to worry about. Just small-town stuff."

"That affects your family."

Sean flinched. "Uh, yeah. I'm sure you've gotten the picture around here. My family has a lot of... I guess now we call them addiction issues or something. When I was growing up, we just called our parents junkies."

It was Juni's turn to flinch. "That's horrible."

"That's my family, Juni." He spread his arms. "I mean, you always asked why I put the brakes on things between the two of us, and that's it. That's why. Nearly every adult in my life is addicted to something or they're a felon, and if they're not, it's just because they're smart enough to not get caught or to take their chances and leave this place." He swallowed hard. "So that's my family."

"But that's not you." She stepped closer.

He took a step back. "It's not me, but..." He stared at her lips. "I have my addictions too. Maybe they're just not as obvious."

"Uh-huh." She stepped closer, and he didn't back away. "You told me once that when things get hard, you run away. That's what you do."

He nodded.

"You're *here*, Sean. You're not running away. Even though no one in this town has ever done anything to earn your loyalty, you're here."

"The kids..." He lifted one shoulder. "They still have a chance."

"I know." She put a hand on his shoulder and felt the heat through his clothes. He felt like he was burning up. She frowned. "Are you okay?"

"I'm fine. I don't get sick."

"I know. I was always so jealous of..." She pressed her fingers into his chest, her eyes going wide when his skin cooled beneath her fingers. "How—?"

"Don't try to fix me." He grabbed her hand from his chest. "I don't want that for you. That's why I always— Go to Costa Rica, Juni. Live your life. Visit your brother on weekends. Be the cool aunt with the cool job. That's what you want."

"While you stay here and throw everything away?"

The expression fell from his face. "Like I said, they're my family."

Juni looked up. "I think you're the most loyal and honorable person I have ever known in my life, and you think no one notices."

He shook his head. "Don't make me a hero. I'm not."

You are. She didn't say it, but she did put her hand on his chest again. It wasn't her imagination. His skin shifted from cool to hot beneath her fingertips. She looked up, marveling at the strange phenomena. "Sean, how—?"

He kissed her.

In her wildest dreams, Sean Quinn had never kissed her like this. His arms wrapped around her, pulling her into his body before he spun her around and pressed her against the cool silver skin of the trailer.

Shivers along her back, her body heating at his touch. Juni was awash in sensation.

Sean's hands gripped her waist, and his mouth was devastating. His lips commanded hers, not a single tentative thing about him. He kissed her like a starving man, as if he knew her mouth and claimed it.

Juni felt branded.

He reached up, one hand curling around the side of her neck while the other slid to the small of her back. He angled her head so he could devour her mouth with his own. His tongue flicked out, teasing her lips until she opened her mouth, and then he took her again, invading her as his fingers fluttered against the sensitive skin on her lower back, sneaking under the edge of her shirt and sliding ever so lightly under the waistband of her jeans.

Her head was swimming. She heard a coyote whoop in the distance, and Sean's head jerked back. He turned, spotted something in the dust, and she could have sworn he hissed.

Juni blinked. "Sean?"

"Sorry." He reached down, picked her up, and Juni automatically flung her legs around his waist.

Was this happening? After so many years? "Sean, what are you doing?"

Wait. He wasn't taking her into his trailer, he was walking to his... pickup truck? She could feel the erection in his jeans, and he was taking her to his pickup truck?

"Fuck me." He groaned.

Okay? Yes please? "Maybe not in the pickup truck?"

His laugh didn't sound happy, it sounded tortured. "Juni, I need to take you home."

"I am so confused right now."

"That makes two of us."

chapter
seven

RATTLESNAKE. There was a fucking rattler under his trailer, and Sean didn't know if it was a wild animal or a cousin. Or one of Lobo's snakes. If Lobo had snakes other than the one who had died months ago.

He yanked open the truck door, plopped her on the seat, and untangled his arms. "Give me a second to get my keys." He pulled away, stepped back, and shut the truck door behind her, making sure the seat belt was clear.

Then he turned, prayed to anything listening that he wouldn't walk crooked from the hard-on in his pants, and slowly stepped back toward his trailer, his eyes sweeping the dusty ground. He kept his senses tuned for any hint of movement in the air around him, but the only sound was the distant rustle of wind in the cottonwood trees. The serpent was either lying low or had already taken off.

Just as well. It put a brake on things going too far with Juni, and the last thing he needed was to follow through on what his body was urging him to do.

Juni needed to leave. She needed to get in her beat-up Volvo, drive back to Venice Beach, and get the hell out of Cambio

Springs. He'd kissed her to distract her when his temperature started to shift erratically.

And because he wanted her.

He'd kissed her and it had been a mistake.

You love mistakes.

Sean yanked the door to the Airstream open, grabbed the keys from the hook, and slammed the door behind him. Then he stared at the dust as he walked back to the truck, hoping and praying that Juni was pissed off at him.

"You told me once that when things get hard, you run away. That's what you do."

He hadn't been lying when he told her that. Things in his pants were very hard, and he was definitely running away. Sean opened the driver door and got behind the wheel, never once giving in to the temptation to look at her.

God, she smelled good. Her arousal was all the drug he'd ever need to get high.

"Sean, what is—?"

"Rattlesnake." He glanced at her, then started the truck. "There's a rattler under my trailer and I heard it. That's why I'm driving you back."

"That's why..." She muttered something under her breath. "We couldn't have gone into your trailer, you know, as an option?"

That was definitely an option. That was probably the better option if his dick had a vote.

His dick did not get a vote.

"Sorry, I just reacted. You don't mess around with rattlesnakes around here."

He would know.

"Right." She laughed under her breath. "Yeah. You don't mess with rattlesnakes."

He recognized that tone of voice. She was moving from confused and emotional to angry. Good. Angry was good.

"Sean Quinn, you're a piece of work." She crossed her arms over her chest.

"Yep." He kept his eyes on the dusty trail between the cacti. "I am."

"You really don't care at all, do you?"

He cared so much he was crying inside. Not that he could tell her that. "Juni, I'm trying to make things right here. I've told you I can't offer you—"

"I'm not fucking talking about me. About you and me. Whatever the fuck we are."

Sean pulled the truck to a stop a few yards from the front of her trailer and scanned the gravel that surrounded it. "We're fucking work colleagues. That's all we can be."

"Actually, we're not. That's what I'm talking about. You are so determined to sabotage anything in your life that goes right, you're going to kill your career."

He whipped his head around. "I don't need you lecturing me about work. I've been doing this long enough to know exactly how—"

"How you're killing yourself?" She glared at him. "You are so blind! What kind of family leader are you going to be if you sacrifice everything you've worked for? How are you going to convince those kids that *they* should dream big when you give up the life you built and end up back here, right where you started?"

He smiled. "Yep, there it is. White trash, dirty Quinns. Don't know why I'm surprised to hear it from you too."

"Stop putting words in my mouth." She was past angry now; she was furious. "There are people who love this town. There are people who *want* to build a life here, and that's a good thing. That's a beautiful thing."

"But not me?" He should have known she would never be happy here. Of course she wouldn't be happy. She was like him. She's fought and clawed her way out of the dust to build a life of her own.

"No, not you." She opened her door. "There's sacrifice and then there's martyrdom, Sean. And if you stay here, you will turn out bitter and angry and you won't be able to help anyone."

"Someone has to step up, and I'm it."

"There he is, poor martyr Sean Quinn." She stepped out of the truck, turned, and put a hand over her heart. "I salute you. I'm sure you're right. You and only you can solve this problem you didn't create."

Fuck off. He didn't say it because he knew all too well that words couldn't be forgotten. "Go to Costa Rica, Juni. Get out of here."

"Oh, I plan on it." She slammed the door shut and stomped to the trailer.

And Sean, because he was addicted to torturing himself, watched every step she took away from him. He hung his arm out the open window of the truck, his eyes scanning the gravel around the trailer to make sure he didn't see any movement.

Juni turned before she walked into her trailer. "Oh, Sean? Make sure you tell the kids in your family that it doesn't matter how much they achieve in life because they will probably end up right back here, taking care of a family and a town that doesn't appreciate them."

"Sure thing. Thanks for the advice." Sean felt dead inside. She hated him and he deserved it.

She blinked hard, and there were tears in her eyes. "Fuck you."

"I'm sorry." He cleared his throat and looked away. "I shouldn't have kissed you. It won't happen again."

He put the truck in reverse, waited to hear her trailer door slam shut, then backed away from her trailer and drove into the desert.

HE DROVE to the overlook behind Old Quinn's house, left his truck at the top of the hill, and shifted, shedding his clothes in the dust and surrendering to his animal form.

Sean shifted into a rattlesnake, immediately feeling the air sink into his skin and permeate his bones. The landscape around him came alive with scent; there was a hint of water in the breeze he hadn't detected in his human form, and a cottontail nest was nearby.

Bold rabbits.

There were very few small mammals who trespassed on Quinn land. They smelled the predators whether they were in human form or animal and stayed away.

He slithered across the tumbled rocks, craving the scent of prey. His bones were cold, and the heat the rocks had captured during the day was the only thing keeping his body from growing stiff. There were pockets of warm air in the rocks, and he had to fight the primitive urge to slide into them and burrow.

His hearing was secondary in this form. He sensed heat and smell more than anything else, and the scent of the rabbits drove him across the rocks and down the backside of the hill toward the hidden warren.

Sean halted when he smelled it.

Wolf.

He froze on the rocks, slithering into a crevice as the larger predator came padding up the hill.

The snake peered out of the rocks, his tongue flicking out to taste the air.

Wolf. McCann. Alex.

Moments after the furry creature came into view, the animal shifted in a trick of shadows and the man appeared.

"Sean, I know you're here."

Alex's nakedness didn't bother Sean. They'd grown up shifting in and out of their animal forms with ease. Bodies were bodies, and Sean had seen nearly everyone in town naked at some point.

Alex McCann sat on a boulder and scanned the rocks where Sean was hiding. "Come on, man. Let's talk."

Sean slid out from between the rocks, but he waited to shift.

"What?" Alex asked. "You're gonna make me wait bare-assed, talking to myself in the middle of the desert while I apologize?"

Sean flicked out his tongue, but he didn't move.

"Fine." Alex huffed. "I am sorry that what we were talking about earlier came across like we don't care about your family. Because we do. *I* do."

Sean waited.

"And yes, I know that making deals with the DiStefanos has been a problem. And I am admitting right now that I don't know how to fix it, okay?" Alex threw out his arms. "Is that what you want? For me to admit I don't know? Because I don't."

Sean finally shifted and walked over to sit on a rock across from Alex. He leaned forward, his body shivering in the cold as a quick jolt of nausea swept over him. It was momentary; then he leaned forward and braced his elbows on his knees.

"I don't know either." He swallowed hard. "But I know I can't keep going like this. Purely on practical levels, if I'm not pulling some money in, at least five families in my clan are going to lose a significant portion of their income."

Alex nodded. "So we figure out a way to get you back to your life and your work."

He shook his head. "How? I've promised the town that I'm going to figure out who Lobo is. I've promised the younger adults that I'll stay."

"They have to understand—"

"They understand that pretty much every adult in our family has broken promises." Sean shook his head. "I have to stick around. I have to be there for them."

"But you don't have to do it alone."

He threw out his arms. "Who, Alex? Marcus was the only one—"

"Maggie." Alex pressed his lips together and let the silence hang between them.

Sean blinked. "Absolutely not."

"You're seeing the negatives, but she's your half sister and—"

"Maggie got Allie's husband killed!"

"Joe got *himself* killed," Alex said. "He's the one who approached Maggie, as far as I remember. Was she wrong to set it up and lie about it? Yes. But hear me out for a minute."

There was nothing Alex could say that would change Sean's mind about his sister, but he clamped his lips shut.

"She does take care of those kids. I talked to Ted about it, and she confirmed. Maggie's the one who's been bringing the kids in for doctors' appointments and signing stuff for school and riding herd on them for *years*. She was a mother to most of her cousins when she was thirteen years old."

"And half of them have juvenile records."

"Is that her fault?"

"Partly!" How could Alex think this was a good idea? Mature, responsible Alex McCann?

"The town failed her," the wolf alpha said. "I am man enough to admit that, Sean. *We failed her.* We used the excuse of keeping to ourselves and not interfering in other clans, but Cambio Springs failed Maggie. Failed the Quinn kids." He frowned. "We failed *you*, Sean."

Sean swallowed hard. "That's still my shirt hanging up in Jena's diner though, right?"

The corner of Alex's mouth inched up. "It's more of a tribute at this point than a warrant, you know?"

Sean took a deep breath and let it out again. His fangs were still on edge, but Alex's humility had done a lot to stem the bloodlust and anger in his system.

"I pissed Juni off tonight." He swallowed hard. "I think she's finally leaving."

Alex grimaced. "I don't know whether to be sad for you or

relieved for the Springs. That girl is too smart and too perceptive for her own good."

"Relieved. Be relieved." He crossed his arms again. "It can't happen, Alex. Not for me. I'm happy as hell for Jena and Allie and you and Ted, but Quinns don't have successful relationships."

"Marcus did. Even after he died, Josie stayed here with the kids. They're thriving; they have lots of friends. Doing well in school. And Josie's going to be running the spa at the resort within a year. She and Allie have gotten really close."

He nodded. "That's good. But Juni isn't that way. She's not settled like Josie."

"Neither are you." Alex stood. "Just think about it, Sean. Think about letting someone else run the family here, because you're right. You need to get back to your life. The money won't last forever, and even if you sell your house at the beach, that'll run out too." Alex held up a finger. "Do not fucking sell that house. You love that place."

Sean had already been looking at how much he could get for it. He hated when Alex read his mind. "Before I can even think about the family or the future, we have to take care of Lobo."

Alex nodded. "I may have an idea about that."

chapter
eight

"SO YOU'RE LEAVING?"

"Yes." She was already packing up the trailer with Lauren's face keeping her company on the computer. "I'll be back in Venice next week, so you and Ryan better get the sex toys out of my room and clean the closet."

"Ha ha." Lauren propped her chin on a hand. "You're sad."

"I'm pissed off at Sean, but what's new?"

"Not that." She sighed. "Are you going to leave me and go to Thailand again?"

"No." It was tempting though. "I let my lease go on the Chiang Mai place when I came back to the States. I want to stay closer to Caleb and Jena."

"And Sean?"

"No, not Sean." She tossed a tote bag full of other tote bags on her small bed. "He is determined to sacrifice his entire life to rescue his family from dysfunction or something, and I have healthier boundaries, okay? I can't change his mind or rescue his career for him, and I'm not going to try."

Lauren frowned. "What do you mean, rescuing his family?"

"There's just a lot of..." Juni sat at the table and sighed. "His parents aren't around. Pretty sure at least one of them is incarcerated or maybe is supposed to be but is hiding? I think other than one uncle, the kids in his family kind of raise themselves, and he's trying to be there for them so they don't grow up and follow the same path as their parents. There's a lot of addiction and dysfunction. Worse than my family. Way worse."

Lauren was quiet for a while. "So he's staying there to raise his younger cousins? That's... I mean, that's a really noble thing, Jun."

"Yes, it is. And I respect that. But he is unwilling to ask anyone else for help, and he's going to sacrifice his entire career in the process, which will put him on a downward spiral that will land him right back here where he started and barely managed to escape the first time." Juni swallowed hard. "Or at least that's what I think."

"Okay." Lauren's expression had shifted from excited to glum. "Now I'm sad."

"Don't be sad!" Juni forced a smile. "I'm coming home and we're gonna go out for sushi and then I'm going to Costa Rica and I'm going to have an amazing time."

"Oh!" Lauren perked up. "And I got the toilet paper commercial." She waved her hands. "Yay. And I also think I booked a spot on *LA Residents*, that medical drama? I'm basically an extra who has one line, but hooray for talking on-screen." She waved her hands again.

Juni forced herself to be excited. "Lauren, that's awesome!"

"I know, right? I'm excited, and Ryan is pretending to be excited."

"He should be *very* excited. The commercial and the speaking role puts you in the union, right?"

"It will. But he's a sound editor with a real job. He doesn't really get the acting thing." She clapped her hands. "But he loves me, and it excited him that I'm excited."

"Good. I'm glad." Juni propped her chin on her hands. "I miss you."

"I miss you too." Lauren touched the screen. "Don't be sad over a boy."

"I'm not sad over a boy. I'm sad about a man I have feelings for, and I'm not going to apologize for that."

Lauren sighed. "Remember, if he wanted to…"

"He would." Juni nodded. "I know."

"Good." Lauren blew her a kiss. "You deserve every good thing."

"You too." She glanced over her shoulder. "It's almost noon, and I promised Jena I'd meet her for lunch, so I'd better keep going. I've been living here for months, and I have accumulated way too much stuff. There's not much to do in this town other that hit the outlet malls every now and then." She pulled out two turquoise-colored shirts that matched the one she was already wearing.

Lauren smiled. "You know, I know that you're not committing yourself to Sean and you have healthy boundaries, but if you want to get rid of some stuff, maybe some of his younger cousins who are kind of on their own might want some cute new clothes. That might be something they could use."

"That is a great idea, and you're right." Juni knew the perfect person to call. "One of Sean's cousins was married to this really amazing hairdresser, and I think a lot of the girls in the family hang at her place a lot. I'll call Josie when I sort through my stuff."

"Great idea."

Speaking of Josie, she could do to have her highlights touched up before she left.

And of course she'd have to let her brother know she was leaving.

Plus there was lunch with Jena.

Not that she was finding excuses to stay in Cambio Springs, but the more Juni thought about it, the more she had to do. It was almost like this town kept finding ways to keep her around.

But being around didn't mean she had to talk to Sean.

Not even a little bit.

JENA DIDN'T WANT to meet at the diner or the resort where she was starting a new restaurant. In fact, she didn't want to meet in the Springs at all, so Juni drove into Palm Desert where Jena had spent the morning at one of the last outdoor farmers' markets before they shuttered their doors during the scorching summer heat.

"It's too hot to operate through the summer." Jena sipped an iced tea and wiped her forehead with a bright yellow bandanna. "There's one on the weekend that moves inside, but there's not much that grows locally out here from June to September."

"That makes sense."

Her sister-in-law smiled. "And Caleb says you're heading back to Venice next week? Getting ready for your big trip?"

"I need to fly to San Juan in a week and a half, so I wanted a few days to settle back into life before I jumped on a plane, you know?"

"I can't lie, I'm going to miss you like crazy and so will the kids, so come back anytime you want. If we've rented out the Airstream, there's always room in the house. Or you could get fancy and stay at the resort if you want. You know Alex will give you the family discount."

She adored this wonderful woman who had married her brother. "I am so happy I got to spend some time with you guys. It's been really wonderful." She was surprised when the tears welled up. "You know, Caleb and I had such a big gap in age that it's been like getting to know him all over again now that we're both adults."

Jena squeezed her hand. "I'll try to ease him into thinking of you as an adult, I promise."

"You've already helped a lot. I think he's finally done patting my head."

"He adores you." Jena smiled. "It feels good that he has part of his family back, you know?"

"I know." She glanced at the menu. "I still haven't called our mom."

"There's no rush. They talk about once a month now, and I think it's good. He feels better about it."

"Is it true she made you guys change Becca's name?"

Jena rolled her eyes. "It's not as big a deal as he makes it. Honestly. We were thinking about naming her Charlotte for his cousin but—"

"Oh no." Juni immediately shook her head. "That was not going to fly. I was barely around the house when that happened, but I know how hard she took it. I'm glad you went with Rebecca."

"Now I can't imagine calling her anything else."

The waiter came and took their order for salads, then left after he'd refilled their water.

"Maybe we need to open a salad place in the Springs." Jena narrowed her eyes. "I bet that would be pretty popular."

"Really?" Juni nibbled on the veggies and dip the waiter had brought them while they waited. "I think of Cambio Springs as a town of carnivores."

Jena nearly spit out her tea. She covered her mouth with a napkin and coughed.

"Oh my God, are you okay?"

"Just... went down the wrong pipe." Her sister-in-law wiped her eyes. "Um... Yeah, you could say there are a lot of meat eaters in the place, but you can have meat in salads too."

"I think you'd have to." Juni frowned, thinking about the Springs. "What was it like growing up there?"

"What was it like growing up in Albuquerque?"

Juni shrugged. "Just normal, I guess. School, family, church when my dad dragged us. I tried to avoid home, and my mom tried to guilt me into staying."

Jena shrugged. "Are you really curious about me or about Sean?"

She sipped her water and didn't know how to answer.

"Sean's family is really complicated" —Jena continued— "because they are utterly loyal to each other if anyone from *outside* the family is threatening one of them. But within the ranks?" Jena shook her head. "They tear each other down. They almost make a sport of it."

That sounded frighteningly familiar.

Juni picked at her salad. "But even with all that history, he came back."

"Yeah, he did. His cousin Marcus was supposed to kind of take over the family from Old Joe Quinn, Sean's great-uncle."

"You make it sound like the mob, Jena."

Her sister-in-law shrugged dramatically. "I mean, that's not... *un*true. In some ways, all the families in Cambio Springs are like that."

So weird. So very, very weird.

"What happened with Marcus? Why didn't he take over?"

"He was murdered."

Juni's jaw dropped. "Oh my God."

"Yes. It was... awful. Absolutely awful. Caleb worked the case, and it was so stressful. And just heartbreaking for Josie and the kids."

"Wait..." Juni blinked. "That was Josie's husband? Sweet, wonderful Josie's husband was *murdered*?"

She nodded. "A domestic dispute with his brother-in-law. Devastating for the entire town, but especially devastating for the Quinns. Marcus was solid as a rock. Successful builder, good family man. He had the steadiest personality, and he wanted to move back with his family."

"To take care of everyone."

Jena nodded. "And then... tragedy. It happened a few years ago. Sean was in Thailand or somewhere when Alex managed to track him down."

Juni froze. "Thailand?"

"Yeah, I think he was visiting a friend or something. Didn't you work in Thailand for a while?" Jena shook her head. "I don't know. He was there, and then the next week, he was back in the States."

From Thailand, where Juni had been living.

Thailand, where he'd left her flowers on her doorstep but hadn't even knocked. Where he'd written her a heartbreaking letter but hadn't been brave enough to deliver it on his own.

You know what I want, but I can't do that to you.
You deserve every good thing in the world.
I'm sorry.

She twisted her fingers in her lap. "So Sean was in Thailand when he found out Marcus died?"

Jena nodded. "Yeah."

"And he came back." Juni swallowed the lump in her throat. "Because there was no one else."

"No one Sean trusted with the kids." Jena picked up her tea again. "You know, I know a lot of people think he abandoned his family, but he sent money back all the time. Ted knew because they talked. He trusted her, so he'd send money back to Ted and she would give it to her mom, who would pass it along to Old Quinn. They had to know where it was coming from, but they didn't say anything."

Juni's heart felt like a lead lump in her chest. Every time she was ready to write this man off as a bad bet, as an inconsistent player, as the ultimate emotional manipulator... another piece of his story unfolded. "No one knew the money was coming from him?"

"Not officially. Sean didn't want them to. You know, he owns two houses in town. From his grandparents on either side. They left their stuff to him and his sister. Josie lives in one of them now, and his sister and a bunch of the girls in his family live in the other one."

"And he lives in a broken-down trailer and fixes it up for rent." Juni leaned forward, rubbing her temple as she went round and round in her head. "I need to say something, and it might not be appropriate, but I feel like I need to be honest with you because you're his friend and we both care about him."

Jena frowned. "Okay, shoot."

"I know Sean is a good guy. What I cannot understand is why he's ruining his career to be here. He could split his time and not sacrifice everything he's built. We are not that far from LA. He has options."

Jena bit her lip. "Things are really complicated right now. It won't be forever, but—"

"What's the endgame? For him?" She sat back. "Because if he's still in this town in another six months, people are going to forget his name. And you can't rebuild a reputation as a hot artist with a unique vision when you're in your late thirties." Juni shrugged. "It sucks—it's ageist as hell—but that's the way this industry works."

Jena took a deep breath and let it out slowly. "Six months?"

"Maximum."

Jena nodded slowly.

"I feel like a bitch for saying this," Juni continued, "but I really do care about him. I know he's emotionally... limited. But I also know he has a good heart and that he respects you and Caleb a lot. Tell him that whatever he's doing out here, he's got six months to figure it out. Or he's not coming back."

chapter
nine

IT WAS Monday night at the Cave, and the bar was closed. Sean gathered with his oldest friends—Alex across from him, Ollie on one side, Ted on the other, and Caleb sitting in the booth next to Sean.

Juni was leaving the next morning, and Sean wasn't imagining it. Caleb was acting friendly again.

Ted raised her hand. "I am officially representing Jena and Allie at this meeting since Allie is on kid duty and Jena had a late shift at the hotel. That means if we're voting, I get three votes."

Sean rolled his eyes. "We're not voting. We're brainstorming, and then I'm going to deal with shit."

The front door was locked, and the night wind rattled the windows. Two overgrown teenagers from the bear clan were stomping around outside, and Maggie and two of her girls were hiding in the bushes. Sean told them to stay out of sight but keep their senses on alert for anyone in the brush.

His sister had wanted to attend the meeting, but Sean knew that wouldn't go well, so he gave her something else to do and was a little surprised when she jumped at the task.

Ollie muttered, "Sean, I'm not really sure why you got it in your head that you're the one in charge of dealing with Lobo, but it's incorrect. If anything, it's my clan's responsibility."

Sean crossed his arms over his chest. "My sister is the one who invited this guy into our business. I'll clean up the mess."

"And it was a coyote from my clan who left the town exposed," Alex said. "This is a problem for all of us, and you don't have to deal with this on your own. That's what this meeting is about."

Caleb raised a hand. "If I can speak generally for Jena and her family too, the Crowe clan is not assigning blame to anyone. However they can help, they will."

"Good." Ted clapped her hands. "So we're all equally responsible and in this. You know my clan will all bitch about it because we're cats and that's what we do, but we need this place to remain secret just like the rest of you, so we will do whatever we need to."

Alex stood up like the student body president he'd been. "First thing on the agenda tonight: Ollie, what do you need to help with perimeter protection for the Springs?"

Sean smirked. "Did you bring a clipboard?"

"Fuck off." Alex couldn't stop the corner of his mouth from turning up. "It's a tactical clipboard."

"If that makes you feel less like a nerd, okay."

Ollie spoke up. "Ted, if you could talk to your mom about asking some of the larger cats to join in patrols, that would be helpful. You guys are better on the high ground around the canyon than we are, and you don't mind going solo. It helps us cover more territory if we can spread out."

"Done." Ted had enough mountain lions and jaguars in the clan to keep an eye on the high ground. "And the wolves?"

Alex sat up straight. "We'll help, but you know how my guys get about solitary patrols."

Caleb muttered, "So much fucking howling."

Ollie grunted in agreement. "You got any coyotes that might want to lend a hand? They'd be better on the perimeter. We can keep the pack closer to town."

"Great idea." Alex made a note. "So that takes care of the perimeter."

Sean cleared his throat. "And there it is again."

Alex, Ted, and Ollie all turned to him.

"What?" Ollie frowned.

Sean was really glad Maggie couldn't hear them. "It didn't even occur to you guys to ask the Quinns to help with patrols," he said. "If you give some of the older kids a task like that, have them reporting to someone responsible, they might be really helpful, and this gang could have reptiles in their group. We'd be able to scent them better than you."

Everyone was silent for a long minute.

"Okay," Ollie said. "Good idea. But they're gonna have to take orders from me, and that's not always a given with your kids."

Sean felt his hackles rise, but he forced himself to take a breath.

"Easy," Alex said. "We all want to—"

"You're right," Sean admitted. "But I'm not gonna get my tail bent if you discipline them or report them to me for discipline like the old man. They're acting up, step on them." He held up a hand. "Not *literally*."

Ollie nodded. "Fine. I'll send you a list of times and locations."

"They might be better during daylight this time of year."

"Noted," Ollie said.

"Okay." Alex looked at his clipboard again. "Now that immediate town protection has been taken care of, let's talk about getting to the root of all this. Caleb, have you found anything out?"

"Not that I haven't already shared," the chief said. "Vegas PD doesn't have anything more than what's on paper. I'd like to talk to someone in Mexico City, but I'm having problems getting anyone to open up. The man is connected."

"And rich." Alex asked, "Is there anything that money can do to help things along there?"

"I don't think so." Caleb scratched his jaw. "I have an old

buddy at border patrol out of El Paso, and I might call him to see if he has a contact I can talk to. Give me a few days to get on that and I'll get back to you."

"In the meantime," Ollie said, "I talked to Razio a couple of days ago, and he let slip the Drifters have a meeting scheduled with the DiStefanos in a couple of days. Something about new routes."

"Lobo is a rival of the DiStefanos," Sean said. "They're not going to know his movements."

Ollie shrugged. "They might know something we don't. I think it's worth checking out."

Ted lifted both eyebrows. "You think they're going to be cool with you just sitting in on a meeting? The DiStefanos know you're not a fan of the drugs they move."

"I'm not gonna sit in on any meetings with those crooks," Ollie said. "But I am more than willing to drive Sean here to their house in Barstow where the meeting is happening."

"Why Sean?" Ted asked.

"Any of you guys able to shift into something small enough to hide in a wall?" Ollie turned to Sean and offered him a nod. "When it comes to surveillance, this guy's about the best there is."

Sean liked the idea. It gave him something to do, and Ollie was right. He could shift into a tiny lizard or snake and no one would be the wiser. "I'm in. It's a good idea."

"So we have the next step," Alex said. "Caleb is going to poke the Mexican authorities to find out more about Lobo's operation in the south, and Ollie and Sean can spy on that meeting."

"And Sean, I'm not trying to step on your toes, but I'm not comfortable with you going by yourself," Ollie said. "I can make an excuse to Razio why I'm in town that day."

Sean didn't object to the backup. "I'd rather not go alone. If I get eaten by a house cat, someone needs to tell my uncle."

There was a knock on the front door. Ollie lumbered over, pushed it open, and Willow McCann poked her head in.

"I'm late," she said. "Sorry. My flight got delayed."

"Willow!"

Alex glanced up. "Hey, sis."

"Will, how long are you back for?"

Sean felt her warmth even before he stood to greet her. "Hey, you."

"Hey." She walked over and gave him a long hug. "How's life in the desert?"

"Eh." He shrugged.

She raised an eyebrow. "Yeah, I see you."

Willow McCann was a celebrated landscape painter who spent as much time out of the Springs as in it, but she always came home. She was also the only water witch in her generation, so she'd been needed a lot during the hotel construction, which meant she'd escaped to her house in Santa Fe as soon as construction was done.

Seeing her made Sean think about his life before.

Willow pulled up a chair and sat next to him. "So what's the plan?"

He nudged her shoulder. "Alex has a clipboard."

"He loves those," she whispered. "Did I miss it all?"

"Mostly." Alex sat down and handed her the clipboard. "Catch up because Ted and I need to go grab Luna from Allie's house before she rebels and refuses to ever babysit again."

Ollie snorted. "Like that'll ever happen." He looked around. "I'll lock up here."

Willow pouted. "Come on, no one's gonna have a beer with me?"

Caleb motioned Sean to let him out of the booth. "I gotta get some shut-eye. Willow, it's good to see you. My sister Juni's leaving tomorrow." He glanced at Sean. "I gotta get up early and help her get back to LA."

"I wish I'd planned better so I could have met her." Willow glanced at Sean. "I've heard so much about her. Hi to Jena, okay? Safe driving tomorrow."

Caleb tipped his hat like the cowboy he was, then walked toward the door with Alex and Ted.

Ollie was behind the bar. He pulled two longnecks out of the fridge before he started cleaning up. "You two have half an hour while I lecture those boys outside about how to do a patrol without waking the dead." He turned off half the lights as he headed to the door. "Then I'm home too, so drink fast."

Sean sat back in the booth, and Willow walked to the bar, grabbed the two beers, and walked back to Sean.

"So." She set one beer in front of him. "Talk to me, Scales."

"YOU JUST LEFT the flowers and a note?" Willow hissed at him. "Sean, are you kidding me?"

"I wasn't thinking. Marcus being murdered meant that any future we had was toast. What should I have done?"

"Not that!" She sat back in the booth. "I remember you telling me about this girl years ago."

He frowned. "When?"

"You said you met someone in Thailand."

"That was... I mean, we were just working together then."

"Okay, sure." She rolled her eyes. "What's the plan?" She looked around the bar. "I can't lie: I love seeing you around here, but you can't stay."

"I have to."

She nearly spit out her beer. "What are you talking about?"

"Who else is going to lead the family if I leave?"

"I don't know, but not you." Willow's eyes went wide. "You're serious?"

"Tell me what options I have." He had already finished his beer and was peeling the label meticulously from around the top of the bottle. "The old man is... old. My parents' generation are either addicts, dead, or gone. Maggie and I are the only older ones who—"

"Okay, there's your answer. Maggie."

"Just like that?" He leaned forward. "She's a criminal."

"But not a felon. They could not prove anything."

He huffed out a breath. "She's a gambler and a thief."

"So was Old Quinn before he settled down and got serious."

"She has made some really shitty decisions, Willow."

"And she paid for them." Willow lifted a finger. "Without a complaint. She respected the hierarchy, and she didn't bitch about her punishment, did she?"

Sean shook his head. "Maggie is not a good option. She's smart, but she's young and she's too..."

"What?" Willow lifted her chin. "Finish the sentence."

Sean didn't want to, but Willow was one of the few people who knew both sides of his life. "She's too much like our dad."

Willow nodded slowly. "You need to recognize that your relationship with Glenn needs to be separate from your relationship with Maggie, because you put them together in your head and they are not the same."

"They're not the same, but they're pretty damn alike."

Willow tipped her beer up and finished it. "On the surface? Fine. Maybe. But there's a lot that separates them too. Would you want everyone treating you like your dad just because you look like him?"

Sean and Maggie's father was a rat bastard who knocked up women and abandoned them. There was a reason he'd run from the Springs when he was seventeen, and finding his father had been part of that motivation.

He was sorry when he found him. "I'm nothing like my dad."

"Don't be modest, honey, you're a sharp-looking charmer when you want to be." Willow leaned back and softened her tone. "And the last thing I'll say about Maggie is that she's a better choice to lead the family than you for one reason and one reason only."

He snorted. "I'm all ears."

"She wants to be here."

Sean couldn't respond to that because Willow was right.

"Maggie wants to be here and you don't."

'Cause he was a piece of shit who abandoned the people he loved.

Just like his father.

Sean wished he had another beer. "I'm not leaving them. Not again."

Willow reached across and grabbed his hand. "It's not wrong to want a different life."

Sean swallowed the lump in his throat. "They need me."

"They do need you, but they don't own you. And they don't need you here all the time because they're smart enough to know that you would hate it."

"I don't..." He shook his head. "I don't hate the Springs. There's a part of me..."

He thought about the taste of the sweet water trickling from the rock, the heat of sandstone on his belly while he lay in the sun, the raucous full moon nights where every animal let their fur or scales out and gave in to their animal instincts.

He thought about Sunday dinners at Jena's house, watching football with Ted, and dancing at the Cave when he was just a little drunk.

"The Springs is always gonna be home to me," Sean said.

Willow squeezed his hand. "You and me? We need this place, but we need to stretch our wings too. We're not like the others, and that's okay. We don't need to be."

"But for now I need to stay."

"When did they stop calling you for jobs?" Willow's voice was curt. Practical.

Just answering the question stung. "The last call I got from my editor was two months ago. She moved me from salary to contract."

"Damn."

Sean shrugged. "She had to do it."

"You need to finish whatever this is, get things set up, and get back to your life."

"It's not that simple."

"It is." Willow let go of his hand. "If you stay here, you'll become as mad and bitter as your mother was. You'll resent every single one of them for stealing the life you busted your ass to build, and it will ruin your relationship with your family, your friends, and with Juni."

He swallowed the lump in his throat. "This isn't about Juni."

"She's part of it whether you want her to be or not. In ten years, I haven't heard you mention a woman more than once or twice. I know Juni's favorite color."

Turquoise blue.

"Willow—"

"Don't argue when you know I'm right." Willow stood. "And whatever happens here, you better keep me in the loop because you know Alex is shit about telling me stuff."

Sean frowned. "I thought you were back."

Willow shook her head. "I'm only here for a few days; then I'm heading back east."

"What are you doing back east?"

She bit her lip. "I'm going back to North Carolina to snoop."

That was where the McCanns and the Crowes had originally come from. "Why?"

She glanced at the bar where Ollie was making "get on with it" faces at the both of them. "I found letters in my grandmother's things. Letters from the first generations."

"From the Springs?"

"No, letters from the family that stayed back east. I found the ones Francie McCann's sister wrote to her, which means—"

"The ones Francie wrote from here might be with her family back in North Carolina."

"The elders will tell you that the McCanns cut off their relatives after the war, but those letters tell me that at least two sisters were writing to each other years later. I want to know what Francie McCann said and why *my* grandmother hid her grandmother's letters."

Sean lowered his voice. "You think they might know about...?"

"About the shift?" Willow shook her head. "I doubt it. Who would believe it? But there were secrets. I'm gonna find out what I can."

Sean rose and both of them walked to the door. "You think this thing with Lobo goes back to the beginning?"

Willow glanced at Ollie, then back to Sean. "I think this entire town was built on secrets, shame, and trying to run from the past. The McCanns were Confederate soldiers. We don't like to talk about that anymore, but it's the truth. They wanted to hide from the war by coming out here. Maybe there were other secrets they were trying to hide too."

chapter
ten

JUNI WALKED down the narrow steps of the Airstream trailer just after sunrise with three duffel bags flung over her shoulder and a bittersweet fluttering in her heart. The air was cool, and the sky was a pearled pink touched with wispy clouds that hovered over the hills in the distance.

She was leaving Cambio Springs—to hell with whatever mysteries her brother and sister-in-law were trying to hide, whatever messed-up relationship Sean had with his family, and whatever prejudices this weird town had with outsiders.

Back to work. Back to life. Back to LA.

Within days, she'd be in San José, Costa Rica, headed to the luxury ecoresort in the mountains. Taking pictures. Eating world-class cuisine. Being wined and dined by hotel staff who wanted to impress her.

It was way, way past time for her to get back to her life.

Caleb and she had loaded most of her belongings in three boxes that they'd packed in his truck last night. Only her clothes and her cameras were left. She'd stuff those in her Volvo, and Caleb would follow her back to Venice in his truck.

She walked back to the trailer to grab her camera bag and shut the door, nearly falling over when a small, child-shaped missile struck the side of her body. Juni looked down to see her niece clinging to her leg with a death grip.

"Auntie Juni." Becca's lower lip trembled. "You going now?"

She narrowed her eyes at Becca. "Oh, you're good."

Jena ran from the back door and plucked her youngest from Juni's leg. "Auntie Juni will be back to visit, Becca. She has to go to work."

Becca cocked her head. "Cook?"

"No, take pictures." Juni leaned over and blew a raspberry on Becca's round cheek. "I can't only take pictures of you, silly squirrel. I have to pay the bills."

She tossed her bags in her car, then gave in to the urge to glance at Sean's trailer.

There was a car parked in front.

Fuck.

She quickly turned away and grabbed Becca from Jena's arms. "Oh, I'm going to miss you!" She squeezed her niece and tried to push down the tears that had everything to do with leaving her sweet family and nothing to do with a strange car parked in front of Sean's trailer.

"It's Willow." Jena caught her look and quickly explained. "It's just Willow. She flew in late, and her place is way out of town, so—"

"It's fine." Juni stopped her. "It's none of my business. I'm fine."

"No, it's just..." Jena huffed out a breath. "They're friends," she whispered. "I don't want you to get the wrong idea."

Yeah, Sean told everyone that he and Juni were "just friends" too, so she knew how that went. "I'm leaving. It has nothing to do with him. I wish him the best. And her too if that's..." She waved a hand. "I'm fine." She handed the baby back to Jena. "Caleb, you ready?"

Her older brother ambled out of the house with two teenage

boys rubbing their eyes behind him. "These guys wanted to say bye."

"Oh." She walked over to hug the two boys. "You didn't have to wake them up. It's cool."

"Love you, Auntie Jun." Bear hugged Juni around her neck and laid his head on her shoulder for a sweet minute. "You're coming back, right?"

"You bet I am. I'm not that far away, kiddo. Just four hours. Maybe you guys can come see me at the beach."

Low hugged her when Bear let go. The boy had sprouted up over the winter, and she only came up to his shoulder now. "That sounds fun. Mom, can we?"

"When your aunt is finished working, we will definitely plan a trip to visit, but work comes first."

Juni heard the squeak from a distance; it was the sound of Sean's trailer door. She didn't turn.

Low kept his arm around Juni. "Make sure you post pictures from Costa Rica. I want to see stuff. I follow Uncle Sean's Instagram. If you send me your profile, I'll follow you too."

"Oh cool. Great idea." She saw Sean from the corner of her eye. He was standing in the distance, but he wasn't walking over. "We better get going." She smiled at Caleb. "Don't want to hit LA when the traffic is heavy."

Caleb glanced across the back acre, his mouth settled into a line, and he walked to the truck. "Yeah. Good call."

Juni quickly hugged Jena one more time, then kissed Becca's teary cheek and waved at the boys before she flung herself into her car, keeping her eyes directly across the dashboard. Caleb got into the truck behind her. She watched him taking his time buckling his seat belt before he flashed his lights.

Ready.

"Just go, Juni." She started her old car, praying that it would turn over without a hiccup; she could see Sean's outline from the corner of her eye.

Along with the car in front of his house.

I told you... She could practically hear her brother's voice in her ear.

Juni plastered a smile on her face as she waved one last time at the boys and Jena, who was holding Becca in her arms. "Just drive."

Her brother put the truck in gear, backed out of the driveway carefully, and pulled onto the main road, Juni following behind him in the Volvo.

At the last minute, she caught Sean running toward the truck and she felt her heart speed up.

Don't stop, Juni.

Do not stop.

Limon Province
Costa Rica

JUNI WAS SITTING on the porch of her bungalow, watching the morning mist over the churning Pacuare River. The jungle enveloped her, the cacophony of morning birdsong, croaking frogs, and the symphony of life that was the rainforest of the Talamanca Mountains.

She'd spent four days and three nights in the luxury resort, enjoying the sprawling suite that overlooked the river along with the private pool, treetop walkways, and sumptuous meals included in her experience.

She sat at her computer, typing up notes from the night before.

> *Species spotted—Numerous colorful and highly poisonous frogs, the biggest spiders I've ever seen in my life, so many snakes.*
> *Pretty sure I heard a jaguar because the guide hustled us away*

after that scream. Definitely glad that Alonzo was there with a machine gun. I get it now.

Definitely recommend the daytime jungle walk for beginners. No one but the hardest-core nature lover is going to like that much animal venom. The birds during the daytime walk will make an ornithologist out of anyone. Gorgeous.

She flipped through her nighttime photos, which were adequate for the magazine feature but nothing near as satisfying as the colorful daytime menagerie she'd experienced the day before.

She'd already photographed her breakfast, so she dug into the hearty plate of gallo pinto with a poached egg over it and fried plantains on the side. She'd already been munching on the fresh fruit accompanying the meal while she sipped the coffee her butler —yes, a butler—had ground the beans for that morning.

The air wafted up from the river, a lush breeze that smelled of green life and damp earth.

"Miss Hawkins, can I get you anything else?"

Juni turned to him. "Nada, gracias."

"Con gusto, senorita."

Juni turned back to her coffee, the third cup that morning, just as a familiar voice sounded in the distance.

"Juniper Hawkins, as I live and breathe. Ha! I've always wanted to say that."

She blinked and turned to see her editor, Rani Prasad, climbing the stairs on the wooden walkway that ran along the edge of the resort. "Rani?" She jumped to her feet. "Hi! What are you doing here?"

Rani motioned behind her where a tall blond man was carrying a clapping girl on his shoulders while a lanky, dark-haired boy walked beside them. "I decided to check up on you and turn it into a family vacation."

"Oh my God, you brought Jay and Tisha?" Juni ran over and hugged her editor, usually not their typical greeting, but everything felt more loose and friendly so far from the office. "You must be Ken." She shoved her hand forward. "I feel like I know you even though we've never met."

The man was tan with wavy blond hair. "I feel the same way." He gripped her hand and gave it a friendly shake. "Sometimes I wonder if Rani talks about you or her little sister more."

Her editor walked over and put her arm around the little boy's shoulder. "On the off chance you ever meet my sister, I will never admit that."

Juni laughed. "This is so fun. I'm not going to lie, this has been an amazing few days, but it would have been way more fun with company."

"That's what I was thinking." Rani smiled a little. "I was really hoping you'd convince you-know-who to come with you."

Juni shrugged. "I tried." She looked up at the little girl. "I am suffering auntie withdrawal, so I am going to enjoy showing you guys all the cool stuff I've seen here! Do you like birds?"

Tisha smiled and nodded shyly.

"Good." Juni's heart ached a little bit. "I can't wait to walk in the jungle with you." She turned to Rani. "Want me to catch you up?"

"I would love that." She turned to her husband. "Ken, can you get these guys settled in? Maybe they want to go for a swim."

Jay's ears perked up. "Swimming sounds cool."

"Sounds good." Ken bounced his daughter on his shoulders. "Who wants to splash around before breakfast?"

"Perfect." Rani motioned to the walkway where two porters were waiting. "We're staying in the family villa next to your bungalow."

"Oh, that looks beautiful, and you have your own pool that overlooks the river."

The porters followed Ken and the two kids while she and Rani walked back to the breakfast table.

"This place is gorgeous." Rani stood at the railing and looked over the river.

"When did you plan this vacation?" Juni sat and picked up her coffee.

"About an hour after you posted your first picture online." Rani turned, leaning against the wooden railing and turning her face to the sun. "So catch me up, Juniper Hawkins. You've been hiding out in the desert with Sean for months."

"Not exactly *with* Sean, okay?"

Rani walked to the table and sat across from Juni. "Make me understand. Because I'm worried about both of you, and it's not just because I'm your boss."

TWENTY MINUTES LATER, Rani was sipping coffee and her face had lost some of its light. "Oh, Sean."

"Yeah." Juni was purposely not thinking about the way they'd parted. Maybe the car was just a friend's, maybe it wasn't. But whatever Sean and Juni were, it wasn't an exclusive relationship no matter what she wanted.

Maybe she needed to get laid.

"I always kind of assumed you two had something going on, but I didn't want to ask. He's not like most of the guys we have on staff. The way they brag about women..." Rani shuddered.

Juni knew exactly what she was talking about. "I know. It was one of the reasons that I wanted something to happen, but I don't think it's meant to be."

"You think he's giving up?" Rani's face was a picture of distress. "I know better than anyone how fucking hard that man worked to build his career. The thought of him just throwing that away—"

"Can we say he's throwing it away when he's trying to hold his family together?" Juni bit her lip. "I know what you're saying, but

I can't judge him. I feel like he got the shitty end of the stick and he's doing a job that clearly no one else wants."

"What kind of family though?" Rani lowered her voice. "Who does that to someone who's worked so hard? Do they not know? Do they just not care?"

Juni pressed her lips together. "I don't think it's intentional. And he's actually really close with my sister-in-law. They grew up together, so I'm hoping he might get enough support from other people that he feels like he can step away."

"If he can get back to LA fairly soon, I can make it work, okay? I'll get him jobs. In fact..." Rani frowned. "If he's gone around eighteen months, I can hint to the rumor mill that he was in rehab or something."

"Rehab? Sean barely drinks."

Rani waved a hand. "I don't have to tell them *why* he was in rehab. It doesn't matter. It could be for online addiction or exhaustion for all anyone cares these days. It'll give him a *reason* that he was gone." She sat back. "Give people motivation to hire him again. Layers. Interest. It could raise his profile, not damage it."

"I don't know. Maybe."

"Maybe."

"But whatever happens..." Juni took a long breath and stared out at the lush forest around her. "I am done sacrificing any part of my life for Sean Quinn. I'm going to work where I want. Travel where I want. Date who I want. Maybe I'll even—"

"Ooh!" Rani's eyes lit up. "Is there someone here you have an eye on?"

"There are a couple of the rafting guides that are pretty damn hot." One had even flirted with Juni when she went on the river her first day at the resort. "I don't know. Maybe." She shrugged. "Or maybe not? That's so cliché, right? Dating a guide?"

Rani smiled knowingly. "Have you *tried* dating since you and Sean met?"

"Yes." Juni nodded. "I haven't been a monk. I've gone on a few dates, but I work so much, you know?" She kept nodding. "It's not that I'm hung up. I just... I work a lot. I'm busy."

"Mm-hmm." Rani sipped her coffee. "Yes. You do work a lot."

Juni stared at the jungle. "I've tried. I really have. It's just... no one is really as interesting to me as Sean Quinn."

Rani sighed. "That is annoying as shit."

"Yeah, it really is."

chapter
eleven

SEAN SAT in the sweltering truck, slouched down in the seat with Ollie next to him. The man was scrolling through his phone like a teenager.

"Are you watching videos on your phone?"

Ollie glanced up. "Power washing."

Sean frowned. "Power washing?"

The bear nodded. "Patios. Rugs. This one guy takes a power washer to car interiors."

"That seems like it'd be rough on the upholstery."

"I thought the same thing, but they always turn out nice." He continued staring at the phone. "We need to wait about five more minutes."

Sean nodded. "And it's just you going in?"

"I told Razio I'd drop off some custom saddlebags that one of my cousins made for one of his guys." He patted the plastic grocery bag set on the bench between them.

"Okay, you're gonna drop those off and drop me." Sean considered a plan. "Then you're gonna have to take off. They'll get suspicious if you're just hangin' around."

"I'll try to grab a beer or something with one of them, but if I can't, yeah." He nodded to the gas station across the way. "I'll park in the lot back there. You gonna be able to make it across the street?"

A real life game of *Frogger*? Yippee. "I'll manage."

"What're you gonna shift to?"

"For the clubhouse, I'm thinking a lizard. That's gonna be the most inconspicuous, and my hearing will be better."

"I'll try not to step on any lizards then."

"After? Probably a snake. I'll be able to move faster over the distance. Shifting to a monitor would attract too much attention." Monitor lizards could move as fast as a sprinter, but they were also not native to the desert. "So look for a snake."

"Got it." Ollie looked over. "So?"

Sean sighed. Shifting into something that small always gave him the shakes. Probably better to have a few minutes to adjust. He eyed the stretch of parking lot between the truck and the warehouse that was the club's headquarters. "Okay, if a bird eats me—"

"Jump in the grocery bag, you idiot. You're not gonna get eaten by a bird."

"Right." He glanced at Ollie. "Stop watching me."

"You've shifted in front of me before."

"Only when I was pissed." He closed his eyes and allowed the warmth to start at his fingertips. He stretched his hands in the sun, reaching for the heat as he felt his body begin to contract within itself.

Sean had no idea how the magic of shifting worked. It made sense that the giant man next to him shifted into a bear, but there was simply no explanation for how a man over six feet tall—even a lanky one—could contract his matter into the form of a tiny lizard.

He just... did.

Within seconds, he was scrambling through the jungle of his clothes, cursing the jeans he'd pulled on that morning for their weight, and skittering up and onto the truck bench next to Ollie.

The man looked down at him, and his voice came to Sean like a muffled boom. "Get in the bag. Time to go in. You good?"

Sean flicked his tongue and licked his eye. It was the closest he could get to flipping Ollie off. Why did people ask him questions he had no way to answer in animal form?

"Yeah, I get it. I'm gonna assume that means you're fine." He lifted a corner of the bag. "Crawl in and I'll try to be gentle setting this down inside."

Sean scrambled into the bag, enjoying the glowing heat inside the plastic.

If there was one form that he truly enjoyed in the summer heat, it was the lizard. In this form, his feet were splayed and wide, his skin the color of the pebbled sand, and his body moved in quick reaction to the environment. The sun made him fast.

Ollie lifted the bag, and Sean skittered to the top near the handles, his feet easily grabbing the smooth leather of the saddlebags. He closed his eyes and explored the scents around him. Animal skin and leather conditioner. Something vaguely chemical overridden by a waxy scent with the faint smell of honey and lemon oil.

Within moments, he could feel the cool shadow as Ollie reached the door of the clubhouse, then a booming knock followed by a creak that echoed through his body as the vibrations filled the air.

"Ollie, man. How's it going?" The unknown man stepped aside, and Ollie walked into a cold room that smelled of mold and beer. The air around him was damp and cool. They used a swamp cooler to combat the heat.

"Razio have time for a beer?"

"Eh..." The man hemmed and hawed. "He's got a meeting with some dick from Vegas."

The bag jostled as Ollie set it on a piece of furniture. "Oh, no worries. I'm around for a while—got some errands for the wife in town—I might give him a call later."

Sean immediately made his move. The plastic bag was perched on a corner of an old sofa stained with who-knew-what and burned by cigarettes. He raced out of the plastic bag and to the nearest dark corner he could find.

Ollie continued, "I brought the saddlebags Coco made. Israel around?"

"Hey, Iz!"

The man's bellow filled the air as Sean crawled behind the back cushion of the couch, up to the back, and then over the edge. He was searching for a wall and an opening. Once he was in the walls of the clubhouse, he could go anywhere he wanted.

"Oh shit." Ollie raised his voice a little. "When did you get a cat?"

A cat? *Dammit.*

"That thing?" The man sounded annoyed. "Tony has some idea that we got rats in the walls. I told him I put poison out, but he picked up this dumb cat from the shelter. You ask me, he just wanted a cat."

Sean made a mental note of the poison and the cat as he slipped into the crack in the drywall.

Ahhh, safety.

The air around him was filled with dust, wood flakes, and the scent of termites and rat droppings. He darted up and down, weaving along the wiring that led from one room to the next.

In this form, he could move ridiculously fast. He raced from one room to the next in the clubhouse, pausing at outlets and holes in the wall to find out who was talking.

He passed the kitchen and quickly moved away from a sparking wire in the wall. He scrambled up a wall, then down a stud to reach the next room.

"...think that's gonna fix it?"

"Dunno, but it can't hurt, right? If I change out the wheel..."

Sean moved on before he heard more. Two of the Drifters were obviously debating something about motorcycles he had no interest in.

He passed a room where a man was having sex with two

women, another one where two men were stoned out of their minds, and another where a man was folding laundry.

Sean paused. The scent of clean laundry was refreshing in a house that mainly smelled like tobacco, weed, and stale beer.

He crawled into a small space between two junction boxes and moved into a wall where a television boomed against the studs, passed that, his ears turning one way, then another to detect voices.

"...way that's gonna keep my guys outta trouble."

What was that?

Sean froze, flicking his tongue to taste the air.

The voices in the room opposite the television continued.

"...don't want to fuck with these guys. The stuff they're getting..."

The voices drifted away when the volume of the television increased.

Dammit. He ran from that wall, around the corner, and found an exterior wall that didn't share any space with another occupied room.

The air was sweltering, but the voices came in more clearly. Muffled but audible.

"...the deal that Cam and I—"

"Cam is out," a deep voice said. "Permanently. It's real important that you realize that, because if you go to his office or some shit like that again, he's gonna call the cops, and you know he may be legit now but he's still got a couple of those guys on his payroll."

"So what am I supposed to do when one of my guys gets fuckin' knifed doing a drop-off? We got no recourse now? He's gonna be fine, but it fucked him up, Carlo."

"Your guys get knifed, you pull out the heavier weapons. We're not asking you to roll over and play dead, Razio."

"This crew is not like the gang we were dealing with before. I don't know what changed down south but—"

"Lobo." The man interrupted Razio. "Lobo fucking changed

it. These people he hired? I have no idea where they're getting their info. And they're fucking everywhere, man."

So Lobo was pushing the old DiStefano crew out of the local drug trade? That made sense, but how did the police not have any indication that he was a player in the criminal world? The DEA had undercover agents everywhere.

"That crew scares the shit out of people, man. I got three grow houses that flat out told me they're done. They want out."

There was a long pause.

Weed might be legal in California and Nevada, but the legal dispensaries had a huge markup in government taxes and fees, which meant the illegal marijuana market was still going strong.

Carlo asked, "Your growers say why?"

"They didn't tell me nothin'," Razio spat out. "I'm telling you, this asshole is stepping over the line. There ain't no live and let live anymore, and with Cam gettin' out, that leaves a huge space in the market. You guys say you're doing protection these days, so what I'm telling you is our small-time guys are getting squeezed."

"And they won't give you a name or anything? You want my people on it, you gotta give me a name. I can't go starting a war over rumors."

"Carlo, they're scared as shit."

"Of who?"

"I can't get them to tell me that. I'm sitting in one guy's kitchen, and he's one of these dudes with one of those big-ass illegal guard cats in the corner of the fucking room—"

"What do they call those things?"

"Savannah cats or some shit."

Sean scooted up the wall, peering through a broken piece of drywall.

Savannah cats were hybrid animals bred from domestic cats and African servals, but they looked mostly like servals. Had Tony Razio seen a savannah cat or a serval shifter in that man's house? If it was a serval shifter, that could explain the man's fear.

A man in a sweat-stained suit was shaking his head. "Fucking freaky if you ask me. Get a fucking dog or something. Those cats freak me out."

Razio continued, "Yeah, and this guy has this freaky-ass cat sitting at his fucking kitchen table, but he's still scared shitless. I don't know who you gotta be to freak out a guy with a fucking guard cat that's nearly as big as a mountain lion, but he flat out said he's out."

A serval nearly as big as a mountain lion? Definitely sounded like a shifter.

"Is your grower out, or is he going with another distributor?"

Razio tugged at his hair. "Man, don't ask me. The last time I was there, the dude was a chill bro who wore his bathrobe all day, carried around a spoiled Chihuahua, and offered me a joint with my beer. Now he looks a decade older and says he's out."

Sean had a bad feeling about the fate of the pampered Chihuahua.

"I'm telling you, Lobo's people got to him. I don't know how, and he won't tell me, but they got to him."

"Fuck." The man in the suit started pacing. "We can't keep losing our small growers. They're the only option that flies under the radar, and I'll leave the fucking desert before I get involved with cartel bullshit."

"I know, man. I don't know what to tell you."

Sean's tongue flicked out and he froze.

He wasn't alone.

The scent of another shifter filled his senses.

Snake.

There was a sour note to the reptile's smell, a sickly thread that made Sean scoot away. Could the other shifter smell him too? Why was it here?

He skittered away, searching for an exit, but he felt the heat of the snake coming closer.

The larger predator was hunting him.

Shit.

He ran through the walls, easily outpacing the less flexible snake who made no attempt to shift. Maybe he only had one form? That would be unusual for a reptile, but more than one shifter who'd had an encounter with Lobo's "crew" reported the sour, sickly smell. There was something deeply unhealthy about the shifters Lobo was using.

He reached the front of the clubhouse, but he didn't hear Ollie anywhere. He knew the plan was to get across the street to the truck, but he hadn't counted on another shifter following him.

He caught a glimpse of the snake closing in from the corner of his eye as he listened for Ollie's voice. It was a sturdy black rat snake, native to the central US and not venomous, but still plenty deadly to a shifter in lizard form.

He slipped into the room, across the threshold, and under the door before anyone in the clubhouse spotted him. A snake wouldn't be able to be so elusive.

Sean ran across the dusty driveway, his feet hot on the burning asphalt. He reached a low stone wall and sped up it, darting into a crevice to scan the parking lot and the clubhouse.

The snake was nowhere to be seen.

He flicked out his tongue to taste the air and sensed another animal, this one coming closer.

Fuck. It was the cat Ollie had mentioned earlier.

He shifted to something larger and sturdier, the stones in the wall breaking loose as the gopher snake emerged from the wall. He was six feet long and pebbled brown, a massive serpent that could eat that cat for lunch.

He curled into a shadow and scanned the road he needed to cross. It was dangerous, but it would be far more conspicuous for a naked man to run across the street and jump into Ollie's truck. He needed to be fast, and he needed to be quick.

A low whine sounded behind him, and Sean turned his head, flicking out his tongue to scent the air.

Coyote. Sour. Sick.

Shifter.

He uncoiled and started across the road, praying that the midmorning traffic would allow him enough time to escape. The coyote was closing in, so the vibrations coming along the asphalt that would usually make him pause propelled Sean forward. He slithered across the road and onto the sidewalk just in time for the truck to miss him, but not in time to escape the coyote's bite.

He felt the animal's teeth close around his tail and Sean turned to strike out, but a quick whip of the animal's powerful jaws flung him into the block wall lining the sidewalk. His head struck the concrete, his vision blurred, and everything went black.

chapter
twelve

"LAUREN?" Juni felt like she was glowing even though she was exhausted. "Lauren, I'm back!" She dropped her backpack on the chair by the door and dragged her rolling suitcase over the threshold of their restored bungalow in Venice Beach.

Lauren's parents had bought the house just after Juni and Lauren moved to LA and just before Venice became the hot new place for the tech bros to live. When they bought the tiny bungalow southwest of the Pacific Coast Highway, there were two rooms, one cramped bathroom, and peeling paint everywhere. In exchange for living there, Juni had helped Lauren fix the place up and learned more about home restoration than she'd ever expected.

Over their ten years there, Lauren's dad had added another bedroom to the narrow bungalow and had talked about adding another bathroom, but Juni didn't know if it would ever happen.

But cramped house or not, Venice felt like home. From the secret walking streets that wound through her neighborhood to the wild art installations woven into trees and the now-posh boutiques on Abbot Kinney Boulevard, she loved the place.

"Lauren?"

Lauren's boyfriend Ryan was the first person she saw.

"Juni!" He walked over and wrapped her in a friendly hug.

"Hey, I thought you were getting back later today. Lauren's at an audition, I think."

"I was able to get an earlier flight, so I grabbed it." She yawned broadly. "I might catch a nap. I'm exhausted."

"Sure, sure." He pointed at the kitchen. "I can make you a coffee if you want. Do you have... jet lag?" He squinted. "I'm not sure if Costa Rica is in a different time zone."

"It's not jet lag—I'm just exhausted." She smiled and patted his arm. "Busy week. I'll pass on the coffee, but thanks."

"Welcome home." He smiled. "Hey, go check out your room."

Juni woke up. "What did you do to my room?"

He was all smiles. "You'll like it. I promise."

Lauren and Ryan had taken the two rooms at the front of the house, leaving Juni the room at the back. With the kitchen and the living space between them, it gave them all some privacy and allowed Juni her own private entrance when she was feeling antisocial.

She walked through the kitchen, passing the kitchen table and the raggedy futon propped by the back door that had been the first piece of furniture she and Lauren bought on their own. To the left, she saw her bedroom door open and more light than usual.

"Ryan?" She glanced over her shoulder. "What did you do?"

He was all smiles. "Just look."

She stepped into her tiny bedroom and immediately saw why he was smiling. "I love it!" The light from the new window hit her first, but it took her a second to notice the door. "Is that...?"

"Yep."

"No way!" She dropped her backpack on her bed and rushed to the narrow doorway, flinging it open to find her very own bathroom with a standing shower, a sink and toilet, and a brightly tiled mirror built into the wall. "Ryan!"

"I am so glad you took those three extra days in San José because this was not done until yesterday afternoon." He was grinning from ear to ear. "We weren't trying to keep it a secret or anything, but when the contractor called me with the estimate and timeline, Lauren thought it would be fun to surprise you."

"I didn't even know you were talking about it."

"The timing worked out. They had all the stuff ordered and ready to go, so when you left, they swooped in and did the work." Ryan rubbed a hand through his hair. "She's gonna be pissed she wasn't here when you saw it."

"Hold on, grab your phone."

"Oh, good idea." He grabbed his cell and stepped back to the door of her bedroom. "Okay, look shocked."

Juni put both her hands on her cheeks and pretended to be surprised.

Ryan snapped a picture while he laughed. "You look more horrified than shocked, but I'll send it to her." He tapped on his phone to send Lauren the picture.

Juni couldn't stop staring at the tiny, brightly tiled shower. It was exactly what she needed and nothing more. "She's definitely going to up my rent after this, isn't she?"

He laughed. "Don't be silly. It's an investment in the house. After all, if we ever kick you out because we decide to have a couple of kids, it'll be nice to have one bedroom with an en suite bathroom."

"If you have kids, you won't be able to kick me out. I'll just camp in the backyard." Her face hurt from smiling. "You two are awesome."

"Well, I think after I took the lead on this project, Lauren's dad might finally realize I don't have any plans to move out and leave his daughter."

"He'll have to smile at you now."

Ryan crossed his fingers. "I'm not counting on it, but I can hope."

Her bed was calling her.

Ryan's phone rang. "It's Lauren."

Juni smiled. Her bed could wait a minute. "Gimme."

 103

He handed her the phone, and when Juni tapped on Lauren's picture to answer the call, she smiled. "Exclusive Escorts, how can I serve you?"

"You're back!" Lauren's voice nearly pierced her eardrums.

"I'm back." Juni looked at the bathroom. "And I love it."

"One—yay, you're home! Two—I'm so glad you like it! Love, love, love it. And three—you need to put your US SIM card back in your phone and call your sister-in-law because she's called me three times in the past twenty-four hours. She said she couldn't get ahold of you."

"Oh shit." Juni still had a Costa Rican SIM card in her phone. "I need to get her on a messaging app for when I'm out of the country."

"Yeah. I don't want to say she sounded panicked, but maybe she sounded panicked a little bit?"

Juni's heart froze. "Lauren, I'm hanging up now."

"Hand the phone back to Ryan please?"

She handed Ryan the phone and fumbled in her backpack to find the small box where she kept various SIM cards for different continents. She pulled out her US card and shoved it in her phone, then turned it on. It immediately began to buzz with messages.

She unlocked it and ignored the notifications to go directly to her voice mail.

Three voice mails from Jena.

Shit.

"Juni, it's me and something happened. Please call me. Sean was... He's injured. There was an accident."

Her heart froze. No. No no no no no.

Juni blinked back tears when she heard the next message. *"Call me. I know it's late, but he's asking for you and he's going in and out of consciousness."*

Fuck sleep. "Ryan, I'm driving out to the desert." She grabbed her backpack. "Do we have any Coke? Red Bull? 5-Hour Energy?"

"I have an energy drink in the fridge. Do you—?"

"I'm stealing it." She was crying when the third message started.

"Juni, I don't know what's going to happen. I thought you were back in the country, but maybe I have the dates wrong. Just please call me as soon as you get this. He's unconscious now and... Just call."

She sniffed and stuffed her things back in her backpack. She headed right back out to her car, thankful that at least she didn't need to pack a bag as she rolled her suitcase through the house, nearly running to the front.

"Juni, what's going on?"

"Sean's hurt. Something happened."

"Oh my God." Ryan tossed her the energy drink. "Should I drive you? Are you okay to drive?"

"I'll be okay." She was already calling Jena. "Tell Lauren I'll see her when... I'm not sure."

Ryan ran over and hugged her, then picked up her suitcase. "Let me get this for you. Call me the minute you get there. Are you sure you're okay to drive?"

No. No, but she needed time alone in her car to think. She didn't want company. She didn't want someone with her.

She just wanted Sean.

"...GOING to the hospital in Indio, right?" Juni had finally gotten ahold of Jena on the phone.

"No, he's at Ted's clinic. She said there's not anything they can do for him at the hospital that she can't do here and she didn't want to move him."

"Jena, that's nuts! Call a fucking helicopter or something. If an ambulance would be too dangerous—"

"Alex already offered, but Ted said... Just come here, okay? The bleeding has stopped, so it's just a matter of waiting at this point."

"I just don't understand why—" Juni bit her tongue. She was

barking at her sister-in-law on the phone, and it wasn't helpful. "Tell him I'm on my way."

"How far out are you?"

"Going through San Bernardino now, so maybe a couple of hours."

"Don't drive crazy."

Impossible.

She'd been berating herself for over an hour, swinging wildly between anger at Sean and anger at herself. How could he be so careless?

Which was irrational. Accidents by their very nature couldn't be predicted.

Why wasn't he in the hospital? Ted sounded like a competent family doctor, but she wasn't an entire staff of emergency room doctors and nurses and surgeons and labs. There was no way she could adequately care for a trauma patient from a small community clinic in Cambio Springs.

But Ted loved Sean just as much as she did.

Did she?

Fuck.

Juni started crying again. She did. Dammit, she'd tried so long to keep from falling over the edge, but faced with the prospect of Sean Quinn not existing on the earth... The truth smacked her in the face.

She was in love with him. She'd been in love with the man for years.

And?

And nothing. It changed nothing except it made the miles between them even more bitter. She shouted at a big rig that changed lanes in front of her so she merged into the fast lane, hoping and praying the highway patrol was taking a break.

She'd been more than ready to leave that damned dusty town, and now all she wanted to do was get back as quickly as possible.

JUNI PULLED into the driveway next to the concrete-block building that was the Cambio Springs Community Medical Clinic. Next to it was the beginning of an expanded building with a taller roof and a larger footprint, but it was far from finished.

There were half a dozen cars in the parking lot, but Juni ignored them as she rushed into the building. Inside, under flickering fluorescent lights and popcorn ceilings, a gallery of strange figures was waiting.

An old man with a handlebar mustache and an enormous cowboy hat. Next to him, a full-lipped young woman a little older than Juni with hooded eyes and deep black hair that reminded her of Sean.

The sister he complained about?

Juni didn't know and she didn't ask.

Across from those two was a collection of teenagers and Josie, her hairdresser and new friend.

The woman with full arms and bright red hair rose. "Hey, Juni. I'm so glad you made it."

"Where is he?"

"He's resting right now, but if you want to talk to Ted—"

"I want to see Sean." She caught a glimpse of Ted walking past a window in the back, and she charged forward. "Ted?"

Josie said, "I don't think that's a good idea!"

The old man chuckled as Juni stormed through the door.

Someone muttered, "This should be interesting."

"Ted?" Juni pushed through the swinging door and halted when she saw Sean in a hospital bed, hooked up to wires with his eyes closed. "Sean."

Her heart flopped down at her feet as he began to shake. Juni walked closer and reached for his hand. He had goose bumps all over his body, and his skin was ice-cold. His color was blanched, and she could see blue veins running under his skin. There was something otherworldly about him.

"Oh God." Juni wanted to cry, but she didn't want to upset him if he could hear her. "Sean, it's me. I'm here. Jena said you were asking for me."

There were bandages packed on his side, and his right arm was in a sling. The skin that wasn't pale white was blotchy red, blue, and green in various shades of bruising, and there was a deep cut that looked like a claw mark along his hairline.

"What happened to you?" She had assumed it was a car accident, but there was no bruise on his shoulder from the belt. No black eyes from an airbag. His face was unmarred except for the deep mark that looked like a slash.

"Juni, what are you doing back here?" Ted barked at her. "Caleb! Come get your sister before—"

"Why is he freezing?" Juni spun toward Ted, who was standing in a hallway next to the door she'd walked through. The building was air-conditioned, but it wasn't that cold. "His skin is like *ice*."

Ted's hair was pulled back in a severe bun, and she wore a white lab coat and a stethoscope around her neck. "Juni, I am taking care of him, okay? Sean has a unique medical condition that—"

"There's no way he should be this cold." This was ridiculous. She was getting Sean to a hospital if she had to call 911 herself. "Why is he still here? Why isn't he at a hospital?"

She felt his hand begin to shake, and she turned to him. "Sean, what's wrong?"

Ted nearly yelled. "Juni, you need to go."

"What is happening?" She pulled out her phone. "I'm calling an ambulance; he's having a seizure!"

"It's not a seizure." Ted was walking toward her, reaching for the hand that held Sean's fingers in a steel grip. "He's getting better. This is part of the healing process, but you need to go right now. He wouldn't want you—"

"Jena said he was asking for me, so I'm not leaving!" She felt frantic. Like she was in a horror movie. Why was no one acting normally? Why did she hear laughter from outside? Was that the Quinn clan? Fuck them! They didn't deserve Sean.

"I'm calling someone to come take him to a real..." Her words died as the fingers in her hand slipped away and she turned back to the bed.

He was gone. Sean was gone. Six foot and some inches of man was simply gone from the bed, and in his place was the coiled form of a diamondback rattlesnake.

"Holy fuck!" She jumped back, and the snake stretched toward her but didn't move farther. "Ted, where is Sean?"

The doctor sighed. "He's right there, honey. That's Sean. He's the snake."

The door squeaked again.

"Oh shit."

Juni turned to see her brother standing in front of the door with Jena beside him. Both of them had wide eyes and their gaze was fixed on Juni, not the live rattlesnake who was quickly slithering under the covers.

Ted plopped an old-fashioned hot-water bottle into the bed and piled a blanket on top of it. "Just huddle in there and sleep a while, dude. It's about time you shifted."

Juni's eyes were everywhere.

Her brother.

The snake.

Ted in her white coat.

The woman with dark hair, peeking through the door.

The snake.

Her breath was coming too fast. Sean had disappeared.

And in his bed was a snake that Ted was talking to like it was a friend.

Sean.

Snake.

Sean?

Snake.

Her head swam, and her vision went watery.

"Someone better catch her."

The entire room went black.

chapter
thirteen

THIS TOWN WAS BUILT *on secrets, shame, and trying to run from the past.*

Not just the town, Willow, the people.

Sean curled in his animal form, the world around him safely distant. He was concealed within a crevice in the sunbaked rocks, hiding from the world around him, secure in his burrow of sleep.

The pain was with him, but it was always with him, a gnawing, hungry thing that ate his entrails and made him run, made him work, made him swerve from any attachment or familial tie.

The pain in his body was a relief, an exorcism of the ache inside.

There was chaos outside his dark burrow, voices in the distance that were shouting and angry.

Better to stay away from all that.

He tried to fall deeper into sleep, but then he heard her voice.

"...no one going to tell me about this? I've been here for months!"

Juni.

A shiver of happiness slid through him, and he felt his tail shake.

"Oh fuck, did it just rattle?"

"Rude."

Dammit, was that his sister? He didn't want Maggie knowing Juni. Juniper Hawkins never needed to know his conniving sister, his bitter uncle, or the rest of his angry family. She was bright and happy and full of life. She didn't live her life in secret.

She didn't belong in the Springs.

"...I know it's Sean. I mean... I know what you're telling me even though it's completely *insane*."

"Juni, I think you're bleeding a little bit. Do you want me to bandage that?"

Bleeding?

Sean's body shifted before he willed it. The snake left the burrow and the monitor lizard reared hissing from the bed, whipping a massive tail across the sheets while arboreal claws tore into the mattress beneath him, shredding the material.

Something crashed, a woman screamed, and Sean's tongue flicked out to taste for danger.

Why was Juni bleeding?

The pain in his side was excruciating, but it barely registered in his primal brain. He flicked a forked tongue, tasting the air for threats.

Juni was there, but her scent told him she was terrified. Of what? Of who?

"Sean!" Ted shouted at him. "She cut her head when she fainted. That's what the bleeding is from. Calm down—you're scaring her."

He sat back on his haunches, his head angling toward Juni. He was scaring her? In this form, his vision was keener than his human eyes. He saw the spectrum of light around her, and she looked like a rainbow.

Blue lit her hair, her lips were bright red, and her skin was a vibrant soft brown the color of sunbaked sand. He settled down, keeping his eyes trained on her.

"Sean?" Her voice was shaking. "Sean?"

She doubted it was him, but he knew the pain would only get worse if he shifted back to his human form.

Juni held out a tentative hand. "Sean?"

She was frightened of him?

Rational Sean broke through his pained animal form. *Dumbass, of course she's scared of you. She's a normal human, not a freaky shifter like you.*

The realization hit him in a wave of fear and shame.

Juni knew what he was. He'd tried to keep his life secret for so many years, but now she knew. If was as if she were seeing him naked. Just as her fingers touched his skin, Sean shrank back, shifting back to his natural form.

The snake retreated to the crevice, hidden in the warm, dark rocks.

"Sean?"

Her voice was farther away.

"Let him sleep. He'll heal fastest in his natural form, okay? He's going to be fine. Let me get you a bandage. He probably got freaked out when he smelled your blood and thought you were in danger, which is why we got to see the big scary lizard."

"What was that?"

Maggie's voice broke through the fog. "We're not like the rest of these guys, okay? Quinns are tricky. We can shift into a lot of different forms, and that one was one of the worst. Monitor lizards are huge, fast, and venomous. If you see him in that form again, I'd run."

Run.

You should run.

Run away, Juni.

The pain sank into his bones, stretching and spreading through his body. It eased as it stretched, dulled by the haze of his system furiously healing.

Run away.

TED WAS SITTING at his bedside when he finally woke in his human form.

"H-how...?" He cleared his throat.

Ted handed him a glass of water. "Drink. You were out for two days."

He nodded as he took a sip. "Any permanent damage?" His voice sounded like he was an eighty-four-year-old smoker.

"You're gonna have a nice long scar on your side since you flipped out and shifted into a monitor lizard because Juni cut her forehead, but other than that, I don't see anything permanent."

A cheerful whistle came from the hallway, and a man with shocking red hair in a curly puff on his head walked through the doorway.

"Oh!" The strange man grinned when he saw Sean. "You're awake and in human form. Excellent. I have so many questions."

The man had a Scottish accent, and he looked like he was five seconds from melting into a puddle. He was wearing an open button-down work shirt over a sweat-soaked undershirt, and his face was the shade of a lobster.

Sean looked at Ted. "Who the hell is this?"

"It's my friend Fergus. He accidentally found out about me in med school. He can be trusted."

"But why is he *here*?"

Ted was scribbling something on a clipboard. "I brought him in for a consult after you shifted into a big-ass lizard and busted up your side again. The shift back to diamondback didn't correct the open wound, and I needed some help treating you."

"Funny thing." Fergus pulled up a chair next to Sean's bed. "I was always a bit of a reptile hobbyist even when I was studying medicine. So when I flunked out of medical school—"

"You brought a *failed* doctor in to see me. Great idea."

Ted rolled her eyes. "Get over yourself. He became a vet, Sean.

He specializes in herpetology and consults with all the major zoos. I needed help."

"I prefer animals to most humans." Fergus was bouncing his knee. "They seem to understand me better."

"Uh-huh."

The vet leaned forward. "I find your family fascinating."

"I bet you do." Sean shifted in the bed. His body ached, but not from injury. He felt completely healed, but he was stiff and more than a little sore. "How long was I a diamondback?"

Ted asked, "Do you remember anything that happened in Barstow?"

He closed his eyes and thought back. "I shifted to a gopher snake to cross the road because they're well camouflaged and they're fast. After that... I remember everything up until that bastard coyote tossed me into a wall."

Ted's eyes narrowed. "It ran off. Ollie wasn't sure if it was a shifter or a normal—"

"Shifter," Sean said. "Definitely shifter. One of theirs; he smelled wrong."

Fergus had blue eyes the size of saucers. "Fascinating."

Sean turned to the strange man. "Why are you here?"

Ted smacked his hand. "Giant-ass lizard, remember? Your family are the only cold-blooded animals in town. I needed help."

"Warmblood."

"Snake."

"Where's Juni?" She knew about him now; he remembered that much but not the details. "Is she still here?"

Did she run?

Is she staying with her brother?

Did they tell her everything?

Everything included Juni living for months in a town full of secret shapeshifters. Her brother being his own kind of strange shapeshifter himself and being married to a woman who turned into a bird on full moon nights.

Everything was Sean lying to her for years about who and what he was.

If she hadn't run screaming before, she likely would when it all sank in. If she could even bring herself to believe it. More than one human—when confronted by the supernatural—simply chose not to believe and put it down to hallucination or a nervous breakdown.

She wouldn't think that way.

You want to believe that. But wanting it doesn't make it true.

"So after the coyote threw you into a wall, you shifted back to human and Ollie had to grab a heavily bleeding naked man off the sidewalk in Barstow and rush him back here."

He cut his eyes toward Ted. "Did anyone from the Drifters see?"

She shook her head. "You were far enough away. He said there's probably a very confused clerk at the Quick Mart, but other than that, he doesn't think anyone noticed."

"The DiStefano guy was there, and they were talking about..." Sean glanced at Fergus, who was sitting rapt and watching Sean. "Maybe I'll fill you and Ollie in on all this when I'm out of here."

Ted glanced at Fergus. "Good idea. You took hours to shift into your natural form after Ollie brought you back. You had some organ damage and internal bleeding that I was having trouble treating in your human form, but once you shifted, it seemed to correct."

"Fascinating," mumbled Fergus.

Ted set down her clipboard. "That's true across the board for us, and I'm still not sure why, but I have to imagine that whatever transformation causes the shift in the first place realigns our bodies into the correct form for the animal, and in doing that—"

"Corrects the injury in the process. At least to a point."

"That's the only thing that makes sense."

Sean didn't really want to listen to the nerds analyze him, so he tried to change the subject. "I shifted into a monitor?"

"Yep." She popped her lips on the *P*. "Because Juni had a little-bitty cut on her head."

Wow, he was way more protective of that woman than he wanted to admit. Fuck. This was not good. His animal half was as territorial as his human half. Maybe more so.

Where was she? Did she even want to see him again? It was one thing to be confronted with a man who shifted into a burly wolf or a sleek mountain lion.

Sean took another, longer drink of water.

He turned into a snake. A cold-blooded, slithering reptile. People had fucking phobias about his animal.

No one had phobias about bears and their fluffy little ears.

Fergus was peering at him like he was a specimen. "Does your shift often depend on mood or is it always a conscious decision?"

Fuck you, Doctor. Sean closed his eyes, hoping Ted would get rid of this annoying-ass scientist. Even if he had helped Sean.

"Our natural forms are the ones that we shift to most commonly," Ted said. "But Quinns, in particular, are highly skilled at adapting to other animals in the same family."

"Any reptile?" Fergus directed the question to Sean.

"Lepidosaurs," Sean said. "No turtles. No crocs."

"But Ted said there is one desert tortoise in your extended family."

"Yes, and he can only shift into other tortoises. No lizards."

"Fascinating."

Ted added, "It's a little like the wolves and the foxes. Though I think that one's a bit more blurry around the edges. They're really different species."

Sean was tired again. "Ted, if you're gonna have academic conversations about me, can you do it in another room? I'm starting to feel like an experiment."

"My apologies!" Fergus rose and clapped his hands. "Lovely meeting you while you're in human form, Mr. Quinn."

"Sean."

"Sean it is." The man seemed to be pathologically cheerful. "I'll say goodbye for now. I'm meeting your lovely sister at some-place called the Blackbird Diner for lunch." Fergus was all smiles. "So delightful."

Wait, Maggie was meeting *this* dude? This walking, talking ball of wholesome-nerd energy? "Uh..."

"I'm off!" Fergus waved from the door. "Ted, can I bring you back a sandwich or some other nibble since you're stuck here with a patient?"

"You're sweet, Ferg, but Alex is bringing me lunch from the hotel when he drops off the baby."

"And I'm missing the adorable Luna!" Fergus cocked his head. "So there's really no way of knowing if she'll shift into cat or wolf until...?"

"Nope." Ted shrugged. "She'll be a cat. Obviously."

"Obviously." Sean smirked.

"Righty-oh," Fergus said. "Either way, she will be a delight."

The door swung closed and the exam room was quiet.

Sean stared at the door. "Did he say he was having lunch with *my* sister?"

"He keeps calling her charming, and I'm trying to figure out Maggie's angle."

"Does he have money? Is he secretly a duke or something?"

"Definitely not, and as for money, Fergus just has the normal veterinary kind, so not really any at all."

Sean narrowed his eyes. "Just make it very clear that he's an old friend and hopefully she won't decide to piss off the cats."

"Okay, sure. That'll work. Probably." Ted stood. "I'll let you sleep."

"Thanks."

"You're welcome."

He caught her hand. "No, thank you. Really. I know I'm a horrible patient, and I know all of us are kind of a nightmare to treat when we get hurt."

She smiled. "Luckily you guys are slippery, so it doesn't happen too often."

"We're not slippery, we're scaly. There's a difference."

"Uh-huh." She started toward the door. "Just so you know, Juni *was* here, and she *was* freaked out."

His smile fell, and a bitter taste hit the back of his tongue. "Yeah, I figured."

"But she was not scared of you, she was scared *for* you."

Sean didn't say a word.

"I'm just saying." Ted glanced at her clipboard again. "There's a difference."

chapter
fourteen

JUNI SAT NEXT to Sean in the clinic recovery room, the same room where she'd seen him shift into a snake the day before. Then a really big, scary-as-shit dinosaur. Then back to a snake.

And now he looked like the beautiful man she knew.

She could hear Ted puttering in the other end of the clinic with the baby strapped onto her chest. There weren't any other patients in the room, and three beds sat empty, their curtains pulled to the side so light filled the room.

He looked like the same man she'd known for years. His hair was the dark black she knew, his skin had its normal color again, and his long, ought-to-be-illegal dark lashes fluttered open as he stretched his arm toward a beam of light.

He saw her as he woke, and his lips curved into a smile.

"Hey." Juni kept her voice soft.

He blinked, recognized her, and his smile fell. "Juni."

"How are you feeling?"

Sean frowned. "How are *you* feeling?"

"Hmm." That was a complicated question. "I don't think I'm hallucinating anymore."

"Okay." His tone of voice signaled caution.

She kept her eyes on a freckle that sat on his shoulder. He had a few freckles, and she'd always liked them. "I had a long talk with Jena. And Ted. And Allie and Ollie."

"Ridiculous fucking names."

Juni shrugged. "I think it's cute. It fits them; they're adorable."

"He's a grizzly bear."

She nodded. "Yes. I did see that. I mean, not right in front of my face because I think he's a little shy about nudity, but he went in the bathroom and came out a bear, so I..." She kept nodding. "Yeah, the bear thing was made clear."

"Jena?"

"Shifted into a hawk." Juni felt like a bobblehead. "Weird. Yeah, I got the full zoological breakdown and then the warning never to drink from the spring at the center of town."

Juni had learned that the spring in the middle of Cambio Springs was the reason the seven original families who had settled there had shifted into animals in the first place. Months of drinking the spring water had turned ordinary humans into something... other.

It was the reason that Sean had hidden who he was from her. The reason she'd felt secrets surrounding her since the time she'd rolled into town.

"Did you and your brother—?"

"We talked, but I'm pretty sure I have *not* gotten the whole story there." She closed her eyes. "Listen, Sean—"

"Are you still bleeding?" He sat up and craned his neck to see her temple. "Ted said you were bleeding."

"I sort of fainted when you first turned into a snake, and I'm not proud of that but—"

"Completely understandable."

"Yeah." She sat back in her chair, crossing her arms over her chest. "I kind of feel like that's a natural reaction to a..."

"An unnatural situation?"

She nodded again. "Yeah. That's a good way of putting it."

He took a deep breath and let it out slowly. "I'm not a bear."

"Nope." She looked out the window. "You are definitely not a bear. Or a wolf apparently. Or a mountain lion."

"Or a desert tortoise."

She squeezed her eyes shut for a moment. "Really?"

"It suits my cousin. It's hard to explain."

"Right." She let out a long, slow breath and kept her eyes on the scene outside, which was nothing really. The clinic was on the edge of town, so the only thing out the window was a Joshua tree in the distance. "I'm going to assume that this is the reason you always put the brakes on a relationship anytime we got close."

His voice was rough when he responded. "Part of it."

"Just part of it?" She swung her gaze back to him. "What else don't I know, Sean? For fuck's sake, what else is there for me to find out, *because I'm about at my limit*." She heard her voice rising, heard the slightly manic tone, but she couldn't help it.

She'd just been informed that shapeshifters—stories she'd only heard about in books and movies—were real. Humans she knew and loved turned into animals, and something weird was going on with her older brother and his entire life—a life she'd thought she was part of—felt like a giant fucking secret.

"Juni—"

"Would you have ever told me?" She blinked. "I mean, my brother lives here. I'm not some random chick you met on a job overseas, Sean. Would you ever have let me in on this... thing? Your life?"

His voice was rough. "You were never supposed to come here."

"Got it." She sat back, uncrossed her arms, and reached for the backpack by her feet. "So that's a no. You would never have told me, and all the times you implied that something might be possible someday if only things were different—"

"What do you want me to say?" Sean tossed off the sheet and swung his legs over the side of the bed, leaving him shirtless and in a pair of thin boxers that left nothing to the imagination. "What? How?"

God, she hated that he was so stunning. She hated that she felt like such a tiny, homely nothing next to him. He was tall and elegant and beautiful, and she was Juni Hawkins from Albuquerque with a too-broad face, a stocky body, dull-brown eyes, and red streaks in her hair.

"You want me to tell you that I would have poured out my family and my town's secrets because I have feelings for you?" Sean spat out the words. "You want me to say that I should've trusted you because your brother lives here? You know who killed my cousin? Josie's *brother*."

She felt something in her chest cave in. "You're comparing me to the man who murdered your cousin?"

"I'm saying that blood does *not* equal loyalty, okay?" He pointed at the door. "You've met my family. They're thieves and con artists who would stab me in the back if they got the chance, but the one thing I know they won't do is betray me to anyone on the outside. *That's* what I know, Juni. That's the way I was raised. Trust..." He put his hand over his heart. "You think I know anything about trust?"

"Right." She swallowed the tears that wanted to clog her throat and stood. "I should go."

"You shouldn't have to live with any of this." His voice sounded desperate. "You should be with someone who doesn't have to keep secrets and doesn't have to worry about mob bosses destroying the single place in the world where freaks like me feel safe. Why would I want to put any of that on you when you could have a normal life?"

She turned at the door. "Who ever said I wanted a normal life? Did I? Or is that what you think I *should* have because you didn't have it?"

He swallowed and looked away.

"From the moment I left home, I have wanted nothing less than an *extraordinary* life." Tears fell down her cheeks, but she kept talking. She had one chance to get this out, because the moment she left him, she was going to fall apart.

"I wanted *you*." She forced the words out because dammit, she was tired of secrets. "You should have trusted me because I *loved* you. You should have trusted me because I've spent years being patient, accepting the scraps of a relationship you gave me—then friendship when there was nothing else. Because I saw the man you are and not the man you think the world sees." She sniffed and couldn't stop the laugh that burst from her throat. "I don't even mind snakes, you ass."

She shook her head and walked out of the clinic. He said her name, but she was done.

Finally she was done.

JUNI WAS THROWING things in her Volvo when Jena came out to talk to her.

"Don't go yet." Her sister-in-law kept her voice low. "Please don't go, Juni."

She dashed the tears from her eyes. "I feel like a joke. I feel like everyone was laughing at me behind my back." She sniffed.

"We weren't." Jena put a hand on her shoulder. "I promise we weren't. We get so used to hiding—"

"I was here for months!" She spun around and confronted her sister-in-law. "How long would it have taken for you to tell me? What about when Becca shifted? Would you have told me then?"

Jena opened her mouth, then closed it. She looked like she was in pain.

"Did you even *consider* telling me?" Juni put a hand on her chest. It ached with the weight of secrets.

"Yes!" Jena blinked back tears. "I told Caleb we should have told you right away. I told him that I didn't think you'd freak out but Sean—"

"What about Sean?" Juni was shouting. She took a deep breath. "Are you telling me that Sean told Caleb he couldn't trust me?"

"He just didn't know how long you would be in town, and he told Caleb that it might be better to wait."

"For him, you mean." Juni grimaced and started packing her car again. "Not for me. That was for Sean. And maybe my brother too, because I know he's not telling me something. I know he's holding back."

Jena pressed her lips together. "If he is, it's because it's something really personal and he's worried about how you're going to see him."

She shook her head. "I don't know what that means."

"It means he loves you and he wants you in his life," Jena said. "And he's worried you won't want that when you know—"

"Jena, stop."

Juni spun around to see Caleb standing on the porch. She marched over to him. "Tell me. Stop this now. Stop hiding things and stop making me question our relationship. I thought I had a brother again."

"You do." He kept his voice low and even. "But when I came here, I was the same as you. I didn't know anything about this place. I drank the water, and it unlocked... something. For a long time, I fought it because I thought it was evil. I remembered my uncle's stories. I remembered Mom and how she hated me after Charlie..."

Died.

Was killed.

Was killed by police.

Was killed by Caleb's gun.

Juni blinked back tears. Charlie had been her bright, laughing cousin, another older brother who teased her and carried her on his shoulder when she was tiny. But even though Juni was young, she'd sensed that there was something deeply wrong in the way Charlie laughed and the shine in his eyes.

"Charlie wasn't your fault, Caleb. He wasn't. Drugs killed him, not you."

Caleb closed his eyes and looked down. For a moment his hat hid his face, but Juni could see the way his body shifted, see the slight broadening in the shoulders and the shimmer that looked like a mirage as the hat tilted up and her dead cousin looked back at her.

Juni gasped and fell back, falling into the side of the car while Jena grabbed her and wrapped her arms around Juni's shoulders.

"What are you thinking?" Jena shouted.

Some forgotten part of Juni's brain brought old words to her lips. Curses for the witch. For something even more unspeakable. She bit them back, hearing her mother's voice in her head and a warning from her uncle.

Once you say a thing, you give it life.

Caleb looked at her through Charlie's eyes, but the voice he used was her brother's. "I can't change this, and it's better that you know."

"You..." She stumbled over the words. "You're a—"

"Don't!" Jena put a hand over Juni's mouth. "You know the power of that word, and you know your brother isn't evil. It's not the same. It's nothing like that."

Charlie's eyes looked back at her, full of sorrow and pain. And in the blink of an eye, he was Caleb again. An angled face instead of rounder cheeks, deep brown eyes watching her with hurt behind them.

The legends of the skin walker, the *yee naaldlooshii*, were some of the most frightening and disturbing stories in Navajo mythology. The skin walker was an evil witch who could take on the form of an animal, and even in some cases, another human being.

Though Juni's mother had separated herself from her Native family, Juni had been fascinated with the myths and legends her older cousins had whispered to her when her mother wasn't around.

She'd only ever thought of them as that. Myths. Legends. Frightening stories for children, not anything close to reality.

Juni's heart turned over, and a punch of guilt hit her in the chest. This was Caleb, who would do anything for her. Caleb, who had tried his best to be her protector, who had welcomed her into his home without question.

Caleb kept his eyes on the ground. "Do you really not understand why I'd hide it?"

Juni ran to him, throwing her arms around his shoulders because of course she did. Of course she understood why he'd hidden the truth. "I don't understand what's happening here. I don't understand any of this. But I love you. I love you, Caleb. You're a good man. A good brother. A wonderful father."

His arms wrapped around her, and his embrace was so tight he nearly crushed her ribs. "Enough." His voice was rough. "No more secrets, Juni. We need to tell you everything. Then you'll understand."

chapter
fifteen

SEAN FELT BACK to normal by the next morning, but his stubborn sister refused to let him go back to a creaky old half-renovated Airstream.

"You have got to be kidding me." Maggie's eyes were cutting. "Just shut up and get in the truck, asshole. You're not gonna hide out in that creaky old trailer when it's hot and you almost died."

"I didn't almost die." He was dressed in the same clothes he'd shifted out of a few days before, and he was more tired than he wanted to admit. His sister didn't need to know that though.

"We turned the old parlor into another bedroom, so there's one downstairs you can take." Maggie started up the truck and put on a pair of aviator sunglasses that reminded Sean of their father.

"Do you ever talk to Dad?"

Maggie jerked her head toward him, then shook it and looked over her shoulder as she started backing up the truck. "That's a question."

"That's not an answer."

"Why the fuck do you think I'd be in touch with Glenn? He never had any use for female children."

Sean muttered, "He didn't have much use for male ones either."

"Last I heard, he was somewhere in Colorado, scamming rich East Coast women out of money at the ski resorts."

"Yeah, that sounds like him."

She shrugged. "He's not bothering me. I don't bother him."

Maggie had lost over fifty grand when Allie's late husband asked her to stake him in a poker match. Joe had won the pot, but then he'd taken off with the money, hiding it in the walls of the resort before it was finished.

Sean's sister had found the money but hadn't told anyone, hoping Sean and his friends would take care of the men who killed Joe and she'd be able to keep all the cash. In the end, Ollie and Sean had found it and Maggie lost everything.

"How'd you get all that money in the first place?"

Maggie frowned. "What money?"

"The money you used to stake Joe in that game."

She rolled her eyes. "This again?"

"I'm just curious."

"I'm not a whore like Dad if that's what you're wondering." She cut her eyes at him as they made their way through town and back to the old two-story house where Maggie lived with three other Quinn girls. "I'm a pretty damn good pool hustler though."

Sean smirked. "Can't hate that."

"It paid the bills for a long time." She turned in to the drive. "Listen, if you're going to stay here, you need to figure out something to do."

"You worried about me getting bored, sis?"

"I'm worried about the fucking money." She tipped her sunglasses up and leaned on the steering wheel. "I know I gave you shit about leaving, but your income filled in a lot of gaps the old man ignored. There are about fifteen kids under eighteen in the clan that don't have parents who are worth a damn. I promised you I'd live on the straight and narrow when I came back, and I do okay doing the landscaping thing at the resort, but my landscaping money isn't going to support fifteen kids even if I do make it stretch."

He hadn't pinned Maggie for being the responsible one who thought about paying the bills, but he'd been gone a long time.

Sean stared at the front of the house, noticing the peeling paint and three beat-up cars in the drive. "I could sell my house in Laguna."

"That's dumb. The money will run out eventually, and you'll have lost an asset." She cocked her head. "You could rent it out though. Or do short-term vacation rentals. Lake Gantry lives in Long Beach now. Did you know that?"

Lake was a distant cousin who shifted into a Gila on full moon nights. "What's he doing in Long Beach?"

"Working. He could probably manage a rental for you if that's something you're interested in, and he's a hustler. He'd do it for a cut of the profit."

He frowned. "You think I should rent my house out?"

"Vacation rentals in Laguna Beach for a house the size of yours average over three hundred and fifty a night, even in the off-season." She turned off the truck and opened her door. "Over five hundred a night in the summer. If you managed to rent it out even half the month, that's over five grand coming in on the regular."

Sean popped the truck door open and eased his way out of the vehicle. "You've thought about this."

"It's sitting there empty, and you're paying the mortgage. You're the one eating into your savings. I'm just saying rent it out, pay the mortgage with that, and whatever is left over you can use as income or help with the kids."

It was a good idea. Even when he was living there, he was overseas half the time. He'd bought the place for a song before prices in the area went crazy, and he'd used every spare minute and dollar to fix it up. The house was only a few blocks from the beach. Maggie was right; it should be an asset.

"Okay, I'll set it up." He walked onto the porch to see clothes hanging on racks all over. "You guys can't afford a clothes dryer?"

She sneered. "You think I'm going to let those girls dry their clothes in the machine when it's this hot outside?" She walked into the house, shaking her head. "I swear to God, rich people like to set money on fire."

Sean walked into the house and saw his uncle sitting at the kitchen table. Two of the younger Quinn girls were sitting with him, both looking a little confused.

"Hey, Uncle Joe." Maggie's voice held a note of caution. "What's up?"

The old man rose. "Just checking on my niece and nephew." He walked over to Sean. "You a hundred percent again?"

"I'm good." He felt Maggie at his side. "What's up?"

"I don't like you helping out that bear. Seems to me like all these shenanigans with the Lobo fella are the wolves' problem if you ask me. Don't have nothin' to do with us Quinns."

Typical. "We all live in the same town. If Lobo has a grudge against one of us, he has a grudge against us all."

"Girls." Maggie nodded at the two younger women. "You two fold that laundry upstairs, will you?"

"Yes, Maggie."

"I have homework."

"Then do your homework first." She walked to the hallway door after the girls ran out, shut it, and opened the fridge. "I think lemonade would be good, don't you?"

Sean kept his eyes on his uncle. "Is it that sugary, powdered crap?"

"Of course it is."

"Sounds delicious." Sean walked over and sat at the table. "You want some lemonade?"

Old Quinn narrowed his eyes, but he didn't move. "We have our own troubles to see to, Sean. Leave this Lobo fella to the Campbells and the McCanns."

Sean looked up when Maggie set a glass in front of him with three floating ice cubes. "Thanks, Maggie."

"No problem." She poured herself a glass and leaned against the counter.

Sean took a long drink. "I already told the town at the last meeting that I'd take care of it. Campbells and McCanns offered to help. We're in it. It's done."

Old Quinn cursed. "Why the hell do something that stupid, boy?"

The sting never went away even when he was long past being a boy. "I'm not being stupid. I'm taking care of business. This Lobo guy is a criminal, and our clan is part of why he was attracted to the Springs in the first place. It's partly our responsibility."

"That's some bullshit right there," Old Quinn said. "McCanns brought him in."

"Not true, and even if it were, it doesn't matter." Sean kept his voice even. "Our kids need this place, maybe even more than the others. You think the world is going to accept a bunch of kids who have scales when the full moon comes out?" Sean kept his eyes on the man across from him. "Uncle Joe, we're taking care of it. It might help if you told us what you know about Efrén Abano."

The old man shook his head. "Don't know nothin' about that man."

"You're lying," Maggie said. "I can smell it."

Sean glanced over his shoulder. "So can I."

"I'm not putting up with this shit." Old Quinn shoved away from the table and stood up. "You kids think you know everything? Fine. I'm out. Maybe I'll go take a long vacation somewhere cool."

Yeah, that was likely. Sean didn't think Old Quinn had left town since 1975. Maybe longer. The furthest that old lizard had gotten was Indio to hit the bingo room at the casino.

"Okay." Sean played along. "You wanted me to take over, so I'm back. Me and Maggie will take care of the kids."

"Fine." There was a note of panic in his voice. "You do that. See if I care."

"Okay." Sean sipped his lemonade. "Maggie, this is delicious."

"I'll mix up some more."

Old Quinn wavered in the doorway of the kitchen before he turned on his heel and stormed out. A few minutes later, they heard a pickup start down the street.

Maggie walked to the window and peeked out. "That old bastard parked behind Nelson's so we wouldn't see his truck. Do you think he'll actually leave town?"

Sean sighed. "He's not going anywhere. Ignore what he says. He likes being around the family too much. He'll stick around, but he is lying about knowing Lobo."

"Yeah, that's not even a question."

He kicked his feet out. "Your turn. What do you know about this guy?"

"I know he's a rich asshole who throws his money around. I know he took a bunch of cash from the cartels to expand into Vegas. And I don't know how he's managed to keep his name completely off police radar, but he's probably paying someone off. Plenty of dirty cops in Vegas."

"Yeah, that tracks." He finished his lemonade and thought about Willow's advice a few days before.

Maggie wanted to be here. She was already taking care of the kids. She was doing more to straighten out her life than Sean was if he was being honest.

"Jena texted me earlier." He tapped his finger on the table. "The gang is having a meeting at their house tonight. You want to come?"

His sister perked up. "You *want* me to come to a meeting of the cool kids?"

"You know as much as any of them about this," he said. "Maybe more. Allie will have to deal."

Maggie shrugged. "Allie and I are cool. She doesn't hold a grudge. The bear is another story."

"Just stay out of Ollie's way and you won't get squished."

MEETING AT JENA and Caleb's house was always an exercise in juggling kids. Three of Allie's were there, but Jena put the two oldest boys in charge of the younger ones and stuck them in the den with pizza and a movie, leaving the adults to gather on the back porch, which sat between the kitchen and the Airstream.

Sean sat next to Maggie with Ted and Alex beside them. Ollie sat in a lump across the way, glaring at Maggie while Caleb and Jena brought chips and salsa to the table. There were burgers on the grill, and Juni and Allie walked out of the kitchen, carrying trays of veggies and buns.

Juni's eyes met Sean's for a moment, and then he looked away.

Maggie muttered under her breath, "Did you know she was going to be here?"

"I didn't." He'd half expected her to be back in Los Angeles, but it wasn't his house and Jena could invite whoever she wanted. "Her brother probably filled her in."

"So it's a real group project now." Maggie smiled. "This should be fun."

Fun? That was one word for it. Not the word Sean would have chosen, but it was a word.

"How about we get started?" Caleb stood, his hands hanging in his jeans pockets. "I've got some news, and then I think it's time we started sharing what we know."

chapter
sixteen

"SO THAT'S what the DiStefanos are worried about," Sean added. "Not *technically* the DiStefanos—I know, Alex—but the people taking over their routes and protection rackets."

Juni watched from the side, sitting quietly next to Jena and taking everything in as her brother's friends talked around her. The conversation answered a lot of the questions she'd had about Cambio Springs since the night of the town hall meeting, but she already had more.

"So Lobo and whoever he's working with are pushing out small producers that the local guys depend on," Caleb said. "We think to clear the way for suppliers from the south?"

Ted spoke up. "That makes the most sense. Cameron DiStefano is out, and he doesn't want anything to do with the illegal parts of the business anymore. That leaves a huge opportunity for new players, and Lobo seems like the front-runner."

"That fits with what I've heard from down south," Caleb said. "There are about three gangs battling for power in Northern Mexico at the moment, and the violence seems like it's being prodded along by someone in the States. The federal agent my buddy put me in contact with didn't have Efrén Abano's name— or the name Lobo—but he said that he'd look into it and that the pattern would fit with what Mexican authorities believe is happening."

"So they think one of these gangs is trying to establish a new corridor in the desert?" Sean asked.

"Yes," Caleb said. "And with the mob pulling back from their territory here, there's a power vacuum."

Everyone on the deck fell silent; Juni could hear the kids in the den listening to a movie with a singing animal of one sort or another. In the distance, a coyote howled.

A regular coyote or a shifter? She'd never know for sure anymore.

Ollie's low voice rumbled across the silence. "That doesn't explain why Lobo cares about the Springs."

"That seems personal," Sean said. "I don't know that poking around law enforcement is going to help with that part."

Juni raised her hand.

Alex smiled at her. "You don't need to raise your hand. Any ideas are welcome. Might be good to get some new thoughts on this since we're all chasing our tails."

Sean muttered, "Speak for yourself, Spot."

"Boys." Ted rolled her eyes. "Juni, do you have a question?"

"Has anyone talked to this guy?" She reached for the beer Jena handed her and tried to ignore Maggie Quinn's piercing eyes. Sean's sister had been mostly silent, but Juni could feel her stare. "Has anyone tried talking to Efrén Abano to ask him how he knows about you guys?"

"I asked," Sean said. "Walked right into his club in Vegas. He hinted at some old grudge, but he wouldn't say more."

"What did he say *exactly*?" Juni persisted. "Do you remember?"

Sean sighed. "He said... 'You only have the word of a traitor that I want revenge, and you only have the word of old men that they've never heard of me.' And that staying away from the Springs was impossible."

"You never told us that before." Alex leaned forward. "So he's saying that the council knows who he is?" He looked at Jena, Ollie, and Ted. "Have we asked the elders?"

Ted said, "You don't think they would tell us if they knew who Lobo was?"

"Maybe," Jena said. "But we all know that sometimes we have to pry the truth from them."

"Maybe we need to be more direct," Ollie said. "I agree with Alex, that sounds like he's got a grudge, and he expects the elders to know what it's about."

"So we start digging." Ted nodded decisively. "We start digging into the history. There are archives in the library."

Jena said, "We need to be more direct with our parents and our grandparents. Ask them questions. Don't let them avoid it. Tell them that the safety of the kids might be at stake and hope they'll listen."

Maggie snorted. "Are you telling us we have to make peace with the old man after we just pissed him off?"

"We need to at least try," Sean said.

Juni guessed they were talking about their great-uncle, the leathery man who had been at the hospital.

"I'll help Ted search through the archives," Alex said. "And there are McCann family histories too. Journals, letters, things like that. I'll get at digging them out. I'm the alpha now; my father can't say anything."

There was a general rumbling about that. Juni raised a hand.

Alex smiled at her. "You really don't need to raise a hand if you have a question."

"I'm just wondering, do all the clans have an... alpha?"

Ted visibly snorted and had to cover her mouth. "Sorry." She cleared her throat and pressed her lips together. "Sorry."

Alex rolled his eyes. "The cats do not, though the clan does have an elder on the council."

"Who is my mother," Ted said. "I'll work on her. But I'm not going to lie, we're secretive by nature, and we've had more than one member banished from the town."

"Banished?" Juni frowned. "What do you mean?"

Ollie said, "Meaning they get sent away. If they've harmed someone in the community. If they've committed a crime and we can't find a solution."

"It's rare," Allie said. "But it happens. Sometimes it's the only alternative to..."

Everyone clammed up.

"To what?" Juni sat up straight.

"Execution," Caleb said. "There was a murderer executed not long after I moved here."

"Executed?" Juni's head swung toward Sean, who was looking at the ground, then to Caleb, then to Jena. "You mean he was killed?"

"She," Jena said. "What are our options, Juni? Send a shifter to human authorities and then face questions we can't answer when they turn into a bobcat on the next full moon?"

"Quinns go to jail," Maggie said. "Happens all the time."

"Because you can all shift to something small enough to hide if you want to," Ollie said. "Hell, most of you could escape a maximum-security prison in a day."

Maggie smirked. "That's true."

Sean and his sister exchanged an amused look.

"Cats, wolves, bears." Ollie shook his head. "We don't have that option. And honestly? If it came to it, I'd rather die than be locked in a cell."

"Agreed." Alex looked at Juni. "It's our way. It's old justice, and there's a reason for it. If you can't deal with that, you should probably leave. No hard feelings. We trust you not to say anything. But know this: Lobo will not be going to jail. Whatever happens, this will be settled by the old laws. Not human ones."

Juni had never heard anything more medieval in her life. Then again, when it came down to it, she could see their reasons.

Could she live with them?

"Willow already found some records," Sean said. "Letters. That's why she went back east. She's looking into the history of the family."

Alex frowned, and the others muttered. No one else seemed to know that.

Willow.

That was the "friend" who'd been at Sean's trailer the day Juni left for Costa Rica.

"What if they don't know?" Allie finally spoke. "I mean, what if there was something that happened to Lobo or his family, but whatever it was happened so long ago that no one remembers it?"

"It's possible," Jena said. "We don't talk about the past much."

Juni's interest was piqued. "Why not? You have such a unique history. I'd think it would be valuable to remember."

"Secrets," Sean muttered. "This town was built on them."

"We need secrets to protect ourselves," Ted added. "And to protect our children. Just like the old laws. Not all secrets are bad, Sean."

"But every secret is dangerous," Juni said. "Right now this guy is using your fear of exposure to intimidate you and control you, right?" She looked around the deck and saw eight grown adults afraid of one individual. "You need to get some dirt on him. Find out some of his secrets." She sat back and crossed her arms. "Go back to Vegas. Make him a little bit afraid, you know?"

The corner of Caleb's mouth turned up. "You think it's easy to scare a drug lord?"

"But he's not a drug lord, is he?" Juni said. "You said he was a property developer or something."

"The problem is," Sean started, "Lobo probably knows who every single one of us is. We can smell shifters when we meet them. There isn't a way to hide that."

Juni shrugged. "So I'll go." She looked at Caleb. "Caleb and I can go. I doubt he'll know what to make of us."

"Absolutely not," Sean snapped.

Juni felt her hackles rise. Well, not real hackles. She was suddenly very aware that there were people in the conversation with *actual* hackles, but hers were only metaphorical. "Sean, you don't get a say in this. This affects my family too, and I'm offering my help. You'd all be foolish to turn me down."

Caleb took a deep breath, but he didn't say anything.

"It's a stupid idea." Sean glared. "You have no idea what you're dealing with. How would you even—?"

"Alex said he's a property developer, right?" Juni looked around. "I just so happen to be a travel photographer. Why do you think he's in Vegas?"

Alex muttered, "He's taking over a hotel south of the city and expanding it. Lake Las Vegas area. Hotel and planned community in the works, folding it into his existing chain in Mexico."

Juni turned to Sean and smiled. "What a surprise."

Sean was about to burst. "This is... It's just not a good—"

"Idea?" Ted asked. "Why not? She's smart and she has a natural in. Juni's idea could work. We'd know more than we know now at least. Right now we're flying blind."

Allie raised her hand. "I think it's a good idea too. If she wants to go." Allie leaned forward. "But you absolutely do not have to if you don't want to, Juni. It could be really dangerous."

Ollie was nodding. "I wouldn't send anyone on their own, but with Caleb—"

"Are you guys out of your minds?" Sean stood up. "Juni isn't one of us. She doesn't have claws. She can't shift and burrow or hide." He spun toward Jena. "She can't fly away. You cannot be in favor of this idea."

Jena raised both eyebrows. "I don't think it's my right to say yes or no. Juni's an adult and she's right—it is a good idea, and Caleb can go with her."

Sean turned to his sister, but Maggie only shrugged. "Sorry,

Sean. I agree with Juni. If we want to find out more, she's probably the best one to go."

"I can talk to my editor," Juni said. "Poke around about the property he's developing and say I want to do a profile. There will be something, and I'll come in looking like a travel reporter wanting to do a puff piece."

"Then I'm going too," Sean blurted. "I think this is irrational, but if Juni's going, I'm going too."

"You can't go," Caleb said. "He knows who you are."

"I'll stay hidden, okay?" He gave Juni a dirty look. "I know how to hide."

"I don't need you to go with me," Juni said. "In fact, I'd really rather you didn't—"

"Don't care." He walked to the sliding glass doors and yanked them open. "If you're going, I'm going with you. It is not negotiable."

JUNI SAT in the folding chair outside her trailer, watching the stars and sipping her third beer of the night. The meeting had folded soon after Sean had stormed into the house. Maggie followed him silently, and the two took off in her old Bronco. After that, the families gathered sleepy children, calmed hyperactive ones, and made their way to dusty vehicles to find their way home.

Caleb wandered out on the back porch, holding a longneck. "Kids are in bed."

She patted the chair next to her. "Join me for a drink?"

Her brother walked over silently and sat next to her.

They sat quietly for a while, and Juni enjoyed that. It was one of the things that had always made her relish time with her brother. The man knew how to be quiet.

After half his beer was gone, he spoke. "I'm backing you up on this plan, but you know I have my reservations."

"I'm somewhat surprised Sean didn't turn into a dinosaur again."

"Jena turned into an eagle once. Claws. Beak. The whole thing. Seriously freaked me out."

The corner of her mouth turned up. "How'd we fall in love with a couple of animals, huh?"

Caleb was silent again. He took another few drinks of beer. "Are you?"

"Am I?"

He turned to her. "In love with him."

Juni sighed. "Yeah, but that doesn't mean anything really. You can love someone and they don't love you back."

"It means something, Jun." Caleb looked up at the sky. "I don't know Sean as well as Jena does, but I don't think him loving you back is the issue. He'd be an idiot not to love you."

He said it so honestly her heart ached. "You're sweet to say that. I can be a pain in the ass though. I'm kind of reckless, and I have a hard time keeping my mouth shut. Not about important stuff like the existence of shapeshifters or anything, but if you and Jena have another baby, do not tell me and expect me to be quiet about it. I suck at surprise parties too. Terrible. And I tend to jump into things without thinking it all the way through, which is why I somehow roped you into going to Las Vegas with me to investigate this Lobo guy, so if you don't want to, you better—"

"Juni, shut up." Caleb sighed. "Stop trying to change the subject."

She didn't say anything, because she was absolutely hoping that her older brother was going to forget that she'd confessed to loving Sean Quinn.

"He'd be a fool not to love you," Caleb continued. "The problem is—especially in this place—you love someone, you get their whole clan along with them. With me and Jena? Well, it's a pretty small family. But there are a lot of snakes out here. A *lot* of them."

"And they don't have the best reputation."

"Unfortunately, they do not." He took another long drink of his beer. "That's no reflection on Sean. But that doesn't keep the baggage from traveling with him."

"I know that." Her heart hurt a little bit. Or maybe a lot. "That's why it doesn't have to mean anything. I know I love him, but I'm not falling into his arms or anything like that. I know that's not how real life works. He always said that's why nothing could happen with us. Even before I knew about him. Like, about all of him. He knows he's not a good bet."

Caleb sighed. "Fuck."

"Yeah, it's not the greatest situation." Juni set her beer bottle down. "But then again, neither is having a supernatural sociopath stalking your town, and I'm willing to help out with that, so who knows what might happen with Sean Quinn?"

Her brother turned to her. "You scare me sometimes. You honestly do."

"You're not the first person who's said that to me, and I doubt you'll be the last."

chapter
seventeen

GOING to Las Vegas with Juni and her older brother was hardly the way that Sean had pictured returning to Sin City, but what could he say? He was apparently a sucker for punishment.

He tossed his clothes into a duffel bag after Maggie and his younger cousins had carefully folded them. "I don't know how long this is going to take. We'll stay someplace cheap unless Juni gets comped somewhere."

Maggie was lounging in an old recliner near the door. "You know the girls folded those nicely for you."

"And all I have is a duffel bag, so they're going to get wrinkled." He rolled his eyes. "I told you they didn't need to wash my laundry."

"Well, they're being punished, so I told them they had to."

He glanced up. "For what?"

Maggie waved a hand. "I'll fill you in when you get back. I already talked to the school about it. It's taken care of, but they're going to be doing a lot of chores. Anything you need done at the trailer?"

"They know how to polish wheels?"

She smiled. "They can learn."

Sean sat on the sofa and looked at his sister. "You're good at this."

She frowned. "What?"

"Managing these kids. Keeping them on track. Riding herd on 'em."

She shrugged. "Someone has to do it. I'm going to talk to the old man while you're gone so I can try to pry family history out of him, but that'll probably just piss him off more."

"Do what you can." Sean rubbed his hands over his face. "I already called Lake about moving some of my personal stuff into the storage area in my garage in Laguna. He thinks I should be able to get some renters in there within a month."

"See? Told you he'd be good at it."

"He might be stealing my speakers, but yeah, I think it'll work. For now." And his house—the one place that had been his sanctuary—would be invaded by strangers looking to party in Laguna Beach.

Maggie could read his expression. "It's only temporary. As soon as this Lobo situation is dealt with, you can go home and get back to your life. Hook up with the chief's sister and go on international adventures together."

He glanced at her. "Yeah, right."

Maggie rolled her eyes. "Why not? Stop being a martyr, you asshole. We don't want your life here, okay?" She gave him a toothy grin, her canines just a little bit extended. "We really want your money more."

Sean couldn't stop the snort. "I swear—"

"You don't want to be here." Her voice was blunt. "You're dying to get away. It's fine. We don't take it personally. You just don't have the stomach for small-town life. I'll take care of things, okay? I'm not a stupid kid anymore. We were doing okay before you came back."

He stared at the floor. "I always thought Marcus…"

"Marcus would have been better than me." Her voice had lost none of the sharpness. "You're goddamn right. I thought he was going to take over the family too. And yeah, he would have been the best." Her voice got rough. "He would have been the dad they all needed. He was tough, but he was kind. He had a family, and he was smart as hell."

"You're smarter."

Maggie said nothing. That meant she agreed with him but she wasn't going to say it.

"You're smarter than all of us," he continued. "And since you've decided to turn away from a life of crime and hustling—"

"I am one hundred percent going back to that unless you start making good money again, by the way. Gardening doesn't pay as well as gambling."

Sean looked up and smiled. "You don't have to worry about getting kneecapped by gangsters though."

"No, I get yelled at by prissy wolves with superiority complexes," she muttered. "Some days I'd prefer the kneecapping."

"You love it."

"No, I don't *mind* it." Maggie leaned forward. "But I love this family. I *love* these kids, and I love the younger ones that have the fucking audacity to put their middle finger up to the past and try to pull themselves out of the dirt." She pointed at him. "And they all look up to you, Sean. So get your head out of your ass, fix this Lobo situation with your little girlfriend, and then go live your glamorous life. Give these kids something to aspire to."

He stared at her. "Does it really matter to them?"

"Yeah. It does. But don't be a fucking stranger again. Not like before."

He stood up. "I won't. And the Juni thing—"

"Oh my God, I don't want to know about your love life. She knows about us now, you're fucking in love with her already, Sean. Just..." Maggie curled her lip. "Go fucking live happily ever after or some shit, okay?"

He raised an eyebrow. "Should I ask about you and the Scottish vet?"

"Fuck off."

"Right." He reached over and patted her head before she could duck away. "Text me if there are any problems with the old man."

"Fine. I'll take care of them myself, but I'll make sure to tell you about it so you feel relevant."

His sister. Just a ball of sweetness personified.

Sean could finally admit that he'd missed the hell out of her.

HE WAS STANDING in front of Maggie's house when Caleb's extended-cab pickup drove around the corner, kicking up dust and gravel before it came to a stop. He closed his eyes and waited for the dust to settle before he picked his duffel up off the porch and tossed it in the truck bed. He yanked open the narrow back seat and mentally calculated how he was going to fold himself in back.

Juni piped up. "Sean, I'm shorter. I can sit in the back if you want."

"No, you can't," Caleb said.

"It's fine." On no planet ever was he going to let Juni sit in the back seat while Sean sat in silence across from her older brother.

"Caleb," he grunted.

"Sean."

He got in and sat behind Juni, stretching his legs across the back while he wrestled the seat belt in place. Once the belt clicked, Caleb backed out of the drive, leaving Sean tortured by the scent of Juni's lemon-scented soap.

She'd always used it, and anytime he caught wind of a woman who smelled even faintly like lemon, he thought of Juni. He'd once spent an entire afternoon at a fancy department store, sniffing every lemon perfume they had, hoping that one of them might match her fragrance. Nothing worked though. They were all pale comparisons.

"How's Maggie?" Juni asked.

"She's good." He cleared his throat. "Some of the kids got in trouble at school again, but she took care of it."

"I think your sister and Mrs. Vasquez have each other on speed dial," Caleb muttered. "But they always seem to work things out."

"She's good with the teenagers," Sean said. "Probably because she was hell on wheels at that age."

"What does she do?"

"Other than herd a dozen slithering Quinn kids on a daily basis?" Sean looked out the window. "She's a really talented landscaper."

"Excellent poker player too," Caleb said. "She's cut back on that some."

"She should try to enter one of those tournaments in Vegas," Juni said.

"Most of the Vegas casinos have banned her," Sean said. "Because she also happens to be really good at blackjack."

"Oh right."

They rode in silence the rest of the way out of town, taking a break when they reached Barstow, where Sean got the chance to revisit the Quick Stop where he'd been thrown against a block wall by a sick coyote.

Sean walked into the store to buy a pack of gum and a soda after using the bathroom.

The guy behind the counter was squinting at him. "Do I know you?"

You probably saw me naked and bleeding a week ago. "Don't think so."

Juni sidled up next to him and put her own drink on the counter, one of the fancy teas she loved in the big glass bottles. "You probably recognize him from some..." She dropped her voice.

"Sexy movies." She winked at the counter guy. "Really big snake, if you know what I mean."

Sean nudged her back and threw a twenty at the guy behind the counter. "Thanks, I don't need change."

His brown eyes were wide behind the glasses. "You sure?"

"I'm good."

"Oh yes, he is." Juni grabbed her tea. "Thanks, honey."

"No problem... pumpkin." He grimaced as he turned and hustled her out of the Quick Mart. "Was that really necessary?"

"I've been waiting to make a big-snake joke for days," Juni said. "The opportunity presented itself and I took it."

He fell into step next to her. "Do you want your brother to murder me and dump my body in the desert?"

"I wouldn't let that happen. Besides, Caleb likes you."

Sean caught Caleb staring at him as he filled the gas tank. He was leaning against the truck bed, his mirrored aviators reflecting the midmorning sun.

He stopped and turned to Juni. "I need you to know that your brother is the natural predator of all my people," he said. "So no. He does not like me, Juni."

She frowned. "Natural predator?"

"He's a cop and I'm a Quinn." He started walking again. "Enough said."

"Hardly." She skipped to catch up with him. "He's not in charge of my life, you know. He knows I'm an adult."

"It doesn't matter—he's your brother." Sean glanced at her. "Besides, when did you decide you don't hate me anymore?"

"I never hated you." She stopped in her tracks.

Sean walked a few steps and turned to see her standing still, staring at him. "What?"

"I never hated you." Her voice was softer.

Would you have ever told me? Would you ever have let me in on this... thing? Your life?

"You were angry with me," Sean said. "And with good reason."

 149

Elizabeth Hunter

He nodded. "I should have trusted you. You've never been anything but honest with me, and I should have known you'd keep a secret."

"You weren't the only one keeping secrets." She blinked back the shine in her eyes and forced out a smile. "Everyone was kind of in on it."

"So why are you still here?" He shook his head. "Honestly, Juni. No one would blame you if you left. It would be a completely normal—and probably very smart—thing to run as far away from this mess as possible."

She wrinkled her nose and sniffed. "What can I say? I'm impossibly curious and also you turned into a giant scary lizard when you thought I was bleeding and I don't know why I'm reading anything into that, but I found it oddly charming."

She rushed past him and walked to the car, effectively cutting off any response he might have been able to put together.

Juni thought that his turning into a monitor lizard was... charming?

Why was that so Juni?

And why did Sean suddenly feel like he could fly?

chapter **eighteen**

JUNI LOUNGED in the plastic chair by the motel pool in Henderson while her editor questioned her on the phone.

"The Lake Las Vegas *Esencia*?" Rani sounded rightfully confused. "It's not our thing."

"But it could be?" Juni was angling to get paid for this if she possibly could. "It's an up-and-coming brand in Latin America. I checked."

"They're a chain hotel, Juni. And a huge one. They're known for all-inclusive tourist traps in Mexico and highish-end—but affordable—resorts in big cities. I didn't even know they were in Las Vegas. What about Desert Haven?"

Juni almost groaned when Rani mentioned the exclusive luxury spa an hour away. "I could do that afterward?"

"They've been trying to get on our list for a couple of years now, and you're perfect for it because they're angling to attract a younger, social-media-savvy guest. Why don't you do Haven?"

"But if I could just do the Esencia first—"

"I'm not going to get approval on that." Rani was blunt. "I have bosses too."

She took a deep breath. "What if you just kind of leaked that I was in the area for Desert Haven, but I had some time to kill before and I was hanging out in Las Vegas with my brother and looking for a family-friendly place?"

"I just don't understand—"

"Please?" She kicked her feet up into the chair across from her and closed her eyes. "Please, Rani? I could use a freebie or a discount is all."

"Seriously?" Her boss sighed. "Okay, but you better be clear that this is your own social media feed only, nothing to do with the magazine. And don't get too in depth or you'll dilute your brand value." Rani cleared her throat. "Maybe make it ironic posting?"

"Sure." She felt someone lift her feet and her eyes flew open.

Sean was sitting across from her, looking dangerous and tempting. He set her feet in his lap, and his eyes were intent on her face when he mouthed, *Rani*?

Juni nodded. "Sean's with me." *And not quite rubbing my feet, but definitely holding them. In his lap. With his thumb in the arch, and why was that sexy?*

"He better not be in any pictures you take," Rani bit out. "Especially at Esencia. I've been insinuating to people that he's in rehab for exhaustion and various unnamed mental-stress issues."

She pressed her lips together to stop the smile. "I promise I won't put him in any pics. Maybe he can do the Desert Haven job with me though." She wiggled her eyebrows at Sean, but her heart was flipping in her chest. Her feet were in his lap. Like, in his lap. Near his crotch. In fact, if she wanted to be evil...

The corner of her mouth turned up, and she angled her foot a few inches toward his dick before Sean caught it up and pinched her heel. "Juni."

His voice was a warning, and she almost burst into laughter at the annoyed look on his face. He was almost smiling though. Just a little bit.

"Are you flirting with Sean Quinn while you're on the phone with me?" Rani asked.

"Absolutely not."

He pressed his thumb into the arch of her foot, and she nearly fell out of her chair.

Fuck, that was so good. "Rani, just drop my name in their publicity person's ear and see what kind of room I can get, okay?"

His teasing fingers slid up and around her ankle, caressing the curve of her leg with a single long finger that made her question every resolution she'd ever made about him.

Lies? What lies?

Who cared if he had complicated family history?

Purely sexual flings were underrated.

"Hang up the phone," he whispered.

"Rani, I'll text you if I hear from them, okay? And..." Her eyes started to cross. "Yeah, go ahead and book me at Desert Haven for a feature next week or something."

"I'll see what they suggest," her editor said. "Say hi to Sean and tell him to get his ass back to work."

"Uh-huh." She tapped her screen and set her phone down on the glass table, which was surrounded by four sad chairs. "You're infuriating."

"I'm not the one with boundary issues." Sean continued to rub her foot. "Aren't you the one who always barged into my hotel rooms? And my hometown for that matter?"

"I didn't actually know it was your hometown because you never told me where you were from."

"I did."

She squinted at him. "You didn't."

He frowned and his hands paused in their work. "I'm sure I did."

Juni sighed. "Sean, I think your idea of our relationship and the reality were very far apart. You told me almost nothing about your life. I was an open book, and you were manic about your privacy."

"Fine. I told you the most important parts though."

She shook her head. "You told me nothing."

"I told you that I wanted you." His voice was a low whisper, and his hands held on to her feet as if she might try to escape. "I told you that you drove me crazy."

"And you told me that I should leave."

"You should have."

"I did."

"But we always seemed to end up in the same place again. And again." He gripped her feet in his strong hands and held them securely, his eyes on her legs. "And every time it gets a little harder to send you away. To be... unselfish."

"No one is asking you to be the sacrificial lamb," Juni said. "Definitely not me."

"So maybe I won't be." He looked up and met her eyes. "Maybe it's time to take what I want and say to hell with the consequences."

She leaned forward. "Is that a threat?"

His eyes dropped to her mouth. "Only if you want it to be."

Juni heard her name in the distance.

"My brother is yelling for me."

"He really needs to learn about texting."

"He's old."

Sean's eyes lit up. "Not that much older than me."

"I always forget you're an elder." She drew her feet away from his lap, but not before she angled her right foot and ran her toe across the evident bulge in his jeans. "You seem pretty young to me."

He stretched out his legs and adjusted himself discreetly. "That isn't likely to be a problem. Shifters don't lose that."

She stopped in her tracks. "Ever?"

He shook his head slowly. "My great-grandfather had a kid when he was eighty."

"Go, Grandpa Quinn." She raised an eyebrow. "And you're telling me this because?"

Sean folded his hands like an obedient schoolboy. "You implied that I didn't share enough." He shifted, and she noticed his erection again. "I'm sharing."

You could share that.

Juni cleared her throat and nodded. "Right. I'm going to go see what the chief wants."

"Fill me in on the plan when you guys decide what you want to do." He looked up and slid a pair of sunglasses over his piercing blue eyes. "I'm flexible."

Now that was definitely a threat.

THE ESENCIA HOTEL RESORT and Spa was a sprawling Spanish colonial-style edifice on the shores of a man-made lake twenty minutes away from the Las Vegas Strip. Far from being populated by massive casinos and high-rises, Lake Las Vegas was a forest of cookie-cutter condo developments, shopping malls, and chain hotels that catered less to high rollers looking for nightlife and more to retired couples and families looking for a quiet retreat.

"Holy shit," Caleb muttered under his breath as they walked into the lobby. "And you're telling me they will just give us two rooms at this place for free?"

"And then some," Juni murmured. "Jena's bringing the kids, right?"

"Becca and Bear, yeah. Low stayed behind." He was still looking around the luxe lobby. "And her dad is coming as backup. You are getting all the favorite-aunt points for this one, by the way."

"Good."

As soon as Juni talked to Rani, she realized that they might need a better cover story than she and her big brother visiting Las Vegas for the weekend. Jena was bringing the kids but would be keeping her distance from anything dangerous. Jena's father would be following in raven form to keep an eye on the family, and Bear

—despite her nephew's name—was already a hefty, near-six-foot member of the wolf pack even as a teenager.

"Miss Hawkins?" A dark-haired woman in a coral-colored suit strode toward Juni seconds after she and her brother crossed the marble-inlaid floors. "It's so nice to meet you."

Mariana Cordova was in charge of "influencer marketing" for the Esencia chain, and she happened to be in Las Vegas for the expansion. Rani said it was a stroke of luck. Juni was just hoping that Mariana was familiar with Efrén Abano and could give them some kind of in.

"Hi!" Juni held out her hand and shook Mariana's. She looked around the lobby that had clearly just had a face-lift. "This is my first time staying at an Esencia, so I'm excited."

"And we're excited to host you," Mariana said.

And my quarter of a million social media followers. Juni smiled. She didn't need to say that part, but she could tell the PR professional knew how this game worked.

Juni gestured to her right. "Mariana, this is my brother, Caleb. We're here for a family vacation."

"Very nice to meet you."

"Likewise." Caleb kept the country-boy high and his voice low.

The executive skillfully guided them through the lobby and toward an expansive bar overlooking a gorgeous stretch of waterfront. "Why don't we stop and get a drink before I go over the promotional package I've put together for you and your family?"

"Sounds great." Juni perched on the edge of a barstool, careful not to jostle her handbag.

He's not in there. Yet.

Sean's initial idea had been to stow away in her shoulder bag in lizard or snake form, but Caleb nixed that. Once they had a room, it would be safe to smuggle him in, but until they knew who or what they were dealing with, it was too risky. He'd have to put up with Caleb protecting Juni from whatever they were walking into.

Mariana's nose twitched a little as they sat, and she looked at Caleb with a smile and slightly narrowed eyes. "I feel like we've met."

Caleb shook his head. "No, ma'am. I don't believe we have."

Juni's radar went up. Was this woman a shifter? She looked down the bar where a burly man with dark brown skin was wielding a cocktail shaker and pouring something green into two martini glasses.

What about him? Was he a shifter? Were all the hotel employees shifters? Could they smell something different about Caleb?

Juni tried to divert Mariana. "Caleb used to be a senior officer in the Albuquerque police department. Are you from there? Maybe you saw him on television at a press conference or something."

The woman blinked and her smile lifted. "That's probably it. I've had a home in Santa Fe for quite a while."

"Beautiful place," Caleb said. "You get back much?"

"Oh no, I work directly with Mr. Abano, the owner of Esencia, so I usually travel with him."

Juni saw her opening. "Oh wow, so is the owner here right now?"

"He is."

"That's exciting."

"I agree." She handed Juni a discreet folder. "In fact, he's hosting a cocktail party tomorrow night, and we're hoping you might be able to attend. It will be on the rooftop bar overlooking the lake. Very hot. Very trending. There will be a DJ, but I can't say who yet." She cocked her head coyly. "It's a surprise for the guests, but I promise you *will* recognize the name. There will also be more than one headliner from the Strip in attendance." She leaned forward. "More familiar faces, of course."

Caleb looked suitably uncomfortable. "Juni, I don't know if—"

"I can go to that stuff." She put her hand on his arm and shot Mariana a conspiratorial look. "You and Jena can hang with the kids, and I'll do the dress-up stuff."

"You're welcome to attend, of course." Mariana's smile was performative at best. "But yes, that is not a requirement of the promotional package." She lowered her voice. "We normally work through vetted agencies, but since this is more informal, I let your editor know that we're looking for a three-post minimum—"

"Mmm." Juni pretended to consider it. "I think two would be more in line with a casual, nonbranded stay like this, but I can do multiple photos in the posts."

Caleb watched her with narrowed eyes. Her brother was old-school and probably had no idea how influencer marketing was arranged.

Mariana nodded slowly. "I think that could work. Can we expect at least three photos from the party? At least one with a recognizable guest?"

"That's absolutely acceptable. There may be someone who I've worked with before."

"There will be at least one model I know you've photographed for the magazine."

"Great." Juni smiled at the man who set the green drink in front of her. "That sounds perfect."

"Would you like to bring a guest?"

Not one that you'll be able to see. "I'll check and see if my sister-in-law wants to come, but it might just be me. No worries—I'm good at mingling, and people are used to me taking pictures."

"We are hiring a professional photographer to cover the event, of course."

"I'll keep it casual," Juni said. "Don't want to step on any toes."

Caleb leaned forward. "So the owner and all the executives and stuff will be at this party, huh?"

"They will." Mariana looked slightly worried. "If you'd also like to attend—"

"Ah, no." He gave her a rueful smile. "I leave all that stuff to Juni. She's the one who brushes elbows with the rich and famous."

"Of course." The woman appeared relieved. "I promise the rest of her schedule will be very light. Lots of time to spend with your family."

"I've heard there's a wonderful art gallery here," Juni said. "I hope I might get the chance to tour it."

Mariana hesitated a little. "The gallery is attached to the owner's private office," she said. "But I'll see what I can do."

"I'm doing a feature at Desert Haven next week, and I'll be touring their sculpture garden and meditation space." She shrugged. "I thought it might be cool to have a nearby collection to reference in the piece."

Mariana laughed a little. "I have visited Desert Haven, of course. A beautiful property. I can tell you though, the art collection here is much more extensive. It would be hard to compare them."

"I'd love to see it firsthand." Juni smiled. "If Mr. Abano doesn't mind, of course."

chapter
nineteen

SEAN WAS LOUNGING on the chaise near the balcony in Juni's room when the connecting room door opened.

"Oh."

Sean turned to see Caleb standing in the doorway. "Hey."

"Juni out?"

"She and Jena went down to the pool with the kids."

"Mmm."

Sean glanced over his shoulder. "Listen, I know you're not thrilled with my staying in Juni's room—"

"Just saying that drawer looks cozy."

Juni's big brother had generously offered his bedside-table drawer for Sean to sleep in while in lizard form, even offering to keep the lamp on at night, but Jena smacked his shoulder and told her husband to butt out.

"I have a feeling your room is going to be a little more crowded than this one, and since the hotel thinks that Juni is here alone..." Sean shrugged.

Caleb went silent, but he was staring at Sean. It made Sean's instincts go wild. Shifters didn't take well to challenges, and that's what his nose was telling him Caleb was heading toward.

Sean sat up and swung his legs around the chaise to face the man. "Should we just do this now while they're gone?"

"Sure, why not?" Caleb leaned against the door. "I don't think you're good for my sister, and I want you to back off. I don't know what all kind of history you two have but—"

"That's right, you don't." Sean was on the verge of his fangs descending. "Juni's a grown woman. I have never chased her."

"You didn't need to, did you? You were a hotshot photographer in an industry she wanted to break into. You didn't have to chase her; your editor assigned her to be your assistant."

"Nothing happened when Juni was working for me."

"Really?" Caleb's eyebrow went up. "Nothing at all?"

Sean blinked, remembering an otherworldly afternoon in Chiang Mai. "I'm not blind. She's impossible to ignore, okay? Even if I was blind, I'd be drawn to her because she's Juni. And I'm sure you've protected her your whole life and you'd probably hate any guy who looked at her sideways, but—"

"Oh, shut it." Caleb shook his head slowly. "You think I don't like you because you're into my little sister? Juni attracts men like flies. You think you're the first man to fall in love with her?"

In love? That was a leap. "Listen, Caleb—"

"I don't think you're *good* for her. She used to meet guys all the time, and she'd laugh and tell me crazy dating stories and it was fine. She's smart and she's got a good head on her shoulders. Other than worrying about sickos—because I'm a cop and that's unavoidable—I never worried about Juni."

"You know I'd never do anything to hurt her." Sean slowly stood. "You have to know that."

"Physically? I'm not worried about that. I know you're protective and I respect what you're trying to do with your family, Quinn. I respect the hell out of that."

Sean halted. "Physically?" Meaning Juni's brother thought he'd hurt her in other ways.

"You turn her sideways." Caleb's voice dropped. "She hasn't dated anyone else—not really—since she met you. She's distracted. Worried. It's like a little bit of her light just... dimmed." He folded his arms over his chest. "And I didn't know what was going on until she came out here and I realized that you and she were involved."

"We're friends, Caleb. I told her ages ago that my life was complicated and we could only—"

"You can *say* that, but that doesn't mean anything when the two of you look at each other the way you do." Caleb hit a fist over his heart. "She's my only sibling, and I just want her happy. I want someone who makes her happy. And the shit part of all this is I think you'd like to. I really do." He frowned and looked at the ground. "I wasn't sure for a while but after... I know you care about her, Quinn, but this is my baby sister. She has gotten left-overs her entire life. Hand-me-down clothes from her cousins, secondhand furniture from college friends, and not a whole hell of a lot of anything from our mom."

Sean felt a knot in his stomach, but he couldn't find the words to speak.

Caleb continued. "I want her to be *first* for someone, you know? She deserves that. She deserves someone who is crazy about her. Who can return all that love and energy and joy she's managed to find in her life. She's worked hard for that joy, and she deserves someone who returns it."

Sean's voice sounded wooden to his ears. "And you don't think I would."

"I think you might want to," Caleb said. "But can you?" He took a step forward. "Figure it out, Quinn. Because we both know she deserves it." Caleb swallowed hard and started to turn. "I'm older than you. And I like to think that I've learned some things."

"Like what?"

"You have to find your own joy," he said. "Before you can give it to other people, you have to find that peace and that happiness in yourself." Caleb shook his head. "If you can't, it doesn't matter how much you want to make someone else happy. You're never gonna be able to."

Find his own joy? What did that even mean? If Sean had to turn into a slap-happy optimist to make Juni content, he was screwed.

Caleb continued, "I'm going to go down and meet everyone at the pool." He stopped, nodded, then walked back into his room, shutting the door and leaving Sean in the middle of Juni's luxurious hotel room.

He'd been on the verge of making his move, trying to see if Juni and he could really make something work, but now he was rethinking everything. Because Caleb wasn't being an asshole, he was watching out for his sister.

I think you might want to, but can you?

"WHAT'S UP WITH YOU?" Juni was fixing her face in the mirror, getting ready for the rooftop party that night. She was wearing some slip of a dress in shining green that reminded him of snake scales or emeralds or something rich. Her hair was artfully mussed, and glittering beads dripped from her ears.

"Nothing." Sean could hear the thump of the DJ when the french doors to the patio were open. "Just thinking about tonight."

The previous look of concentration turned to worry. "No, you've been weird since this afternoon. What's up? Did Caleb say something rude to you about staying with me? I'll talk to him. He can be nosy as hell, and I am not a teenager anymore. He has no—"

"No." Dammit. He was turning her around again and getting her to question herself. Again. "Caleb didn't say anything about you and me sharing a room." Mostly true. "It's me, okay? I'm just in my head right now." One hundred percent true.

Juni frowned. "What are you worried about? Abano trying something? It's going to be a huge party, Sean. And totally public. He's not going to try anything when we're surrounded like that even if he has figured out I'm connected to Cambio Springs."

"You're right." He ignored the twist in his gut. He wanted to go over and kiss her. He wanted to bite the lipstick off her full lower lip and nibble on the curve of her ear. "I..." He cleared his throat and pushed down the desire that flooded his system. "I want this to work, but I'm kind of worried that we're not going to learn anything new."

She shook her head and went back to applying something glittery on her cheeks. "From what I can tell, none of you guys know much about this guy, so it seems like anything we learn might be part of the puzzle."

"You're right." His eyes skimmed over her body, the shimmering green outlining her soft curves and teasing the length of her legs. She was short, but her legs were fucking beautiful.

"I know I'm right." She winked at him in the mirror.

"And you look amazing."

"Thank you." Her cheeks turned a little rosy beneath her tan. "Are you sure you'll be okay in my purse?" She peeked inside the clutch. "I don't want to squish you."

Sean smiled. "You won't. I'll be in lizard form. I have very little scent in that form, and I'm pretty tough."

"Sean?"

"Juni?"

"Can I ask you a personal question?"

"I'm sharing now, remember?" *Tell her the truth. Whatever it is, you will tell her the truth. Even if it's painful.*

Juni turned to him and narrowed her eyes.

Oh God, this is going to be bad.

She lowered her voice. "If your tail breaks off when you're a lizard, do you lose anything in human form?"

Sean blinked. "What?"

"That's probably too personal, right?" She waved a hand and started to turn. "I don't know why that popped into my head."

He burst into laughter. "My tail?"

She put down her makeup brush. "Okay, now I feel silly, but lizards can lose their tails and regrow them, right? Did I remember that wrong?" She turned back to the mirror. "I just wondered—"

He was at her back so quickly she gasped.

Sean closed his eyes and indulged in her scent, trailing a finger down her neck as the soft skin heated under his touch. He felt her body come alive, and arousal was the sweetest perfume.

He placed one hand on her hip and the other on the counter next to her, pressing the front of his body against the round swell of her backside. "Were you worried about me losing... anything vital?"

She arched her back and cuddled her backside into his growing erection. "I know it's not an exact science, but you don't have a tail."

He lowered his head and trailed his lips along the curve of her neck. "Then you'll be very relieved to know that I do not lose anything in human form. That's not the way it works."

"Good." Her heart was racing, and she reached for the hand on her hip and placed it on her rib cage, just under her breasts. "What if you turned into a snake and I wore you around my neck tonight?"

Fucking God, that was such a sexy image. "Gonna have to wait for the right venue for that one. Might put Lobo on guard." He dragged his lips across the back of her neck. "But maybe..."

He closed his eyes and let the shift take him, transforming into the emerald-green tree python he'd been picturing in his mind when he saw her dress. Within seconds, he had curled around Juni's ankle.

She gasped and looked down. Sean waited, watching as her expression shifted from shock to wonder.

She blinked round brown eyes, and the corner of her mouth tilted into a smile. "Wow."

He curled around her leg, moving slowly so she could get accustomed to the sensation of him in snake form. His body hugged her leg, the end of his tail flicking against the back of her knee while he climbed her, arching his muscled form up her side, around her waist, sliding between her breasts as her chest heaved.

"I'm not scared. Fuck me, Sean. How is this sexy?" Her head tilted to the side, and he flicked out his tongue to taste the air.

The fragrance of her arousal was everywhere. He could feel her racing heart on the surface of his skin, so he happily slid up and around her neck, resting his scaled body along her shoulders.

Sean angled his head and looked at them in the mirror. Juni's lips were flushed and parted as she watched him rest his head on the coils of his body, which he'd draped over her tattooed shoulders like an emerald-green cape. In python form, he was an excellent climber, and it was one of his favorite animals. He had excellent vision and senses like this, and he wished he could join her at the party as her python necklace.

Juni reached up and ran her fingers along the smooth scales of his resting body. "You're amazing."

No, you're amazing.

"I don't think I had strong feelings about snakes before this, but now I'm definitely a fan."

He flicked his tongue out and tasted the air, tickling the back of her ear.

She giggled a little. "Are you playing with me?"

He did it again, flicking the end of his tail along the underside of her breast as she gasped.

"Naughty."

She didn't look displeased though. Her eyes were sparkling, and all the shadows were gone. Her face was bright and she was smiling.

Mission accomplished.

She deserves joy. She deserves fun and laughter and love.

Maybe.

Maybe if Juni could enjoy the weirder parts of his life, he could make her happy.

If he could keep her safe.

If he could make her laugh.

Find your own joy.

Sean stared at Juni's delighted face in the mirror, watching him with fascination and wonder.

Maybe joy wasn't as far away as he thought.

chapter
twenty

"JUNI!" Mariana waved at her from a table by the elevator. "So glad you could make it."

As per contractual obligations. Juni smiled and hitched her purse securely on her shoulder. "Mariana, so nice to see you." The party was already in full swing, and the music was thumping. "This is great."

"Thank you." The PR rep looked more than pleased with the turnout. She held a martini glass filled with something ruby-colored in her elegantly manicured hand and surveyed the crowd. "I think you'll find a few familiar faces. Would you like some introductions, or would you rather mingle?"

"I'd love some introductions later." Juni was hoping Mariana's introductions might lead Juni to the boss. "But let me grab a drink first."

"Of course." She lifted her glass. "Make sure you try one of the signature cocktails tonight. This one has cactus fruit in it."

"Sounds yum." Juni made her way through the crowd, careful not to let her purse bump against anyone as she walked.

She'd left the zipper partway open so Sean could hear what was going on. He claimed he didn't need it, but after he'd shifted from the stunning green python he'd morphed into before the party and into the tiny form of a fringed lizard, she didn't want to take chances.

"I'd really love it if you had a way of talking to me," Juni said quietly. "But until I learn to speak reptile, I'm shit out of luck."

She didn't even know if he could hear her over the raucous noise of the party, but he'd insisted on coming with her.

Juni saw a model she'd worked with a few months ago sitting at a tall table, talking with a dark-haired man in a suit. "Blythe!" She lowered her voice. "Blythe Hanson is here. She's sweet."

The model waved back and motioned her over to the table as the man moved away.

Juni abandoned the idea of a club soda with lime and walked over to the familiar face.

"Hey!" The young woman had been doing a swimsuit feature in Bali with Juni in March. "It's so great to see you here! I didn't know you'd left Asia."

"I have family that lives not too far from here. I'm visiting."

"Same." Blythe grinned. "I'm from San Diego."

With her dark tan, golden-yellow hair, and liquid blue eyes, Juni didn't find that surprising. "Awesome."

"I got this invite, and I wasn't sure about it, you know?" The model leaned closer. "But the money was so good. Good to see you here. Is the magazine—?"

"No." Juni shook her head. "I just happened to be here. Doing an editorial at Desert Haven next week, and I wanted to hang with my family." Someone bumped into her and she cringed. She took her purse off her shoulder and set it on the table. "Do you mind...?"

"Not at all." Blythe set her drink next to Juni's hard-sided snakeskin purse.

It was her own private joke, but she made herself laugh with it. She thought Sean might have rolled his eyes when he crawled inside, but she wasn't sure if lizards could roll their eyes.

"Oh, have one of these." Blythe flagged down a waiter. "The purple one is good."

"Cool." Juni grabbed the martini and sipped it. "Oh, that actually *is* good."

"Right? Usually it's some dreck to promote an actor's new tequila project."

"Or rum." Juni sipped the drink, which tasted of fresh fruit and vodka with a hint of sage.

"Is it rum now?" Blythe rolled her eyes.

"I think that's the new trend."

"Ladies?" A photographer grabbed their attention. "May I?"

"Of course." Blythe slid off her chair and angled herself toward Juni, who put on a neutral face and held her drink.

The photographer got his shot and drifted away.

"I never know how to pose for those things," Juni said. "I'm used to being on the other side of the camera."

"You could model, you know. For magazines." Blythe hopped back on her chair. "You have such a unique look, and you have amazing style. You know, a lot of designers like working with models who aren't cookie-cutter like me."

She managed not to spit out her drink. "Stop. Nothing about you is cookie-cutter. And I'm good on the lens side, thanks. I don't have the patience for skin care that you girls do."

The model laughed. "It is a lot." She leaned forward. "I have to get a picture with the DJ before I leave."

"Contract thing?"

"Yeah, and we share an agent. She's kind of pushing the rumor that we're dating."

"Who?"

Blythe motioned to the DJ on the platform overlooking the pool where dozens of bikini-clad women were swimming. "DJ Cruz. The guy in the lucha libre mask?"

Juni craned her neck and saw a muscular young man in an

open shirt and a black-and-silver mask ruling over the soundboard. "Have you seen him without the mask?"

Blythe nodded. "It's not a bad view. Who knows, maybe our agent is actually playing matchmaker?"

"I heard that the... owner of the hotel is kind of hot." Juni looked around the rooftop, but she didn't spot anyone who looked like Efrén Abano. "Is he here?"

"Oh yeah, going for that big money score." Blythe winked. "I can see it."

"Oh, it's not like—"

"There he is!" Blythe waved at someone. "Efrén! Come meet my friend Juni."

Shit shit shit.

"Oh cool. He's coming over." Blythe smiled. "I wouldn't call him hot or anything, but he's not bad and he's superrich, so he can hire a stylist."

"Uh-huh." Juni pushed her purse to the center of the table and "accidentally" spilled some of her drink, hoping that whatever was in it would mask the possibility of Efrén Abano—who was a shifter—smelling Sean in her purse. "You know, I was mostly joking about the—"

"Efrén!" Blythe hopped off her chair and double-kissed the cheeks of the dark-haired man who was suddenly standing before them. "Okay, so you have to meet Juni. She's an incredible photographer; I worked with her in Bali this year."

Juni looked over, prepared to meet the devil incarnate, but was faced with a perfectly average-looking man of Latin heritage and medium height.

"Juniper Hawkins," he said. "Of course." He smiled, and his eyes glittered in the flashing lights of the party. "I feel like we've already met."

"YOU MUST TELL me how I can get a feature in your magazine." Efrén Abano had stolen Juni away from Blythe and tucked her into a luxurious corner table with a view of the rooftop party.

They were in the VIP section of an already VIP party, and Juni was feeling out of place.

"Oh." She tried to downplay. "I'm here on my own, and I'm not an editor in any way—"

"But you know people." He smiled. "I think you are the eyes of the future, Miss Hawkins. Your features always attract attention, and your social media following is most impressive."

She saw multiple movie headliners and musicians, most of whom were drinking signature cocktails. Contract work, but clearly well-paid if Abano was paying for these faces.

Paying for all these faces and yet clearly sucking up to her. For the magazine? For other reasons?

"Well..." What was she supposed to say? She was wildly conscious of the purse sitting on the table, though she was trying to treat it as an afterthought. "Thank you very much. I think I just lucked out, moving to short video before a lot of influencers. It was good timing."

"And skill. And knowing the right people."

Efrén Abano was dressed in a stylish suit and wearing a watch that probably cost more than Lauren's house. He also had no accent, which surprised Juni a little, because according to everyone on the internet, he was born and raised in Mexico. His English wasn't only impeccable, he sounded like a West Coast native.

Abano leaned forward, his eyes warm and... flirtatious? "I was so happy to be able to invite you tonight. I think we know some of the same people."

Juni was trying to figure him out, but it was hard to match the pleasant facade to the gang boss she'd heard about who was trying to ruin a small town in the desert.

"Oh really?" She sipped her drink. "Who is that?"

"Sean Quinn."

Juni blinked but managed not to flinch. "You know Sean?" She forced her face into a smile. "That's so cool. How do you know him?"

"I'm familiar with his work."

"Oh right. I mean, of course. Who isn't? I was able to work with him when I was first starting out, and I learned a lot. Really talented guy."

Oh God, oh God, oh God. Did he know? How could he know? *Shit.* Wait, was Efrén Abano trying to mine Juni for information about Sean while she was trying to mine him for information about his motives?

"I think Sean Quinn is also from this area, is that right?"

Juni bluffed. "Last I heard, he had a place in Laguna Beach, so I think he's more Southern California based? But that might not be right."

Efrén nodded. "I heard through the grapevine that he's taking some time off for personal reasons." He frowned a little. "I hope he's all right."

"Oh..." Juni widened her eyes. "You know, we're friendly, but I'd hardly say he confides in me or anything. We're not that close."

"You've worked in several projects together, have you not? That wonderful profile of the safari camp in Kenya. That profile of—"

"Have you been to Kenya? Isn't that place amazing?" She had to get control of the conversation. "I have to say, I'm so curious about you."

Abano smirked. "Are you?"

"*Professionally.*" She turned on the charm. "I know the Esencia resorts are incredibly successful in Mexico and Latin America. What made you want to expand your reach into the US too? I think the Latin American market actually has more growth potential than the US."

He raised an eyebrow. "I suppose that depends on what you consider growth."

"Oh?"

He lifted his chin. "You know, I also have family roots in this area."

"Really? Here in Las Vegas?"

He smiled a little. "Not far from here. I think we always have that urge to prove ourselves, don't we?"

"To our families?"

"To those who... rejected us. Those who saw us as less somehow. I'm sure you understand."

Juni forced another smile. "I've tried to leave my high school bullies behind. Onward and upward; that's my philosophy."

"I think you are far from average, Juniper Hawkins. And nonaverage people have a harder time fitting in." He sipped his drink. "You come from Albuquerque, but you don't go back often." He caught himself. "I mean, do you? Go back often?" He slipped into an accent. "I think I phrased that incorrectly."

No, you didn't.

Juni turned on the charm again. "You know, there just aren't many photography jobs in New Mexico. At least not compared to LA."

"No, I imagine not. And sometimes the memories of the past aren't the finest companions."

Juni felt an undercurrent of threat behind his words. "I agree." She lifted her drink. "I can see you're going to be successful with this place. It's absolutely beautiful."

"I hope your family is enjoying it."

"We are. The kids..." She smiled. "I'm the favorite aunt now."

"It's so important to think about the future, isn't it?" His eyes drifted to someone in the distance. "We all have those we care for. Those under our protection."

Who did Lobo think he was protecting? Did he consider

himself the "alpha" of his gang? Did he see it as a gang or something else?

Juni smiled innocently. "Well, I don't think I have to protect my family from much here. It seems very safe." Was she doing enough to play the clueless bystander? She'd gained some insight into Efrén Abano, but she still had no idea if her ploy to remain the innocent was working. "I think you're doing a great job with security."

"Of course." His smile was a little disappointed. "So tell me again, how can I get a feature in your magazine?"

Juni leaned forward to pick up her drink, and in the process she knocked her clutch over and much of the contents spilled out. She gasped in panic as she saw the edge of a tail disappear back into the bag and felt the air around her electrify.

She looked at Abano, whose nostrils flared. His eyes narrowed on Juni, and he started to lean forward, one arm outstretched. Juni scooted back, scooping her lipstick, phone, and sunglasses back into the clutch as she slid out of the booth and stood.

"I need to go to the ladies' room." She backed away from Abano, keeping her eyes on the darkly furious man who was glaring at her. As soon as she felt herself surrounded by the crowd, she turned and walked to the elevator where a uniformed attendant held the door for her.

"Thanks. I'm claustrophobic and I don't want company." She shoved him out of the elevator and punched the button for the sixth floor.

"But miss—"

"I'll hyperventilate if you're in here with me!" She jammed her finger on the Door Close button repeatedly until the silver doors blessedly slid shut.

"Damn, damn, damn." She needed to get out of the hotel. Abano knew she had a shifter with her, and it was only a matter of time before they were surrounded.

chapter
twenty-one

SEAN LET the shift take him, and seconds later he was standing naked in an elevator with Juni, who was shaking in her brilliant green dress.

"Stay calm."

"Shit." She was staring at the buttons, and her voice sounded like she was on the verge of tears. "He knows about you. He smelled you. How is that possible? He's going to know about you, he'll go after Jena and Caleb and the kids. He might—"

"Stop." He quickly wrapped his arms around her from behind. "We'll get them out. It's going to be fine."

"Becca is probably asleep. Jena and Caleb might be—"

"Call your brother." Sean waited at the door, willing the elevator to go faster. "Call him now."

She reached down and took the phone from her purse with trembling fingers. "You're naked."

He hadn't even thought about it. "If anyone sees us, they'll think it was a *really* great party." The elevator doors opened, and Sean bolted toward the room only to have to wait for Juni to catch up because he didn't have a key.

"—were fine until I knocked over my purse and he smelled

Sean and he knows now. There's no way he doesn't. I could see—" She broke off, mumbling as she waved the card in front of the lock. "I don't know, but we need to get out."

The door opened and Sean pushed her inside, following her but keeping the lights out. "Tell Caleb to get everyone up and out of here and to tell Jena's dad."

Sean ran for the balcony to see if there was a raven outside watching. He grabbed a blanket off the sofa near the french doors and poked his head outside to see a massive man wrapped in a towel already knocking at Jena and Caleb's balcony doors.

"You were watching?"

Thomas Crowe was a tall man with dark features and a severe expression. He cast his eyes at Sean and jerked his head in a nod. "Was watching both of you."

"Juni already called her brother."

"My grandkids are in his hotel." Thomas looked furious. "The baby can't shift yet."

"Juni and Caleb can't shift either."

"Caleb can."

Oh shit. Caleb *could* shift, and it was unlikely that Lobo's people would be able to identify the baby on sight. A plan immediately popped into Sean's head. "Have Caleb shift to a new face and take the baby. Bear can shift to a wolf. Do they have a collar? Could they sneak him out as a dog?"

Thomas frowned. "Unlikely, and that kid's natural form is massive. He's better staying human."

Sean cocked his head at something in the distance. Thomas did the same.

"Cats," they both said at once.

There were at least two creeping down the balconies above them, slowly moving from floor to floor.

Jena opened the balcony doors. "Dad?"

"Inside."

They both went back into the room. Sean locked the balcony behind him.

Juni was throwing things into her bag. "What's happening?"

"Jena's dad was watching. He's next door now. There are shifters coming down the balconies; don't go outside."

"What?"

Sean pulled on a pair of grey sweatpants and walked to the connecting door, opening it just as Jena opened hers. "How fast can you leave the hotel?"

"We're ready. Caleb packed everything and shifted into his mom, which is super weird, but he looks like a seventy-year-old woman carrying a baby and Bear is carrying all their stuff and calling him grandma." Jena was clearly alarmed but calm. "They're headed to the car right now. Bear will stay with them and shift if he needs to."

"Did you self-park?" Sean asked.

"Always." Jena looked over Sean's shoulder. "Juni."

Sean could feel her panic and turned. "It's going to be fine."

"This is all my fault," she was whispering, and her eyes filled with tears. "What's coming from the balconies?"

Thomas appeared behind Jena, pulling on a black T-shirt. "Is she ready to go?"

"What are we doing?" Juni asked.

Sean focused on Jena first. "Get them out of here. Find some-place clear and fly away. Don't use the balconies—he's already covering them."

"I'll take the stairs to the roof," Jena said. "He'll be expecting us to go down."

Sean nodded. "Assume that they're watching, but if you stay in public areas, I think you'll be safe. They won't want to make a scene with the party still going strong."

He spotted an older woman passing with Becca in her arms, and Bear waved with a bright smile and the confidence of a teenage boy. "See you back in the Springs, guys!"

The door closed, and Sean turned back to Juni. "Okay, I think the direct approach is going to work best for you, especially this time of night. I'm going to stay human. Thomas stays human too, and we both escort you out. No talking to anyone. No explanations. We get in a taxi and go."

Juni was shaking her head. "They'll be watching."

"If we can get to the lobby, they won't try anything. There are a million people watching; he's not going to create a scene, because someone will call the police and he doesn't want that."

Sean heard a quiet thump on the balcony outside and saw the shadow of a mountain lion beyond the sheer curtains. It was joined by a smaller cat, a stocky bobcat or lynx of some kind. The two padded back and forth on the balcony but made no attempt to come in.

"We need to go before they block the hallway." Sean grabbed Juni's bag from her and looked at her feet. "Shoes."

"Oh fuck!" She kicked off her heels and ran to put her flip-flops on. "This is all I got."

"Then let's go."

She was still in her shiny green dress and he wished she'd changed, but speed was more important than hiding now. Sean opened the hallway door and looked left and right. Jena ducked under his arm and headed to the stairs.

"Jena," Thomas called.

She turned.

"Be safe."

Jena nodded and disappeared into the stairwell.

Sean took Juni by the hand and walked toward the elevator, her duffel bag thrown over his shoulder. Thomas brought up the rear.

They waited by the bank of elevators for one to open, and Sean braced himself to shift quickly if he needed to. If Lobo's people were inside, they would have a fight. If the elevator was empty, they might just have a chance.

Ding!

Ding!

Two cars arrived, one after the other. The first was nearly at capacity with a laughing group of partiers from the rooftop bar, and the other opened on three stone-faced shifters in black.

Sean shoved Juni in the elevator with the party guests and nudged Thomas in behind her.

"Go!"

"Sean!"

He hit the Close Door button and walked toward the three shifters, taking two steps before his human form dissolved in a shower of light and he transformed into the most vicious lizard he could conjure.

The Komodo dragon whipped its tail around, hissing at two wolves and a large red fox that charged him. Their long legs made them agile and fast, but the dragon dwarfed all of them in size. At nearly ten feet long, the thick-skinned reptile was not only massive, it was venomous.

They snarled at the lizard, but they could smell his poison. One slice of a serrated tooth and bacteria and anticoagulant would flood their veins, killing them slowly over the course of a few days.

Sean stalked toward them, his heavy neck holding up the venomous jaws of the animal while the wolves backed down the hallway. This standoff wouldn't last forever. More shifters would come, and it only took a couple of large cats to surround them and end the fight.

The fox yipped, and a wolf snarled in warning. Sean herded them toward the second bank of elevators in the resort, which overlooked an open-air atrium filled with tropical plants and a waterfall.

Scaring the warmbloods had been satisfying, but he needed to find Juni. Even now he hissed in rage that these three had distracted him from protecting her.

His lizard brain was focused on the prey in front of them, imagining the sweet tear of flesh if he got his teeth into a juicy haunch. His human brain battled to think past the lure of the hunt and focus on Juni.

He listened for her, but all he could hear was the rush of water from the artificial waterfall in the lobby.

They rounded the corner into the open-air portion of the sixth floor, and the wolves and the fox backed away from the glass edge of the landing, hiding in the overhang of the floor above.

They didn't want to be seen.

He could see a keen-eyed owl perched on a balcony two floors up and knew the bird was watching him. Damn.

Sean hated owls, the silent bastards.

He swung his head back toward the wary canines and edged his body toward the atrium. He would need to be fast for this to work, and he was going to be utterly exhausted if he managed to survive.

Get to Juni.

In the space of a blink, the Komodo disappeared and a tiny draco lizard slipped under the glass edge of the railing and flung itself into the atrium.

The silent owl took flight, aiming for the outstretched "wings" that Sean extended to glide across the expanse of the artificially lit tropical jungle in the hotel lobby.

The raptor missed by inches, and the draco landed in the climbing vines that crawled up the side of the acrid-smelling, chlorinated waterfall.

He swiftly shifted to a small emerald-green python, sliding beneath the broad leaves of the foliage and down, down, down to the first-floor lobby.

He could hear her now. He knew her steps. Thomas had cleverly hidden her in the crowd of partygoers they'd ridden down the elevator with, so Juni was laughing and mingling while Thomas scanned the lobby, probably looking for him.

Sean saw a covey of black-clad security heading toward them, and he could not allow them to take Thomas and Juni out of the public space. He slithered through the tropical flower beds and watched them near the doors, looking for an opportunity.

Which presented itself in a passing cart of yellow-and-white-striped towels an employee was pushing toward the pool.

Sean slid out of the flower beds and into a corner of the lobby, shifting back to human and grabbing a towel as the cart passed. He wrapped the towel around his waist, ran barefoot to the crowd of partygoers, and grabbed Juni's hand.

Someone gasped when they saw him, and a woman burst into laughter.

"Don't ask!" Sean shouted in a bright voice. "And don't make bets when you're drunk."

The crowd seemed to follow them as Sean pulled Juni toward the glass doors, and Thomas walked with them, carrying Juni's bag and scowling like someone's angry dad.

"Fucking fool," Thomas grumbled as they walked out into the scorching desert air.

"Sean, are you—?"

"Questions in the cab."

Lobo's people were still following them, but none of them were in animal form. An elegant brunette in a cream-colored suit walked out the doors with a half dozen men and women in black uniforms behind her. She crossed her arms over her chest, and her eyes narrowed at Sean and Juni.

"I know her," Juni whispered. "That's his publicist."

"She's a shifter."

The VIP party was just starting to break up, and most of the guests were waiting for the valet or private cars in front. No one seemed to object when a naked man wrapped in a pool towel laughingly pushed to the head of the line and ran toward the first cab that pulled up to the hotel.

Sean opened the cab door and shoved Juni into the safety of

the cab; then Thomas jumped in front and Sean walked around to the other side, his eyes locked on the woman in the cream suit.

There was something distinctly feline about her, though Sean couldn't say what it was.

She met his stare, cocked her head, nodded at him a little, then flicked her finger at the people following her.

Sean finally broke eye contact when he ducked into the back of the cab. "Go, go, go."

"Where we going, man?"

"Anywhere but here."

He finally looked at Juni, whose eyes were wide and terrified.

She whispered, "What happened to you?"

"I'm fine." Sean slid his arm around her shoulders and glanced at Thomas, who was already on his phone, talking to Caleb to find out where they were.

"Sean?"

"I promise." Sean looked down at Juni, and seeing her safe made everything fall into place.

She was it. She was his life. His joy. Making her safe and happy was the only thing that mattered.

His life had been in danger, but the only thing that could make him focus was the idea of getting back to Juni. Seeing her safe under his arm brought Sean such a hit of primal satisfaction he felt goose bumps rise on his neck.

He smiled, and the warmth of it drove away the cold fear that had taken over his body when he thought she was in danger. "I promise, Juniper. We're okay."

Sean leaned down, pressed his lips hard against hers in a lingering kiss, then pulled her into his chest. He wanted to feel her skin warm against his before he started to get the shakes.

He kissed the top of her head. "So that was exciting, but I have a few ideas about our second date that don't involve pursuit by hotel security, okay?"

"Sure." She wrapped her arms around his bare torso as

Thomas read off an address to the driver. "By the way, did you happen to see a really big lizard while you were walking around upstairs?"

"A really big lizard?" He watched the lights of the city race past the window. "As a matter of fact, I did."

chapter
twenty-two

"'WE ALL HAVE those we care for. People under our protection.'" Juni was sitting at Jena's kitchen table again, but this time she was the center of attention. "Clearly Lobo considers himself not just a gang leader but a protector of some kind."

"Whatever that means to him," Alex muttered.

They were sitting inside because while the sun had set, the heat hadn't abated much. Summer was reaching into the canyons and mountains around the Springs, baking the small town with unrelenting heat.

Becca was asleep upstairs while Low and Bear were in the den, watching a movie and remaining suspiciously silent.

Juni leaned over to Caleb. "You know the boys are listening in, right?"

Her brother shrugged. "If they're old enough to help us escape a hotel owned by a sociopathic shifter, they're old enough to know what's going on," he muttered.

He'd been wearing a stormy expression since they drove out of Las Vegas, and it wasn't because their family vacation was ruined. Jena had been trying to calm him down, but Juni felt horribly guilty. It had been her idea to bring the family to the resort, and they'd ended up fleeing in the middle of the night while literal wolves stalked the corridors outside their bedrooms.

"At least we learned something from all this," Ollie said. "We got some confirmation about shit that was only theoretical before."

Allie said, "There's still a lot we don't know."

Sean nodded. "But I think all of us have been working around the idea that Lobo was distantly related to someone in the Springs, right? A shifter who fathered a child he didn't know about, or someone who left and disappeared. What he said to Juni confirms that."

There were nods and murmurs of agreement around the room.

"His saying he had family roots in the area confirms it, but it doesn't explain his anger," Jena said. "He hates us. He hates the whole town, and he's tried to kill Sean on multiple occasions now."

Maggie piped up. "He's not the first person to want to kill Sean. He can be pretty irritating."

"Thanks, sis." Sean rolled his eyes. "Nice to feel loved."

"No problem."

Juni watched Alex's face because there was something going on there. There was a darkness behind his expression that seemed to be hiding a larger anger or worry. "Alex, you and Ted were going to look through the archives, right? Did you find anything about someone who might have been sent away? Someone who could have been related to Lobo?"

"There wasn't much." Ted was the one who answered. "And I checked with my mother. It sounds like most of the people who have been banished over the years eventually came back, or their families did. We're drawn here; it's instinctive."

"That's true," Allie said. "Even families who move away tend to come back every year or so. We don't do very well if we're away from the spring too long. It makes us weird."

Sean kicked his long legs out. "We're all kinda weird anyway."

Juni was still looking at Alex. "Has anyone questioned the older members of the town council?"

Alex looked up and met her stare. "My dad is hiding something."

Ted looked at him with a frown. "You didn't tell me that. What makes you think that?"

He shook his head slowly. "I can just tell. I knew the early records of the Springs were spotty, but there were some big gaps, and when I asked my mom and dad about it, my dad ducked the question, tried to change the subject. He kept talking about how to get the human police involved in taking out Lobo. Didn't seem to even register that this is something we have to take care of ourselves."

"If we get human authorities involved," Ollie said, "it could blow back on us. That guy gets arrested and put in custody, what happens on the first full moon night? What happens to the other shifters Sean mentioned?" The big man shook his head. "Absolutely not. We take care of Lobo ourselves."

"It's more than just him though," Sean said. "Two wolves at least and a big-ass fox. Two large cats. We know his old second was a snake."

"So that's three types of shifters at least," Jena said. "And there could be more."

"There was an owl too."

"Four types of shifters."

"The woman I met who organized the promotion contract," Juni said. "I'm pretty sure she was one because she felt off about Caleb." She turned to her brother. "Remember that? Her name was Mariana Cordova."

Caleb said, "She said she was from Santa Fe, but she traveled with Abano. Seemed pretty cozy with the man."

"I agree," Juni said. "She was more than just a publicist."

"That's the woman who was in front of the hotel when we were leaving?" Sean asked.

Juni nodded.

"So she is a shifter." Sean nodded. "My gut instinct is cat, but I don't know why. And she had at least six people with her. That was minutes after I shifted and got down to the lobby. I didn't even have clothes on. So those guys weren't the ones chasing me on the sixth floor."

Ted smirked. "I'm not going to lie, I am somewhat sad I missed this."

"Me going scaly in a fancy hotel or me getting chased by three scruffy mutts?"

"Both. Definitely both."

Juni felt her phone buzzing in her pocket. She pulled it out to see Rani's name on the screen. "Shit."

Sean glanced at the phone. "You haven't talked to her since you bailed on the hotel?"

"How exactly am I supposed to explain this?" She answered it and stood. "Hey Rani, I'm at my brother's house. Let me get to a quiet place."

Juni walked out the sliding glass doors and shut them behind her. "So about the Esencia thing—"

"What the hell happened?" Rani sounded pissed. "I told you it had to be presented as a personal thing, but you tore out of there in the middle of the night and people saw you, Juni."

She winced as she walked across the deck and opened her trailer door. "Are there pictures online?"

"There were pictures of you *and* Sean on a couple of timelines and he looks naked."

"Okay, so—"

"It's a good thing Blythe Hanson likes you so much. I talked to her and she promised to get the word out to delete those pics, but what the hell? Also I heavily hinted that Sean's been having mental health issues, so he better be okay with that."

The trailer door cracked open behind her, and she saw Sean's head poke in.

Still Rani? he mouthed.

Juni nodded. "I'll tell him and I'm sure he'll understand."

He was going to be pissed.

"And now I've got the head of PR for Esencia calling me and trying to get your contact details? What the hell is going on?"

Sean held his hand out for the phone, but Juni shook her head.

"Are they giving you a headache about this?" Juni rubbed her eyes. "Whatever the cost of the room was, I'll cover it. I don't want them harassing you."

"I don't care about the room, Juni. Besides, I told them that the magazine wasn't involved in any of this and they had to take it up with you. They don't have any leverage with me. I'm just worried about what happened."

Sean held his hand out again, and Juni turned her back. "I don't want to get into details, but the owner of the hotel got me into the VIP section at that party, and he made me very uncomfortable."

Rani was silent.

"I don't want to make any kind of formal complaint," Juni continued, "because nothing really happened."

"Juni." Rani's voice was scary. "Did he—?"

"He didn't do anything." She turned, and Sean's face was stormy. "It was a vibe and my alarms were going off, so I listened to my gut and got out of there."

"Good." The editor let out a long breath. "Okay, I understand."

"I did not feel comfortable hanging in that hotel after that because I knew I wasn't going to return to that party, so I got my family out and we left. That's all I can say."

"Do you want me to say something on my end?"

She knew Sean could hear Rani on the other end of the phone because his eyebrows went up.

"No," Juni said. "In fact, is it Mariana Cordova calling you?"

"I think that was her name, yes."

Juni went with her gut. Again. "Give her my number. Tell her to contact me directly."

"Are you sure?"

"Yep." Juni wasn't a shrinking violet, and she wasn't going to take a hit to her professional reputation. Besides, if Mariana was who Juni thought she was, none of this would ever get out to the public. "I'll deal with it."

"Okay." Rani sounded unsure. "I can help if you want."

"Absolutely not," Juni said. "This is my mess."

"What was Sean doing there?" Rani asked. "And why was he naked? Is he actually having some kind of breakdown?"

He started to open his mouth, but Juni slapped a hand over it. "It's a long story, but no, he's not having a breakdown. I woke him up in the middle of the night, so it's not his fault."

"I have so many questions."

"It's late." Juni glanced at the clock. "Do you mind if we catch up tomorrow?"

"Tell Sean I'm putting out hints that he'll be back in two months, so he better get his shit together."

Juni felt a spike of frustration. "You know, I'm not his agent." He nipped her fingers, and she pulled her hand away from his mouth. "Rani, I need to go."

"I'll talk to you tomorrow."

"Bye." She hung up before Sean could say a word. "I'm not in the mood for you right now."

"What?" His eyes went wide. "What did I do?"

"I'm making excuses for you." She shook the phone in his face. "To my boss! I am making excuses for you to my *boss*." She tossed the phone on the counter and turned to take off the heavy earrings that were making her ears ache. "I'm done with covering for you and making excuses, Sean. From now on, I'm going to tell Rani if she wants to talk to you, she needs to call you herself."

"I never asked you to make excuses for me." Now Sean sounded pissed. "Why would you?"

She spun on him. "Because I care about your stupid career, you idiot! Because I care about *you*. Because I don't want you to throw everything you've worked for away, and I don't want to think we have no possible future together because you plan on being stuck in this town for the rest of your life like a shitty martyr!"

Sean stepped forward and grabbed her shoulders, bending down to kiss her. At the last moment, Juni ducked away.

"Why?" Sean asked.

"I'm not doing this again." Juni felt like crying. "You're going to kiss me and tease me and I'm going to think that it means something, and then you're going to change your mind or second-guess yourself and you're going to leave and I'll be dangling my heart in the wind like an idiot *again*."

"No." He stalked toward her. "I'm not leaving. Not anymore."

"Bullshit." She was going to cry, and it pissed her off. "Sean, please—"

"I love you."

Juni froze.

Sean's voice was barely over a whisper. "Please don't tell me to leave." His eyes were wide and his shoulders tense. His jaw was locked, and she could see a muscle near his ear jumping with nerves.

He was bracing for rejection.

She walked toward him, not letting her eyes waver on his. "You love me." She didn't doubt him for a second. Sean Quinn would never have let those words slip out of his mouth unless he was sure.

"You don't have to love me back," he said quickly. "I know I've jerked you around and I'm probably not the best bet, Juni. I understand all the reasons you would be really smart to stay away from—"

She threw her arms around his shoulders and kissed him, stopping the flood of words that hurt her heart.

He *was* the smart choice. He *was* the best choice ever because he was the best man she had ever known and he tried so hard to hide it.

She pulled away from his mouth. "I love you too. So much."

Sean let out a shaky breath, then bent down, put his arms around her waist, and lifted her in his arms. "No more waiting."

chapter
twenty-three

THIS WAS HAPPENING. This was really happening after so many years of waiting and wishing and keeping the tightest of leashes on his craving for her. Juni was in his arms and she loved him.

She *loved* him?

Sean couldn't stop touching her. He lifted her in his arms, and Juni wrapped her legs around his waist. They were pressed together, but he wanted more. He wanted skin. One hand slid under her shirt at the small of her back and he felt her, soft and warm.

She tore her mouth from his. "Bed."

"This is a trailer. Rocking happens."

"Don't care."

"Mine," he said. "Not yours." Her trailer was right behind her brother's house, and Sean was not holding back. "Juni—"

"Fine, fine, fine." She unwrapped her legs and wiggled down his body, brushing against his very hard erection. "Car?"

He grabbed the keys from his pocket. "Grab your stuff."

Juni frowned. "Stuff?"

He leaned down, cupped her cheek, and kissed her again. "Get whatever you want for the night, because once I have you alone, I'm not letting you come back here for a while."

Her cheeks were flushed and her lips swollen. "Right." She lifted a hand. "Uh... good idea." She started to throw random things in a canvas grocery bag.

Sean had no idea what she'd packed, but minutes later they were sneaking out her door and running to the truck that was parked on the side of Caleb and Jena's house.

He opened the passenger door, and Juni jumped inside. "You know, you have a trailer too."

"Yeah, but mine is more than ten steps away from their house."

He parked the truck behind his trailer, under a stand of cottonwood trees that created a private feel to the half-restored Airstream. She was out of the car faster than he was, and Sean nearly ran to keep up with her, grabbing her around the waist and pushing her up against the side of the cool metal like the night he'd kissed her and the snake had interrupted them.

"Tell the truth," she panted between furious kisses. "Did you kiss me that night to distract me?"

"Yes." Sean ran his lips down the side of her neck and licked at the skin blooming with heat. "And no."

"What does that mean?"

He yanked the door open and took her hand. "Juni, there hasn't been a moment since Chiang Mai that I've been around you and *haven't* wanted to kiss you." He grabbed her bag and tossed it on the narrow table by the door. "It's more a question of when I gave in to temptation." He turned to see her standing by the door, staring at him. "What?"

Shit, was she changing her mind?

Please don't change your mind.

"Juni, what—?"

"Really?" Her voice was a whisper.

Sean took in her wide, dark eyes.

Quinn, you asshole. What did you do to this woman?

He dropped his keys on the counter and fell to his knees in front of her. "Juniper Rain Hawkins, if I have ever given you cause to doubt yourself or doubt how much I wanted you, I am the biggest ass in the known universe and I am so sorry." He put his hands on her hips, kneading the soft curve where her waist turned out.

She looked down at him, brushing the hair back from his forehead. "That's a pretty good apology."

She ran her fingers through his hair, and Sean laid his head against her soft belly, inhaling the scent of her skin with a tinge of lemon from her soap that morning.

He closed his eyes and turned in to her hand. "I wanted you so much I couldn't sleep." He pushed his hands back to cup the curve of her bottom, sliding his fingers down to the back of her thighs, then up again. "I was an asshole half the time we were together because all I could think about was how much I wanted you and how you deserved so much better than my sorry ass."

She was wearing jeans, and he needed them gone.

Sean took the button off her jeans between his teeth and tugged. "Off."

Juni's breath caught. "So take them off."

He looked up just as one hand slid between her thighs. "My hands are busy." His teeth tugged at the waist. "Off." His hands left her thighs and slid down the inside of her legs, reaching her knees and gently nudging her feet apart.

Slowly, Quinn.

He'd been dreaming of having Juni naked beneath him for years. He was too likely to rush if he didn't remind himself to take his time and savor. He was starved for her, his mouth watering at the scent of her arousal.

Juni flicked the button of her pants open, then pulled down the zipper, revealing a pop of bright blue panties with butterflies on them. "I don't really have sexy underwear."

Sean's mouth was hanging open at the sight of her, and his

erection was screaming. "Yeah, this is good." He reached up, yanked her jeans down her legs, and groaned at the sight of her bare thighs and the narrow triangle of blue cotton. "Oh my God."

She stepped out of her jeans, and the scent of her arousal was everywhere. "Should we—?"

He leaned forward, his hands cupping her bottom as he brought her cotton-clad pussy to his mouth. He licked over the cotton, dipping his tongue between her thighs and licking up the taste of her already-soaked panties.

"Oh fuck." She braced one hand on the counter and another on his shoulder. "Yes."

He couldn't wait. He pulled the panties down her legs, tossed the scrap of cloth over his shoulder, and opened her thighs to bare her sex. He draped one leg over his shoulder, bent his head, and feasted.

"Sean." Her voice was high and needy. "What... I mean...?"

He pulled his mouth away and looked up. "You don't want—?"

"Yes!" She grabbed his head and pushed his face back to her pussy. "I don't know what I'm saying. I can't think. Yes. Just... yes."

Thank fuck. He licked up the delicious center of her sex, teasing the sensitive flesh as she dug her fingers into his shoulder, holding his hair in an iron grip.

He was in heaven, surrounded by the scent and taste of her. He could feel the tension building under his lips and tongue, so he slowed down, savoring the sweet flesh, licking up her center like she was his own personal dessert.

"Oh, you better not."

He smiled against her skin. "Don't rush me."

"Sean!"

He peppered her pussy with teasing kisses. "I've been thinking about this for a very long time."

"So have I." She let out a strangled breath that was half groan. "Make me come."

"Who's stopping you?" He gave her a few more teasing licks. "Come already."

She arched her hips into his face and he gave in to temptation again, burying his mouth between her legs as he teased her opening with his thumb.

She was drenched.

"Oh fuck." She was nearly crying. "I can't. I can't."

He reached under her shirt with his other hand and flicked his thumb over one hard nipple, teasing it as her back arched.

She convulsed around him, her pleasure flooding his senses. He pulled away, putting her foot on the floor and standing to lift her and bring her to the bed. She was limp in his arms, her body soft and her arms thrown around his shoulders.

Sean placed her on the bed and quickly stripped away his clothes. Juni had pulled off the rusty-red tank top she'd been wearing with her jeans and was grappling with her bra until Sean reached over, rolled her to the side, and unclipped it.

"You should skip underwear," he said, sliding into the bed behind her and pulling her back into his chest. "It just gets in the way."

"Clothes too?"

"Clothing is always optional when you're hanging with shapeshifters." He leaned over and sank his teeth into her shoulder. "I don't have condoms, so we don't have to—"

"Birth control." She held up her arm. "I'm good for five years, and I tested after my last partner."

His cock nearly jumped. "I'm clean too. I haven't really... It's been a while."

Juni looked over her shoulder, reached back, and closed her hand around his cock. "Hmm. Poor guy. Have you been ignoring him?"

He closed his eyes and bit his bottom lip, trying to garner some hint of control. "He's been pretty focused on you for a while." Sean reached around, lifting her knee and pulling it over his leg, shifting her body to open for him.

Juni turned her head to the side, and Sean took her lips as he slid into her.

She let out a long sigh and arched back, taking him deeper. "Yes." Her voice was a whisper. "Sean, yes."

His head was swimming, and he pressed his forehead to her shoulder, closing his eyes as he reveled in the feel of her body caressing his. She was heat and sensation, a wave of pleasure that left him mindless as he started to move.

He wrapped his arms around her, teasing and playing with her delicate breasts with both hands as his hips drove into hers.

Sean wasn't going to last long—it had been too many years of craving her like a forbidden drug. He wanted her to come again. He reached down, teasing her body with his left hand as she started cursing in a low whisper.

"I can't."

"You can." He closed his eyes and kissed the back of her neck. "Juni—"

"Fuck!"

Her body exploded around his cock, and Sean felt the climax barrel through his body. He released, his arms embracing her from behind, holding her to his chest as he came.

Mine.

He wasn't giving her up. Not ever. He didn't care what he had to do, but Juni was his and he would spend the rest of his life making her happy. And making her come because that was awesome.

"Oh my God." Juni was panting. "Oh my..." She could barely catch her breath. "I've never come twice like that."

He pulled out, flipped her over, and gathered her into his arms. "Then we'll have to start catching you up." He took her mouth and settled into a long kiss, stroking her tongue with his own, brushing strands of hair back from her cheeks, petting her skin as he turned her tiny frame around. "I love you so much."

"I don't know what to do with my limbs." She felt boneless under him. "Please don't ask me to move for the next hour or so."

"Fair enough." He lifted her arm and draped it over his shoulder. "I'm gonna take a quick nap; then I'm gonna make you come again."

"Oh my God."

"I didn't get to see your face last time. I really want to see your face." He was already falling asleep. "I better lock up before I pass out."

"Yeah."

He pulled away and she flopped onto the bed limply, naked and soft in the tangled cotton sheets. The lamp over the kitchen sink was the only one lit, and it made her soft brown skin glow with a gold light.

"I'm really not joking about the moving thing," she muttered with her eyes closed. "You fucked me boneless."

And he was hard again.

She opened her eyes, saw him standing at attention, and blinked. "Wow, you weren't joking about the recovery thing, huh?"

He quickly locked the doors, peering into the darkness and listening for anything lurking around the trailer.

Nothing. The night patrols would be guarding the town perimeter. Juni was within reach. His family was defended.

Rest.

He felt his shoulders relax as he turned back to the bed.

Juni was there, watching him with sleepy eyes and a lingering smile. "Hey."

Sean felt happy in a way that felt alien. But good. "Hey."

She scooted over. "Come and sleep."

Sean walked toward her, got into the bed next to her, staring as she fussed with the sheets and pillows.

"I'd ask if you have a blanket, but the sheets are probably enough with this heat." She pulled the cool cotton over them and fluffed the pillows. "Your bed is small like mine, but the mattress is good. Do you have a fan in here?"

Sean lay next to her, watching her face as she made them a nest.

Juni caught his stare and smiled. "Am I fussing?"

"Yes."

"Sorry, I'll relax. I just—"

"I like it." He couldn't stop looking at her face. He was staring, but he couldn't seem to stop. "Move your stuff into here. Take over the trailer. Do whatever."

She smiled. "I'm not going to take over your trailer."

"You can take over my house then. Want to move to Laguna? Do you like balconies? I have two balconies and a roof garden I never use."

Juni blinked. "We don't have to plan everything right—"

"Just saying." He was grinning like an idiot. Juni might not realize it yet, but she would completely run his show. Whatever she wanted, he'd give her. Whatever made her happy, he'd do it. "Get some sleep." *Because I'm going to wake you up as soon as you get some rest.*

She settled down into the bed, and Sean wrapped his arms around her, holding her like he'd dreamed of for years.

"Sweet dreams."

He pressed his lips to her temple and closed his eyes. They had all night and the rest of their lives, but Sean had a vivid imagination and years to plan.

They weren't going to be getting much sleep that night.

chapter
twenty-four

JUNI WOKE when the light hit her face. She blinked her eyes and stretched, only to run into a very large something in the bed next to her.

"Ow." Sean lifted his head. "That's my nose."

Her breath caught, and the marathon from the night before popped into her head.

Sean. She was in Sean's bed.

And she felt like she'd hiked a mountain the day before.

He frowned. "Juni?"

"Just... processing."

He lifted an eyebrow. "Okay."

Sean Quinn had been the impossible dream for so many years she didn't quite know what to do with the reality. Her body felt deliciously used and sore. That hadn't been just sex. That had been...

Wow.

He was staring at her with an amused expression. "Do you need coffee?"

"Coffee would be good." Jena banged on her trailer door most mornings when the coffee was ready. Had she already called for

Juni? Had she realized she wasn't home? Were they worried? Did they know?

Juni sat up, holding the sheet to her body, feeling oddly shy. "Did I bring my phone? I should let Jena know I'm okay since I'm not in my trailer and—"

"She already texted me." Sean yawned. "She said to tell you to give her a call when you're ready for the day."

So her sister-in-law knew that something happened. "Oh. Okay. Good."

"I'm not hiding that we're together." He propped himself up on his elbows. "So don't even think about it."

Together. She and Sean Quinn were... together.

I don't know what that means.

"I think Jena wanted you to go with her to Palm Springs later," Sean continued. "To get Willow from the airport."

Willow McCann.

"Ah."

Sean cocked his head. "You realize she's just a friend, right? I don't know if you remember last night, but I told you—"

"I love you."

His smile was crooked. "You can say it again if you want to."

"I love you." She turned to him, still holding the sheet over her body. "And you love me."

"Yes." He reached for her and dragged her into his arms. "I love you and you love me. And we're together." He started nibbling along her ear. "Which we always should have been, but you stubbornly insisted on keeping things professional for all those years."

She closed her eyes and smiled. "I know. I'm so stubborn."

"Just an absolute" —he bit her earlobe— "stickler for the rules. Everyone talks about it."

"Rigid." She nodded. "Inflexible. I hear it all the time."

"I'm not surprised." His lips continued traveling down her neck. "I like to think that we could work on your flexibility together."

Her eyes were starting to cross. "Really? You'd do that for me?"

"I would." His hand slid under the sheet. "It would be a sacrifice, but I would."

Juni was easing down into the sheets, her skin starting to flush even as the light from the windows warmed the trailer. There was a fan on the other side of the small bedroom, and the cool air washed over her in a gust as Sean's mouth trailed from her neck, across her collarbone, and down between her breasts.

But before she could get lost in the moment, his head popped up.

"What is it?"

"Someone's coming."

She blinked and tried to clear her head. "Uh... what?"

"It's Jena." His shoulders relaxed. "Sorry. She probably got impatient with the time and all."

"What time is it?"

"Ten?"

Juni's eyes popped open. "Ten in the morning?"

"We didn't get much rest last night—I wanted you to sleep in."

She bolted out of bed. "I never sleep this late." It was summer, so unless you attacked the day before it got too hot, you were going to lose any and all motivation to do anything other than nap. "I need to talk to Rani. I need to call the office."

"I need to talk to Rani too." He scooted to the edge of the bed and pulled on a pair of loose pants over his boxers. "But you should stay here and sleep." He dropped his voice to a whisper. "No clothing necessary."

Juni snorted. "Right." She pulled on a tank top and her discarded jeans. "I need a shower."

"Shower here."

"My clean underwear is at my place, and someone is knocking at your door."

"Jena."

"How do you—?"

"Sean?" It *was* Jena. Of course it was. "You can't keep Juni to yourself forever. Ted and Allie and I want to take her into town when we drive in to get Willow."

Sean walked over and cracked open the door. "No. She's mine."

"Sean!" Juni held back a laugh.

"I know you're probably feeling very grabby right now and don't want to share her—hi, Juni!—but you can't keep her prisoner," Jena said from beyond the cracked door.

"I was not planning on hiding in his trailer all day." *Even though I would like to for several reasons.* She slid on her sandals and walked through the tiny kitchen to the door by the cozy dinette. "Sean, you need to let me go back to my house."

He turned with a frown. "Why?"

"Because I need to shower and clean up and charge my phone and eat breakfast and I don't think you have any food over here."

He narrowed his eyes. "Can I come over there?"

Juni glanced at her sister-in-law, who was trying to hide her smile. "Um... I guess that's fine. If you want to make coffee at my place—"

"Good idea. I'll make breakfast too." He swung open the door and walked out, scanning the front of the trailer yard even though Jena was the only one there. "It's clear."

Juni grabbed her keys and her phone with its dead battery. "Okay." Was he being clingy? Was Sean Quinn actually going to be... clingy?

"This is normal." Jena spoke in a low voice. "Just go with it."

"Really?"

"He's going to be like this for a while. It's a territorial shifter thing."

Okay, so that kind of made sense. "So I'm his territory now?"

He was walking ahead of them, his eyes scanning the path that led from his trailer to hers.

"No, you're not his territory," Jena continued. "You're his

mate. And his girlfriend. He'll get over the animal instincts after a while, but because it's new, just go with it." She cocked her head. "It's so cute to see him this way. I didn't think I ever would. Snakes can be very standoffish."

"I would not have expected Sean Quinn to be a stage-five clinger."

"Oh no, this is mild by shifter standards. Be glad he's not a wolf because they actually growl and they will snap at you if they think you're doing anything even slightly dangerous like... climbing a ladder. Or walking on a sidewalk without holding their hand."

"For real?

"Very much for real."

That would drive her crazy. "What do snake shifters do?"

"Poison anyone who looks at you sideways."

Juni froze. "What?"

"Kidding!" Jena laughed. "Mostly. But uh... they are just as territorial as the rest of them." Jena looped her arm through Juni's. "You should have fallen for a bird or a cat if you wanted space."

HE WAS GLARING at the back of Ted's car when the women pulled away from the house. Juni waved from the passenger's seat and saw Sean pull out his phone. A moment later, she got a text.

Can you share your location with me so I don't go crazy?

"Oh my God." Juni blinked. "He wants me to share my location."

"Oh yeah, that's normal," Allie said. "Especially right now. Things are new, and Lobo's people are lurking around town."

"Are they?" Juni sat up. "What happened?"

Ted was driving. "Two of my cousins snagged some of Lobo's people last night, a coyote and a bobcat. They tracked them through the canyon, cornered them, and they shifted back to human and tried to run away but—"

"Someone had already called Caleb," Jena said. "So he's holding both of them at the jail. A man and a woman—well, teenagers really. Maybe a tiny bit older? They haven't said anything yet."

Juni's mouth dropped open. "But we actually caught two of them? Like, two of Lobo's people?"

Ted nodded. "They're expanding the patrols at night."

"And the bears are digging more tunnels," Allie said. "They love tunnels."

Jena sat beside Allie, shaking her head. "I hate tunnels."

"You can't fly in them, so that makes sense, but I find them comforting." Allie patted Juni on the shoulder. "Just share your location for now. He'll share his with you, and then you can both breathe just a little bit easier when things are scary."

They were driving on the interstate, headed west into Palm Springs and the airport where Willow was landing in a few minutes. Juni had no idea how they were going to cram another person in the car, but maybe Willow was as slender as her namesake tree.

Juni glanced in the back where Jena and Allie were sitting. "How are you both so calm?"

Allie shrugged. "I only stress about things I can change. Until I know what I can change about this, I'm just rolling with it."

"And she has fangs," Jena said. "And claws. Nice sharp ones."

Allie winked at her. "I'm really good at hunting down snakes if Sean ever starts to annoy you."

"I'll let you know." Juni smiled. "So why did you all really want me to join you today? It doesn't take four people to get one woman from the airport."

"We just wanted to gossip," Ted said. "And we wanted to ask about the sex."

Uh... what?

Allie nodded. "We grew up with Sean, and he flirted with us all and played the aloof, distant asshole at times—"

"He's very good at being an aloof asshole," Jena said. "Kind of his signature move."

"True," Ted added. "But I always had this suspicion that he'd be the sweetest boyfriend when he finally fell for someone."

Juni stared at Ted. "I'm not going to tell you about the sex, so strike that from the agenda immediately."

"Not even a little bit?" Ted whined. "Come on, I have an infant and hardly any sex life at all right now because we're exhausted. I need to live vicariously."

"No." Juni looked over her shoulder. "Sex talk is predicated on the *sharing* of sex talk, and I love you, Jena, but I do not want to hear about my brother."

Ted curled her lip. "You know what? That's a good point."

Jena nodded. "Completely fair."

Allie sighed. "Oh well. We'll all just have to keep wondering, though I will say that Juni has a really nice glow this morning, so that's good."

They were shameless. She liked them. "Wasn't Sean like a brother to all of you or something?"

Allie burst into laughter.

Ted shook her head. "Definitely not."

"Sean had a reputation for being a really great kisser," Jena said. "So let's just say he got a lot of practice time in."

"For educational purposes," Allie added.

"Right." Juni had so many questions, but she had a feeling she didn't want the answers. She turned and watched the highway again while Ted continued driving.

"So while Jena and I were in Vegas, you guys were poking around here, right? What did you find?"

"Before we start with all that," Jena asked. "How much do you know about the founding of Cambio Springs?"

"Not much," Juni said. "I know that there were seven families that came out from back east, but that's about it."

"Seven families officially but five different clans. They migrated in the late nineteenth century after the Civil War was over. The McCanns were Confederate soldiers," Ted said. "They don't like to admit that, but they were."

"And my ancestor Thomas Crowe was a scout for the Confederacy," Jena said. "He was a Cherokee from North Carolina—his family hadn't moved west to Oklahoma, but he hated the federal government—and he knew the McCann brothers. When the war was over, he packed up and left the Carolinas with them."

"They picked up more people along the way," Ted said. "My family was originally from Texas. One brother and his widowed sister and all their kids. They were running out of land. They brought cattle with them."

"And Ollie's family were free Black Americans from the north who had already started west," Allie said. "And the Quinns…?"

"Were thieves," Jena said. "Well, Rory Quinn was. He was a pickpocket, but they saved him from drowning and brought him along."

"Seven families who became five clans," Allie said. "They reached the desert here and settled in the little valley at the mouth of the canyon where the spring is. There are a lot of springs in the area, but there were no permanent settlements at this one. They set up camp and started farming a little. There was space to graze the cattle, and they thought they could mine out here, maybe find silver in the hills."

The car crested the rolling hills of the desert and headed down the slope, the vast, flat plains of the Coachella Valley before them.

"Instead, after months of drinking from the springs, they discovered they could shift into different animals," Jena said. "Wolves and coyotes."

"Foxes," Allie said. "Bears."

"Big cats," Ted added. "And, of course, the snakes and reptiles."

"And birds!" Jena smiled. "The best shifter of all."

"Biased much?" Juni smiled. "So all the families have stayed here after all these years?"

"For the most part," Jena said. "Some people move away and only come back to visit. Some people move back when they have kids so the kids can be around other people like them and not feel weird."

"Alex left and came back," Ted said. "It's not that unusual."

"But sometimes people are banished too," Juni said. "And that's where Lobo probably came from?"

"That seems like the most likely explanation," Allie said. "But we're starting to feel like the elders might have a few secrets they haven't shared."

"Or they've forgotten," Jena said. "We're talking about a hundred and fifty years at least. That's five generations."

"Town records?" Juni asked. "Journals? Archives?"

"Willow found letters from her great-great-grandmother," Jena said. "That's why she went back east. There was something in there she wanted to track down."

"And then there's the quilt," Allie said. "My mother had a collection of quilts that goes back to the founding. One of them is a family tree quilt, and there's a name on there we didn't recognize."

"Early," Ted added. "Like, within the first generation born here."

Juni nodded. "So we're not talking about too many new people at that point."

"The first generations of kids kind of married who was around," Jena said. "McCanns married Vasquezes or Campbells or Crowes."

"Quinns have always tended to marry out of the clans," Allie said. "But this was a McCann quilt, and there was a woman who married in who didn't have a familiar name. She was listed as S. Abila."

"S. Abila." Juni nodded. "So someone in the McCann family married someone who wasn't a shifter. It was bound to happen, right?"

"It definitely would eventually," Allie said. "Except this woman's quilt square was decorated with two symbols. A wolf and a fox."

Juni turned to Allie. "So she was already a shifter?"

"That's what it looks like," Jena said. "The problem is, we don't have any records of an Abila family living in Cambio Springs. And at that point in time—"

"None of the McCanns had shifted into foxes," Allie added. "See, foxes and wolves aren't really alike. They're not like coyotes or dogs."

"But McCanns occasionally produces fox shifters, right?" Juni looked at Allie. "I mean, you are."

"I am." Allie smiled. "But what if the fox gene doesn't come from the McCanns? What if there was another family we never knew about?"

"Abila," Juni said. "I can't be the only one thinking that doesn't sound far off from—"

"Abano?" Ted asked. "Nope. You're definitely not the first one who noticed that. I asked my mother and got nothing. Alex asked his father and he got zip."

"And Willow?" They were pulling into the airport in Palm Springs. "Has she found anything yet?"

Jena rolled down her window and waved at a long-haired woman standing on the curb in the distance. "I think we're about to find out."

chapter
twenty-five

SEAN SAT BACK, stunned by what Willow had shared with the group.

"There were eight families," Willow said. "Not seven. There were eight. The Abilas were the last to join, east of Santa Fe."

Alex shook his head. "And why do we know nothing about them?"

Willow shrugged. "The letters Francie McCann wrote to her sister mention some kind of rift between families, but she was vague. There was definitely something between the Abilas and the Quinns though."

Juni was sitting next to him, and he was tempted to lift her up and place her directly in his lap, but that might have been going too far. He glared at Ollie on the other side of Juni, and the big man shifted away, hiding a smile behind a cough.

Good. Fine. That was fine. He knew he was being overly protective, but it was Juni and she didn't have claws or teeth.

"And so an entire family was just..." Juni's voice was soft. "Banished? Run out of town? How? Why?"

Sean flashed to the image of his uncle, a cagey smile always lurking on his face. "I knew he knew more than he was letting on."

Maggie nudged his foot. "The old man?"

"Yeah, I knew it." Sean sighed. "So we have to assume that Efrén Abano is descended from this clan who was banished and that's why he hates the town."

"And especially the Quinns," Juni murmured. "He'd hate your family most, right?"

"If we were the reason they were forced out, yeah." Sean nodded. "That makes sense."

"But this was generations ago." Allie turned to Ollie. "Have you heard anything about this? Anything from your grandfather?"

"Nothing," Ollie said. "Not a word."

"It was a long time ago," Willow said, "but the fact that none of us have ever heard of any of this feels suspicious."

"So what are they trying to hide?" Jena asked.

"Francie's letters were from the early 1900s, and Allie's family still has that quilt. Foxes still pop up within the McCann family, so I think it's safe to say that clan members who'd married into other clans were allowed to stay."

"They wouldn't turn the children away," Ted said. "They couldn't."

"But would the adults have allowed them to stay?" Alex asked. "If I were being banished, I sure as hell would take my kids with me."

Sean was imagining what it must have been like, an entire family of shapeshifters formed by the springs, changed by the water, who were then banished from the very thing that had given them supernatural powers.

Powers and weaknesses.

"They would have had to hide the children," he said. "They would have had to go someplace that no one would find them."

"Sounds like they went to Mexico," Juni said.

"On their own," Maggie said. "Shit. No wonder Lobo hates us."

"That's no excuse," Ollie said. "This guy tried to hunt Allie's *kids*. He entrapped and killed their dad. He murdered his own people after they'd been captured. He's been terrorizing people up and down the desert—"

"Drug dealers and growers." Sean shrugged. "Not that it makes it right."

"I don't give a shit about the drug dealers and the mob," Ollie said. "But I do care about our town and our people."

"Lobo's gang tried to kill Sean," Juni said. "Didn't you say that coyote tried to eat you?"

"To be fair, it's not the first time a coyote has tried to eat me," Sean said. "Usually it's one of Alex's cousins though."

"Hey," Alex said. "Don't antagonize the younger kids with the rattles and the hissing and they won't snap at you."

Juni shook her head. "You guys sound like you had the most feral childhood imaginable."

Ted nodded. "Feral is a good word for it."

Caleb cleared his throat. "Okay, getting back to business: How do we draw Lobo out? How do we get him to the Springs so he's in our territory? I'm done trying the legal way because I'm not getting any traction from law enforcement. Abano is too well-funded. Too slick, and he's made too many allies who are aboveboard. The police aren't going to do anything about this guy."

Juni raised her hand.

"Again with the hand raising," Alex muttered. "We're not in school."

"Maybe we don't try drawing him out," Juni said. "Maybe we try negotiating."

Sean shook his head. "That's what I had in mind when I went to see him, but he said leaving the Springs alone was impossible. His words. *Impossible*."

"But he's not the only one in the family, right?" Juni looked at Maggie and Sean. "Families have arguments."

"Not all of Lobo's people are Abilas," Sean said. "I mean, he's found others. Maybe he's tracked them down over the years.

Maybe that's been his goal all along, finding shifters who have lost connection to the Springs."

"God knows that Quinns have probably fathered more illegitimate children than the average shifter," Maggie said. "There's no way we could ever track them all down."

"But maybe Lobo has." Alex narrowed his eyes. "He's the head of this group. This *clan*—if we want to call it that—but I guarantee he's not the only leader."

The image of a dark-haired woman with keen eyes and a crisp suit popped into his mind.

"Mariana Cordova." Sean looked at Juni. "The woman in charge of marketing. You said she smelled something different about Caleb?"

Caleb said, "She said she recognized me."

"But that could have been a cover," Jena said. "You do smell different than mundane humans like Juni."

Sean scoffed. There was nothing mundane about Juni. "I'm positive that woman is a shifter, and I'm guessing she's a cat."

"I saw her with security," Juni said. "Outside the hotel. She had like half a dozen people with her who all looked pretty scary."

"I'm going to guess that Mariana Cordova is definitely in Lobo's inner circle," Sean said.

"And?"

Juni said, "Lobo doesn't want to negotiate, but what if Mariana does?"

Alex raised both eyebrows. "Go around the boss and speak to the lieutenant?" He nodded. "It could work."

"I have her number," Juni said. "I can try calling her directly. She might hang up on me, but she might listen too."

"And in the meantime," Caleb said. "I've got two shifters back at the jail, and neither one is saying a word." He looked at Sean. "Maybe they could use some encouragement."

"You have an idea?"

"I have an idea," Caleb said. "But I need Alex's help, and yours."

SEAN WALKED into the old concrete-block jail with a large grey wolf padding next to him. He nodded at Jeremy McCann, the deputy sheriff, who had his feet kicked up on the desk. The minute Jeremy spotted his alpha in wolf form, he kicked his feet off the desk and sat up straight.

"Boss."

The wolf huffed at Jeremy but kept walking.

Sean hadn't been back in this building since he was in his teens, but not much had changed. It had been updated with shifters in mind, so the old iron bars were covered with a layer of plexiglass to keep the smaller shifters in, and heavy-duty reinforced concrete would contain a rampaging bear if that was necessary.

Usually the jail was empty, but that afternoon Sean saw two sweaty young people sitting next to each other on the benches. They were both dressed in cast-off clothes and had no shoes.

The young man wore his scruffy brown hair down to his shoulders. He had a sprinkle of silver in the brown and golden eyes that told Sean he was definitely the coyote shifter of the two.

The woman across from the coyote was trying to keep her chin up, but Sean could see the fear in her eyes.

Cat.

She might be pissing herself on the inside, but she'd never show it.

Despite their silence and evident fear, they sat close together, nearly huddling in the cold cell.

"My name is Sean Quinn," he said to the two silent prisoners. "I'm the leader of the reptile clan here in Cambio Springs. This is Alex McCann, alpha of the wolves."

Alex bared his teeth and let out a low snarl, staring directly at the young man on the bench.

The young man began to tremble; then his body went into shakes.

Alex walked to the bars and growled deep in his throat.

"Kyle." The girl put her hand on the young man's arm. "He's not gonna hurt you. Relax. He can't hurt you."

"That's very incorrect," Sean said. "He both can and would hurt your friend. You were caught on our territory, and we're not the human police."

The woman's eyes flashed. "What do you want?"

"The better question is what do *you* want?" Sean crouched down, digging a hand into Alex's raised ruff. "Alex here is sick and tired of his people being messed with. We've had to patrol our borders for over a year now. We have scared kids and families. Lobo killed one of our people, tried to kill more, and sent a reptile assassin to try to attack a family who had already lost their father."

Marcus Ashford, Lobo's first enforcer, had nearly killed Allie and her entire family trying to find a quarter of a million dollars he'd lost in a poker game. That was Sean's first introduction to Lobo's gang, and it hadn't engendered much good will.

"Ashford was a maniac," the young woman said. "None of us liked him."

"*You* went after me in Vegas." Sean sniffed. "Yeah, pretty sure you were one of them."

The girl's eye twitched, but she said nothing else.

"We have a community to protect, and anyone working with Lobo isn't to be trusted."

The woman snorted. "And this is coming from a Quinn?"

"You've met my sister? Maggie?"

Her eyes narrowed. "Yeah, I met Maggie Quinn a time or two."

"I'll ask her if she remembers you." Sean dug his hand into Alex's fur, and the wolf's body vibrated with anger. "But we're not talking about Quinns—we're talking about wolves."

Kyle's body was shaking, and sweat poured off his body. He

was desperately trying not to shift, and it looked like he was losing the battle.

"Kyle, don't!"

Alex growled again, barking at the young man, who shattered into a reddish dust behind the bars of the jail cell, emerging as the scrawny coyote that Caleb had captured the night before.

The woman sprang to her feet. "Get him away from Kyle!"

Alex charged the bars, barking and snarling at the cowering animal.

"He's not going to hurt him," Sean said.

"Are you blind?" She ran up to the cell door and pounded on the plexiglass. "Get him away from us! Get him away!"

Jeremy McCann came strolling into the cellblock from the front desk. "Ma'am, your friend isn't going to get hurt by my alpha unless he defies him."

Her face got paler. "We're not part of your pack."

"That's exactly the problem." Sean stared at the girl. "He's in McCann territory, and he's a canine shifter. He'll submit to Alex's authority or he'll die."

She pounded on the bars. "Fuck you!"

Sean shrugged. "You can yell all you want, but this is between the wolves."

"Kyle is not a wolf!"

"Doesn't matter." Sean kept his eyes on her. "You feeling okay?"

The girl didn't look okay. She was sweating and her face was pale. Her hands were shaking. "I'm fine."

The deputy frowned. "No, you're not."

"Jeremy, call Ted."

"We just need the water, okay!" She gripped the bars of the cell. "Lobo said that when we take over the town, we'll be able to drink from the spring. The sickness will go away after that."

Sean froze. "What sickness?"

There was a high whine, and Sean smelled urine. The coyote

had rolled over onto his back, peeing in submission under Alex's snarls. The wolf immediately stopped barking, letting out an inquisitive whine that had Jeremy running for the keys.

Sean kept his eyes on the girl. "Tell me about the sickness."

"Some of us shift... wrong." She was shaking again, and even though the door was about to open, she went back to the bench and slumped against the wall. "Lobo's going to kill Kyle." Her face crumpled into tears. "We're both dead now."

Sean leaned against the bars as Jeremy unlocked the cell door, allowing Alex to rush into the cell. The wolf nosed the coyote under his chin, and the younger animal lifted his head and let out a whine. Alex allowed the coyote to sniff him, standing protectively over the young male, who scooted away from the puddle of urine, sliding on his belly until he was under Alex's nose again, baring his throat and looking away.

"He submitted," Sean said. "Your friend is safe, but you're not looking good." He walked into the cell and crouched next to her. "What's your name?"

She shook her head, and he could see the tears in her eyes. "Doesn't matter. We're dead now."

"No, you're not." He looked over his shoulder. "Jeremy, tell Ted to bring water from the fresh spring. They both need to drink."

The girl's eyes went wide. "No. He said you don't let outsiders drink the water."

"We don't let *mundane* humans drink the water," Sean said. "But you're shifters, and if I'm right, your family was as much a part of this place as my family is." He put a hand on her shoulder. "That means that the fresh spring belongs to you too. What's your name?"

She slumped against the wall, her eyes wide with confusion, fear, and maybe even a little hope. "Sadie. My name is Sadie."

Sean squeezed her shoulder. "Nice to meet you, Sadie. Let's get you feeling better. Then we can talk."

chapter
twenty-six

THE GIRL NAMED Sadie couldn't have been more than twenty-one or twenty-two, but her eyes were old. She had red-brown hair, amber eyes, and tan skin that was slowly gaining more color as she scarfed down the cornbread and chili that Jena had brought from the diner.

Her eyes darted around the room, taking everything in. She was wary, and not without reason.

They'd moved the young people from the jail to the clinic after Ted insisted on checking them out. Three wolves were in the waiting room along with Ted's cousin Rafael, who shifted into the biggest black cat Juni had ever seen in her life. There was a giant black bear parked outside in front of the window, sitting in the shade of a paloverde tree.

The boy named Kyle had come into the clinic as a coyote but shifted back to human when Alex entered the room. He was also eating and drinking like he hadn't seen food in days.

Both the kids were unnaturally thin, but as they ate the food and drank the water from the fresh spring, color started to return to their cheeks.

Juni felt like an outsider, but Sean didn't want to let her out of his sight, and they were trying to figure out whether Juni's idea had merit. Were there any of Lobo's gang who might be open to reason?

Jena and Caleb went to the waiting room with the guards, leaving Ted, Alex, Juni, and Sean with the two young people.

Alex asked, "Where did he find you?"

Sadie answered. "Lobo?"

Sean nodded.

She swallowed and took a long drink before she spoke. "I was born outside El Paso. Just this cruddy little town with like three hundred people in it. My mom... she never talked much about my dad, just said that he'd taken off."

"Did he know she was pregnant?"

Sadie shook her head. "She said he didn't. She wasn't a bad mom, but when things started to... happen..." The girl looked down. "She was afraid of me. I took off after that. Ran away. I thought something was wrong with me, and I was really scared, but I didn't know what to do." She looked at Ted. "You know. When you're a cat, sometimes it's easier to just be an animal."

Ted nodded. "I understand."

"It was safer to be a bobcat than a girl, but I was always scared. Sometimes I'd shift when I could find clothes and go into towns, but the longer I was living as a cat, the harder it got to stay human. Until I met Lobo. Well, one of his people."

"Where was that?"

"New Mexico." She took another bite of chili. "He has a big compound there."

Sean nodded. "How did they find you?"

"I don't know how I knew, but there was one night when I was out hunting and this mountain lion was in the hills. I saw her tracks and I was trying to keep away, but when I smelled her..." Sadie shrugged. "I knew. Somehow I just knew because she didn't smell like a wild cougar. She smelled like me."

"You're most likely related to her in some way," Ted said. "All the cats came from two families."

Sadie watched her carefully. "Do you know who my dad is?"

Ted shook her head. "I don't. It could be any number of men in the cat clan, but if you really want to find him, we can try. Shifters don't do DNA profiles, but there are other ways."

"She looks like a Vasquez," Sean muttered.

"Yeah." Ted smiled and touched the girl's hand. "You do."

"Huh." The girl was skeptical to say the least. "Anyway, she found me, shifted, and told me I wasn't a freak and I wasn't alone."

"Who was it?" Juni asked. "Anyone we might know?"

"Mariana," Sadie said. "She took care of me."

Juni filed that away. "She took you back to Lobo's compound?"

"Yeah." Sadie glanced at Kyle. "Kyle was already there."

"I was born at the compound." The boy's voice was barely over a whisper. "Lobo says he's my uncle, but that didn't mean he was nice to me or anything. If anything..."

"He's stricter with the foxes and the coyotes. He trusts the wolves more." Sadie looked at Alex. "He's a wolf, but he doesn't shift much. Only on full moon nights."

Alex kicked his legs out. "An alpha wolf can make other wolves submit to him. Foxes and coyotes are more likely to go their own way. They're not tied to a pack. He won't trust anyone he can't control."

Juni muttered, "Fits most bullies I know."

"He's not a bully." Sadie's eyes were sharp. "Bullies push you around and take your lunch money. Lobo *kills* anyone who crosses him."

"He killed a young man we sent back with a message," Sean said. "Before you came to town. This was after Allie caught the snake shifter who killed her ex-husband."

"I don't know about any of that," Sadie said. "But Kyle nearly died from a snakebite, and Lobo refused to call a doctor. Mariana was pissed."

 221

"Regular snake or shifter?"

"Shifter. He keeps a few snakes around, but not many. He doesn't trust them. Treats them like shit."

Alex and Sean exchanged a look. "That's probably why Ashford was willing to go behind his back to try to get that money."

"There are a few birds in the gang, but it's kind of the same thing," Sadie said. "He doesn't trust them, but he does treat them better, so they hang around."

Juni pulled up a chair and sat across from Sadie. "You said Mariana was pissed when Lobo didn't call a doctor for Kyle. Did they fight?"

Sadie nodded. "She's the only one who can argue with him. They're related, I think. Not sure how because she's a cat like me."

"Cats and wolves can come from the same family," Ted said. "If one parent is a wolf shifter and the other is a cat, the kids can be either."

"I didn't know that." Sadie's color had returned, and her cheeks bore a ruddy color in the warm tan skin. "I don't know if Lobo and Mariana are brother and sister. They don't act like it."

"If you had a problem," Juni said, "would you go to Lobo or Mariana?"

Kyle snorted. "That's a no-brainer."

"Mariana isn't nice, but she's practical," Sadie said. "If you can show her that it's good for the group to help you with your problem, she'll help you. She has big plans for the hotels and stuff."

Sean glanced at Juni. "That's good to know."

"She won't cross Lobo though," Sadie said. "No way. She's loyal."

Juni had a feeling that pushed hard enough, that might not be the case. "What kind of thing pisses her off the most?"

Kyle spoke. "Wasting people. Efrén got pissed at me once and told one of the snakes to shift and bite me and that made Mariana mad. She said, 'That's a waste, Efrén.'" The boy shrugged. "I'm a good tracker. I have a really sharp nose—that's why we were sneaking in. I tracked the fresh spring, and we were going to steal some of the water and take it back for him."

Not the warm fuzzies that Juni was hoping for, but then again, she had a feeling that warm and fuzzy wouldn't survive long in Lobo's gang.

"You didn't come back," Alex said. "I'm sure they were expecting you. What will Lobo do next?"

"Send more people," Sadie said. "Trust me, he really wants that water."

JUNI FLIPPED the business card with Mariana Cordova's phone number on it. Sean, Alex, and Ted were still interviewing the young shifters and making plans on where to keep them—both the kids were actually voting for the jail again because it felt safe—but Juni kept thinking about Mariana.

Bright, fashionable, publicity-conscious Mariana Cordova. Public relations and promotions. She was the face of Efrén Abano's organization while he was the bully behind the scenes.

Juni didn't care what Sadie said, Lobo was a classic bully. Only instead of lunch money, he wanted control of the spring that made shifters stronger.

Mariana, on the other hand...

Juni couldn't see a woman with Louboutin shoes and Chanel suits living happily in Cambio Springs.

She took out her phone and called the number. Seconds later, a voice answered.

"I haven't seen the Instagram posts from the party yet."

"Bill me for the room," Juni said. "Kind of got distracted when your goons were chasing my family out of the hotel."

"Trust me, we had no intention of driving you out. We wanted to talk to you."

"Is that so?" Juni kept her eyes on the door to the exam room. "So talk now."

"Are they alive?"

Juni frowned. "Who?"

"Kyle and Sadie."

Juni made a note that Mariana knew the two kids' names. "Of course they're alive. We're not monsters."

"We? So you're grouping yourself with these shifters now? That's very interesting. Are you in love with the Quinn?"

"That's none of your business. Are you in love with Lobo?"

"Don't be ridiculous." The tone of utter disgust was enough to confirm their relationship for Juni.

"So you're a sister or a cousin?" Juni said. "Something like that. I understand family loyalty, but he's going to end up killing your business. He's already screwing things up, and you know it."

Mariana was quiet on the other side.

"Wasting time on intimidating small-time drug dealers in the desert," Juni said. "Parking valuable people at grow houses just to put pressure on the leaders here? One, it's not working; people from the Springs don't like the drug trade either, they just try to ignore it. Two, you're pissing off the Italian mob, which is going to cost money you don't want to spend. Three, it's a waste of your resources when you've been busy building a legitimate hotel empire that could make you a lot more money than the petty drug trade."

"I highly doubt you're interested in my well-being or the health of our enterprises," Mariana said. "What do you want?"

"I don't want anything." Juni said a silent prayer of thanks that they were on the phone and the woman wouldn't be able to detect the lie. "But I do want to get out of here and not have to worry about my niece and nephews getting bitten by a snake in their sleep. So why don't you put your very creative mind to work and figure out what needs to happen?"

"You're saying there's a deal that can be worked out?"

"I'm sitting in a medical clinic right now, watching two of your people eat healthy food and drink water from that damn spring that's making them look like kids again instead of strung-out addicts. The doctor here—who's a shifter and a cat like you—is practically shoving that water down their throats to make them feel better."

Juni waited to let it sink in. There was complete silence on the other end of the call.

"Mariana," she continued, "I don't know what fiction Efrén Abano has been feeding you, but no one in this town is going to keep your people from drinking the water here."

"Our people were banished."

"No, your great-great-grandsomethings were banished," Juni said. "And no one here even remembers what your clan did. You weren't enemies to anyone here until Lobo made you enemies."

There was a long silence.

"Are you still there?" Juni asked.

"I'm listening."

Juni kept going. "So the question is: Are you going to hang on to a grudge that died three generations ago instead of making a deal to end this standoff and get your people healthy?"

Mariana said nothing, but Juni knew she was still there.

"I'm going to hang up. You have my number now. Call me when you want to talk."

"Kyle and Sadie?"

"They're staying here for now," Juni said. "They think Lobo will kill them if they go back. Are they right?"

Her silence confirmed Juni's suspicions.

"The guards aren't going away," Juni added. "The whole town is on alert. We can't trust Lobo when he's clearly been aggressive. Can we trust you?"

Mariana hung up.

Juni walked back to the exam room, and Sean turned to look at her. "Hey." He narrowed his eyes. "You did something."

She smiled. "You have a minute?"

"Always."

They walked outside, past the guards in the waiting room, and Juni nearly jumped when she saw another large black bear leaning on the railing outside, snoring a little bit.

"Jaden!" Sean barked.

The bear started, letting out a low growl.

"Ollie know you're sleeping on the job?"

The animal grumbled.

"I know it's hot, but you gotta stay awake." Sean walked past the looming animal and walked Juni to his truck. They got inside, and he immediately turned on the air conditioner. "Fuck." He sighed. "I'm so ready to leave this place."

"I called Mariana Cordova," she blurted.

Sean's mouth dropped. "When?"

"Just now."

"And?"

"And I told her how Sadie and Kyle were. She asked. Told her that Lobo was probably wasting their money and resources. Took a leap there, but I'm pretty sure I'm right. Told her that no one was going to stop them from sharing the water."

"I don't know about that," Sean muttered.

"Not Lobo," Juni said. "Not anyone who's been aggressive. But you tell me: Is anyone in the Springs going to stop an orphan shifter from drinking the spring water so they can heal themselves?"

"No." Sean sighed. "Alex will be pissed you called her."

"I'm not one of Alex's minions."

Sean grinned. "No, you're not, and I do love that about you." He put the truck in gear. "Let's go on a little trip."

"Where?"

"Out to the ancestral pile, and I do mean pile. It's time for you to meet the old man properly."

"What old man?"

Sean glanced at her. "My uncle."

"The one who was mean to you?" She stared at him. "Why?"

"Couple of reasons." He persisted in smiling. "I want him to meet the woman I love." He reached for her hand. "But also, that old bastard has the longest memory of anyone in Cambio Springs. If anyone knows why an entire clan was banished from the town, it'll be my uncle Joe."

chapter
twenty-seven

SEAN HADN'T BEEN out to the old Quinn house in weeks. When he pulled up to the turnoff, he started having second thoughts, not about confronting the old man about the past but about exposing Juni to the truth of his family.

Now or never.

If she stayed with him, she'd have to meet the old man at some point. Better now than later. She needed all the information about who he really was.

He felt her hand close around his. "I'm not going to promise to like him, but I promise I'll give him a chance."

Sean blinked. "I don't care if you like him; I care if he scares you off."

Juni laughed. *"Really?"*

He frowned.

"Sean, you did about everything possible to scare me off all on your own. You think an octogenarian shapeshifter is going to tip me over the edge?"

He stared at the driveway. "I think he's in his nineties now."

"Even scarier."

He glanced at her and let his foot off the brake. "You say that now."

They drove up the bumpy driveway, over the new gravel that Sean had paid for, and up the tracks to the adobe brick house with a wooden porch that wrapped around, overlooking the edge of Cambio Springs in the distance.

"Hmm." Juni was smiling as she looked at the old place. "It's cool. Needs some work, but that porch is great."

Sean blinked. "It's a pile."

"It's an old house." She rolled her eyes. "They're all kinds of run-down. The desert is hard on old stuff. But you give it a fresh coat of white paint and add a pop of color on the porch, it'd be really pretty."

"Pretty?" He had to admire her optimism.

Sean parked the truck in the driveway underneath the shade of a desert willow. The breeze rustled the twisting leaves of the tree, and he could see a clutch of lizards hanging in a lower branch, taking in the cool wind from the higher elevations that swept down the hill.

Juni spotted the lizards. "Cousins?"

Sean squinted. "Maybe one or two of them." He turned and grabbed her hand. "Let's do this."

"Can you try not to sound so ominous?"

"No." The path wound up through the boulders that tumbled down the hill, dotted here and there with a few surviving scrub brushes.

"Hey!" Juni pointed at a twisted bush. "It's a juniper."

"We planted them especially for you."

"I figured." She squeezed his hand. "You know I'm fine, right? I'm not going to run off."

"Juni—"

"Whoa." She froze, yanking on his hand, her eyes staring at the ground. "Snakes."

He'd already heard them, a greeting party of four rattlers slithering over the rocks and between the bushes, their familiar Sshaped figures dancing across the dust until they curled in front of Sean, flicking their tongues and staring.

"Hey." Sean didn't know which kids they were, but at least two of them were Maggie's girls. "Is the old man home?"

The rattlesnake party unfurled and slithered up the path, racing each other to the base of the porch where an old man was sitting in a pair of red long johns and nothing else.

"Oh, for fuck's sake." Sean grimaced. "Can you put on some clothes?"

"I did." Old Quinn pointed to the red long johns. "I was naked until I heard your truck. Whadya want?"

"Uncle Joe, you can't be naked around the kids. You're gonna embarrass them."

The old man looked down at his chest, which was tan and sprinkled with silver hair. Ropy muscle covered his upper body. "You may be embarrassed of your natural Quinn good looks, Sean Patrick, but I believe in healthy self-esteem."

Juni snorted.

"Jesus," Sean muttered.

"Better not let your Aunt Rachel hear you swear like that."

"Aunt Rachel hasn't left her convent more than once a year for forty years, Joe. I doubt she's minding my language. Put a shirt on."

"Well, hell." The old man pushed to his feet. "I was sunning myself on that rock not five minutes ago. Hold your horses, Pious Poppy."

Old Quinn ambled into the house, opening the screen door and letting it clap back behind him. The rattlers on the path had scattered into the rocks, hiding from Sean.

"Hey!"

One of the rattlers poked their head up from a boulder.

"If anyone is missing school today because of all the shit going on in town, you're gonna hear from me and Maggie."

At least one of the snakes darted behind the house, and

minutes later Sean saw one of his younger cousins running toward a dirt bike parked next to the garage.

"Sorry, Uncle Sean," the boy muttered before he jumped on the bike.

Juni was watching everything with an amused expression. "Your family is not boring."

"You have no idea."

"THE TOWN WAS FOUNDED by seven families." Old Quinn was slurping on a cup of weak coffee doused with sugar. "Everyone knows that."

Sean leaned back in his chair. "How do you know?"

"'Cause that's what they told us." His eyes glinted. "Why? You heard different?"

"Who are the Abilas?"

The corner of his mouth turned up. "You been listenin' to Mexican gangsters, boy?"

"I've been listening to my friends," Sean said. "And that name has cropped up more than once. Who were the Abilas?"

He shook his head. "People come and go over the years. This place ain't new. Devin's people were here first; then the Native groups headed closer to the river and they left this place. Said it was cursed if you ask my grandfather."

"Your grandfather who was the first generation born here?"

Old Quinn scratched his beard. "Was he? I don't know if he—"

"You fucking know he was, old man." Sean was losing his temper. "Who were the Abilas?"

The old shifter narrowed his eyes and looked at Juni. "You know why he's so goldarned eager to leave this place? Because his mama was a bitch. And she was my own niece, so I can say that, but she was too influenced by her old man, who was a corrupt son of a bitch who nearly got the whole family run outta town."

"Like the Abilas were run out?" Juni asked.

Old Quinn cut his eyes to Sean. "She's as bad as you."

"Just give us the story and stop lying about it," Sean said. "We already found Francie McCann's letters to her sister, and she names the family. Doesn't say what happened, just that they were run out."

The old man sighed. "You really like pickin' at scars, don't you?"

"This time the scar is picking back. Lobo is from this family." Sean leaned forward when his uncle didn't flinch. "But you already knew that."

"Not hard to figure out." Old Quinn gulped his coffee and set his mug on the table. "You tell me, was it seven families or was it really five? Because the cats and the wolves stick together."

"And the Abilas?"

The corner of his mouth ticked up. "Some folks aren't equipped to be black sheep. Edmund Abila was one of 'em. He wanted his family on the same level as the wolf or the cat clan." The old man shook his head. "Wasn't gonna happen."

"Tell me what did happen."

Old Quinn furrowed his brow. "The bears, the snakes, the birds... We're all side players in the politics of this place. The bears are the noble protectors, the birds don't really give a shit about any but their own, but they're loyal, all in all."

"And the Quinns?" Juni asked.

The old man grinned. "We're the strangest of all. Different from the warmbloods. But we're fine being on the outskirts, aren't we?" Old Quinn nodded at Juni. "You know all about that."

Juni smiled at him. "There's safety in being on the edges." She rested her elbows on the table. "You can see everything going on."

"And the more you don't care about power, the more you can get what you want," he continued. "One way or another."

"Sneaking around?" Juni asked.

Old Quinn shrugged. "Making do with the expectations assigned to you. Everyone expects a Quinn to be a villain."

"Times are changing," Sean said. "We're not playing that game anymore. Not me. Not Maggie. And definitely not the younger kids."

Old Quinn smirked. "You're still Quinns. We're not like the others, Sean."

"That doesn't mean we have to be on the outside." Sean leaned toward his uncle. "*You* chose that. Maggie and I are choosing different."

Old Quinn looked out the window. "The Abilas were foxes. Desert foxes, kit foxes, red and grey and sandy. They were some of the best trackers in town. *Fearless.* Independent. They took *pride* in being separate from the wolves. The only problem with that... We're people first, aren't we? As much as animals. Can't control who your kids take as a husband or wife."

"The wolves and the foxes started to intermarry?"

"McCann boys sure do seem to like those independent foxes and cats, don't they? Wolves like a little challenge, especially the stronger ones, and over a couple of generations, the McCanns and the Abilas became so intertwined a lot of people kind of forgot that the Abilas were a separate clan. Until Edmund came around."

Sean watched his uncle with suspicion, never sure what was the truth and what was a lie. "Do you remember this?"

Old Quinn shook his head. "This all happened before I was born. My granddad was on the town council that banished them, and it was all because Edmund married that wolf."

Sean glanced at Juni. She was riveted to his uncle's every word.

"Explain," he said. "Edmund Abila married a McCann woman?"

"She was a sister of the McCann alpha at the time, and it pissed her off that her brothers and cousins all looked down on her husband. In another time, she'd have been alpha herself, but back then the men ran things."

Juni asked, "What was her name?"

"I don't know. No one said it, but they called her the she-wolf, and according to my grandfather, she and Edmund tried to take control of Cambio Springs. Not equal to the other families. Above them. Running things. They came to the Quinns, tried to get my grandfather in his corner, but Danny Quinn was Rory Quinn's favorite grandchild. Our kind may not like the wolves, but we like traitors less. Danny went to the elders, told them Edmund's plans."

Sean frowned. "And the elders banished an entire clan because of it?"

Old Quinn raised an eyebrow. "All of them. Edmund and his wife. Their children. Their brothers and sisters. Every man, woman, and child in the Abila clan. Every single fox that wasn't married into another clan? They all had to leave."

Sean was gobsmacked. "Why?"

"Who was going to trust a fox after their leader tried to take over?"

Juni asked, "What about people who had married into other clans?"

"They could stay." Old Quinn nodded. "Sure they could stay. But they had to pledge loyalty to the McCann alpha."

"Fuck." Sean felt his stomach drop. For an independent shifter, pledging loyalty to a clan they weren't part of would be gut-churning.

Old Quinn shrugged. "Over time, you didn't see many of them anymore. A lot of them left, even after they'd pledged to the McCanns. More than one family broke. And the Abilas weren't spoken of. People tried to pretend a whole founding family up and left. The ones who stayed? They kept quiet about who and what they were."

Juni shook her head slowly. "So the town elders banished an entire clan because the McCanns insisted?"

"Everyone insisted. All the remaining families. The Campbells, Crowes, Vasquezes and Leons. Us too." Old Quinn shook his head. "Like it or not, this world's a brutal place and our kind need a firm hand. The McCanns had the clearest hierarchy. If they could keep control of the foxes that remained, they could stay. Otherwise...?" The old man lifted his shoulders again. "The Abilas lost their seat at the elder table and their place in Cambio Springs."

"And the Quinns kept theirs," Sean said.

"*We* hadn't betrayed the town." Old Quinn looked at him. "We may be more... creative than the rest of these shifters, but this is our home and we're not giving up one inch to the warmbloods just because we're different."

Sean said, "Sounds like if Edmund Abila hadn't been power-hungry, his family could have lived peacefully."

"Of course they could have," Old Quinn said. "One bad leader lost the Abila family everything they'd built here—not that it was much to begin with—but they had a home. A place."

A place to call home was a valuable thing. Sean had traveled the world, but he always knew he could come home. What would it do to an entire clan to be cast out like that? What would it do to the children? To the elders?

"None of them ever came back?" Sean asked.

"Over the years a few tried. Some were accepted if they were willing to bow to the McCanns. Most of them?" The old man shrugged. "Disappeared into the great big world."

Juni was frowning. "So the foxes were the ones banished... but Lobo is a wolf."

Old Quinn nodded. "A direct descendant of Edmund and his wife, no doubt. Remember, she was a McCann."

"Then where did the cats come from? The snakes?" She looked at Sean. "They have birds with them too. Efrén Abano has collected a whole bunch of shifters in his group."

"You telling me you don't think none of the people who take off from the Springs and wander around the world ever father kids they don't know about?" Old Quinn shook his head. "You know it's not right, but it happens. I suspect this Lobo fellow saw an opportunity. Round up the strays and make them your army."

"Strays?" Juni scowled. "These aren't strays. Most of them— like this Sadie girl—are scared and confused kids with no idea what's happening to them. They're not strays."

"Hey, I don't mean it as an insult. Any stray shifter is welcome in the Springs if you ask me. I'm not afraid of change, girl." Old Quinn looked at Sean. "It's the warmbloods who have a problem that way. Especially the bears."

"Bears hate change," Sean muttered. "But we have to do something."

"Lobo is bad news," Old Quinn said. "But not all the Abilas were. Lots of them just wanted to live their lives. I suspect most of Lobo's people are the same."

"The kids he sent said he's definitely a wolf," Juni said. "But also that he avoids shifting."

"He must have inherited his ancestor's blood *and* her ambition." Old Quinn shook his head. "Be curious to see what the man comes up with next. Might be fun."

WHAT LOBO CAME up with next was four shifters—two reptiles and two foxes. This time they were caught sneaking out of the canyon with bottles of water. Four teenage boys, naked as the day they were born and as thin as Kyle and Sadie were.

The getaway Jeep parked at the end of the wash was able to escape, but Maggie and Allie rounded up the others in animal form, herding them toward the wolves who were waiting at the fresh spring, and four more of Lobo's shifters were taken to the jail where Ted checked them out, gave them spring water to drink, and Jena fed them.

"Six." Sean leaned against the wall of the Cambio Springs police station, listening to the hubbub inside.

Alex and Sean were standing in the shade of the building, tossing ideas back and forth.

"He just gonna keep sending kids we can feed?" Sean squinted into the distance. "He running short on lunch money? What the hell is this?"

Alex kicked at a rock by his foot. "You said your uncle told you the Abilas were banished because they challenged the McCanns?"

"They challenged the whole town, according to him."

Alex pursed his lips. "But at that time, did that mean the McCanns? It's not a real good feeling, knowing that your family ruled an entire community with an iron fist because they happened to have fangs."

Sean smiled and allowed his fangs to fall down. "Hey, I got fangs too; get over yourself."

Alex smiled, but he shook his head. "Things have to change. I'm not my father. And I'm definitely not my grandfather."

"Neither of those men would have been confident enough to marry a cat who was gonna challenge every damn thing you say every night of your life."

"And twice on Sunday," Alex muttered.

Sean decided to be direct. After all, Alex was in a changeable mood. "Juni called Mariana Cordova."

Alex blinked. "The PR lady?"

Sean shook his head. "She's more than that. I think she's the public face for a reason. She's the power behind Abano, and Juni thinks they're family."

"You said she's a cat?"

He nodded.

Alex was a little red in the face, but he bit his tongue. "I wish she'd asked me before she did that."

"She had a hunch and went with it. She's not one of your people that has to ask permission to fart."

"Fuck you." Alex huffed out a laugh. "Fine. What did the cat say?"

"Not much, but she seemed open to listening."

"Good." He nodded. "That's good."

"Juni said she's a businesswoman. Abano is wasting her people and her resources."

"And she's ready for a change?"

"The young people—the ones here, the ones he has working for him—they've been told a pack of lies."

"About the fresh spring?" Alex nodded. "There are lots of shifters who don't live in town. They're still connected. They're still safe here. They're all welcome to drink the water."

Sean felt a weight lift off his heart. "I'm glad as fuck you said that, because Juni basically held out the olive branch to Mariana Cordova."

"It's a smart move," Alex said. "At the end of the day, the only people who have really been harmed by Lobo and his people were Allie's ex and the Italian mob."

"Lobo has to go."

"Without question." Alex glanced in the windows of the old jailhouse. "But that doesn't mean *all* his people do."

"Ollie won't like it."

"Ollie doesn't like change, but the Campbells are practical and they want the town safe. Plus he's a softie. He'll come around when he sees these half-starved kids."

If Lobo's army consisted of scrawny shifters who were undernourished and sick, he had to know he couldn't take on an entire town of protective wolves, cats, bears, snakes, and birds.

"This isn't a deal our grandparents would have made," Sean said.

"No, it's not." Alex looked at Main Street in the distance. "But like you said, things are changing. We don't have to be ruled by the past."

chapter
twenty-eight

JUNI WOKE up with the sun on her face and Sean stroking her hair. She stretched and rolled into his chest, burrowing her face in the comforting scent of his familiar cologne.

"Good morning." She kept her voice to a whisper.

"You slept hard."

"You wore me out."

He responded by letting out a low grumble of pleasure. "I like wearing you out."

"Good."

It had been a passionate night after a contentious meeting with the elder council and Sean's closest friends. There was an air of desperation hanging over the town, a raw tension from those who knew a confrontation was imminent whether they wanted it or not.

That morning, mothers and fathers with small children were leaving to visit family or friends out of town. The school was shut down until further notice. Calls were made to shifters in the area who could drop everything and help defend their clans. Juni could already hear traffic rushing by on the main road.

An unexpected "water main break" had shut down the

Cambio Springs Resort, sending guests home with apologies and generous vouchers for future stays while the place emptied out and reservations were rescheduled.

She kept her eyes closed and stretched one leg over his hips. "So what are we doing today, Brain?"

"Thought we might try to take over the world."

"I don't know." She blinked her eyes open and looked up. "That sounds like a lot of work."

"Good point. Maybe we'll just let Alex and Ted do it so we can go on vacation."

"I like that idea better."

He wrapped his arms around her and pressed her close. "What time did you call her?"

"About ten last night."

Juni had called Mariana Cordova's number last night after the meeting with the elders and told her that the olive branch had been officially extended.

To her. *Not* to Efrén Abano.

"Did she give any indication—?"

"No."

"Not surprising." Sean stroked his fingers up and down her back. "You think it'll be soon?"

"I think she's a woman who likes to take care of business. That one does not have a lot of tasks hanging around on her to-do list."

"Guess we have to be ready for anything then."

"Yep." Juni looked up. "I guess so."

So until Mariana made a move, the Springs would be suspended in a defensive posture. Jena was taking baby Becca to her sister's house, but the boys insisted on remaining in town. Ted's mother had taken their newborn daughter to an uncle's house in Los Angeles, leaving Ted and Alex in grim waiting mode.

Allie had taken her younger kids to the Campbell family compound in Big Bear except for her oldest, who was already working with the McCann pack as a tracker.

Sean hadn't asked Juni to leave, but she knew he probably wanted to.

"My uncle likes you," he said.

"I like him. With reservations."

Sean chuckled. "That's exactly how you have to like my uncle."

"Maggie can handle him."

Sean was silent.

"She can." Juni looked up to see his lips pressed together, as if he was holding in a retort. "I'm telling you she can. And probably better than you can. Give her some credit."

"She's sneaky."

"So is he."

"True." He started playing with her hair again. "Do you think I'm doing the right thing?"

"Yes."

Sean and his sister'd had a long talk the night before. It was overdue and more than a little emotional, though neither of them would ever admit it.

She put her hand on his cheek and drew him down for a firm kiss. "You're doing the right thing. Don't make the same mistake the McCanns made and think that a woman isn't strong enough to hold a clan together."

"It isn't that she's a woman, it's that she has a record. Literally a criminal record."

"Not a felony though." She frowned. "Right?"

"Only because they couldn't find the evidence."

"See? She'll be fine." Juni watched him carefully. Sean knew he needed to leave. Needed to give the leadership of the clan over to someone who *wanted* to be in the Springs full time, but he was feeling guilty. "It's the right thing to do. And you'll always have a place here. We both have family here. Wherever we go—"

"We?" He smiled.

"You think you're getting rid of me now?" Juni rolled her eyes. "Besides, Rani already has your reentry planned."

"I'll have to remember to look exhausted."

"Maybe you can dress in all white or something. Dye your hair. We could go to Burning Man and dance in the desert."

"So I can do psychedelics with all the rich kids?" Sean's shoulders were shaking. "Can you imagine a snake shifter tripping?"

"Never mind. No mind-altering substances for you."

Sean rolled her to her back and started to kiss her. "You're the only mind-altering substance I need, Juniper Hawkins."

"You say the sweetest things."

IT DIDN'T TAKE LONG for Mariana Cordova to make her move. The first vehicles were spotted at the north end of the canyon three nights later. Jena was on patrol, flying over the Springs in raven form. She reported to Alex that there were six vehicles parked—two black Suburbans, three Jeeps, and a sleek black Range Rover with blacked-out wheels and trim.

With one call, every shifter remaining in the Springs went on alert.

At the first coyote howl, Juni had gone to her assigned position. She was perched on a ridge along the south edge of the canyon, Bear guarding her in wolf form. The large animal was looking down at the canyon and whining.

"You need to be quiet," Juni said. "Or your mom is going to send you home."

The large grey wolf sighed deeply and set his head on his paws.

A black raven landed on the rocks next to them, and Jena emerged from the darkness, throwing on a blanket that Juni had set out for her.

"Lobo is with them." She looked across the black chasm below. "I figured that it was him in the biggest car, but I couldn't be sure until I saw him."

"He's really here?"

"Yes. And he's shifted." Jena looked grim. "I guess this is a big enough fight for him to show up in animal form."

"What does he look like?"

"He's the biggest damn timber wolf I've ever seen in my life."

Juni's eyes went wide. "Bigger than Alex?"

"Yeah." Jena wrapped the blanket closer around her. "Size isn't everything, but with wolves..."

"It matters, right?"

"Yeah." Jena reached down and dug a hand into the heavy scruff at her son's neck. "He keeping quiet?"

Juni looked at Bear's big brown eyes. "He's been great. Best guard wolf I've ever had."

Bear whined at the back of his throat.

"He wants to be in the fight," Jena said quietly.

Juni shook her head. "He's a kid."

"So are some of the shifters with Lobo." She looked at her son again. "Some of those kids don't look any older than fifteen or sixteen. More in their twenties, and only a few over thirty, I'd say."

"Lobo probably gets rid of anyone who might be a threat," Juni said. "Younger kids are easier to manipulate. Did you see Mariana?"

"Yes, but she hadn't shifted. Yet. She looked annoyed with Lobo. She was bitching at him, but I only caught a little bit before this owl swooped down close and tried to grab me."

"Big white barn owl?"

Jena nodded and tossed off the wrap she was wearing. "I need to go report to Alex. I just wanted to check on you two. Stay here and stay safe."

Bear whined again.

"Absolutely not" was the last thing Jena said before she shattered into a spray of gold and a midnight-black raven took her place. She slipped silently off the edge of the ridge and floated into the darkness.

"Your mom is pretty badass."

The wolf beside her huffed.

SEAN SAW the raven before Alex did. "Jena."

Alex was dressed in grey sweatpants and a black T-shirt, easy clothes to leave behind. He lifted a hand and snapped at one of his people. "Blanket."

Jena landed on the other side of the truck and transformed, grabbing the camping blanket that someone threw at her. "Six vehicles, I'd say about thirty shifters that I could count, but that's probably not counting birds or snakes."

"Lobo?" Ollie asked. "Is he with them?"

"Yes." Jena hesitated. "Some of them weren't in animal form. There were guns. A lot of guns."

It made Alex pause. "How about Lobo?"

"No, he *has* shifted, and he's big."

"Had to rally the troops," Ollie muttered.

Sean had to agree. It was one thing to wear a suit to a board meeting, but if you were leading a group of shapeshifters into battle, you wanted teeth and claws.

Alex was staring at the hood of the truck. "So most of them are in animal form, but some are human."

Jena nodded. "I'd say he had about six guys who were in tactical gear, armed to the teeth."

"Fuck," Alex muttered.

Sean kept his voice low. "You want guns, I can get you guns. But bullets do damage that is hard as hell to repair, even for our kind."

Jena was shaking her head. "There are so many kids in his group, Alex. Most of them are so young."

Alex looked at Sean. "How certain is your girlfriend that this Mariana is going to flip?"

"Not certain. At all. The woman has her own agenda, and

she's not confiding in Juni." Sean looked at Ted. "You prepared for bullet wounds, Doc?"

Ted's face was blank. "I'll do what I can, but it's not ideal. Bullet wounds kill faster than fangs and claws. Shifting doesn't repair that kind of wound. Lobo's guys start shooting and we'll lose people. Maybe a lot."

An idea sparked in Sean's mind. It hadn't been the original plan, but it was better. He thought about the warm ground of the canyon and the shadowed walls where serpents could hide. "Alex, send me and Maggie in first."

"What?" Alex lifted his head. "Why?"

"Because snakes are hard as shit to shoot. Especially in light like this."

Jena nodded. "He's right. Let the Quinns go first. Sean and Maggie can take out anyone armed. Leave the bigger animals for the rest of us."

Alex was staring at the mouth of the canyon where they'd placed their scouts to alert them when anyone approached the fresh spring. "I don't want this night to end in a bloodbath if we can possibly avoid it."

Ollie's voice rumbled in the dark. "Jena said they're kids."

"I know." Alex looked at Sean. "Lobo is here and he's in wolf form. Mariana is with him. I'm guessing that if this woman is going to make a move, she's going to do it in the heat of the fight. Lobo will be focused on *us* as an enemy. He won't be looking for threats from his own people."

Sean nodded.

"If I were her," Ted said. "I'd make my move then. Take him out and then grab his people's attention when they're confused."

"So our goal is to give her time to make her move," Alex said to Jeremy, who was standing on the alpha's left side. "Spread the word among our people, but remind them that all of us defend ourselves and each other. That's not negotiable."

Jeremy nodded. "So we let them advance if they want to?"

"Have your forward wolves put up a fight," Sean said. "But fall back before anyone is too seriously wounded. We don't want them thinking it's too easy or they'll get suspicious."

Alex nodded. "Good point." He looked at Ted. "All the cats in place?"

"We have the high ground all along the canyon, and the birds are watching the sky."

"And the snakes go first," Maggie said. "The snakes should always go first." She bared her teeth, and Sean saw her fangs extended, dripping with venom.

She started marching away, and Sean grabbed her by the arm.

"Be careful," he said quietly. "The majority of our fighters are just kids."

"You think I don't know that?" She wrenched her arm away. "It's their home too."

Maggie stalked off, and Sean hesitated only a moment before he followed her. She walked to a clutch of Quinn teenagers and a few young adults. A few of the younger kids had fled the town with adults, but the majority of the Quinns had stayed. Most of them were pale with dark hair and light eyes. Angled cheekbones and pointed chins were common; Quinn blood was strong.

There were over two dozen snake shifters who had shown up to protect the town, and Sean felt a surge of pride in the lifted chins and defiant eyes of his family.

"We're Quinns." He spoke quietly, knowing they could hear him in the darkness. "Maggie is going to tell you the plan. Protect each other. Take your natural form and hide if you get hurt." He put a hand on the rocks. "This desert is *ours*. More than any of the warmbloods, we're at home here. We're *strong* here. We know this canyon in our bones, so don't be afraid just because they're big." He grinned. "Because we're Quinns."

Maggie stepped forward. "Whatever your natural form, I know all of you can shift into damn near anything you want."

Scattered laughter in the canyon.

"Lobo brought guns and warmbloods. I don't know if they have scales. Remember, we're immune to venom and the others aren't, so we move up the canyon fast and quiet, taking out anyone with a gun that might rip through a wolf or a cat."

"How lethal?" a voice called from the back of the group.

Maggie looked at Sean.

"Rattlesnake venom will take a warmblood out, but it'll take a long time to kill them," Sean said. "We're all fast in that form and it's good in the sand, so let's keep in rattler form unless things get sticky. We want to incapacitate, not kill. But use your own judgment and protect yourself and each other no matter what."

Low murmurs of agreement.

Maggie added, "Our goal is to take out Lobo and knock out anyone who's shooting. We're not here to beat up on a bunch of brainwashed kids, okay? Most of these people have been fed a bunch of lies and told they're rejects. That they're not wanted." She looked around. "A few of you know what that's like."

The young people nodded, their expressions telling Sean they understood.

"Lobo told them they were outcasts. That no one here would accept them. It's not our job to prove Lobo right tonight. Fuck him."

The kids laughed a little.

"But we're not idiots either. None of our wolves, cats, or bears are fighting with guns, so we level the playing field. We take out the firearms, but that's it."

A few of the older snakes looked annoyed.

Sean stared down one ornery-looking teen with a clutch of kids gathered around him. "You know and I know any one of us is capable of killing any one of them." The boy looked up and met his eyes. "But we're not murderers. We don't kill unless we have to. Understood?"

The young man nodded. "Yes, sir."

"Yeah, we get it."

"Got it, Mags."

Sean glanced at the truck where Alex and Ted were waiting. He heard a long howl in the distance, and Alex gave him a nod.

"Okay, Quinns." Sean turned, but nearly all the people had disappeared and a small army of rattlesnakes was hissing and curling at his feet. "Let's go protect our town."

"I CAN'T SEE anything up here." Juni was frustrated. "Bear, why don't we get down closer and—"

The wolf growled when Juni got to her feet.

"Oh, come on!" She huffed out a breath. "I'm not saying I'm going to fight anyone, I just want to see what's happening."

It wasn't like she was entirely inexperienced with wildlife photography. She'd captured a bloody showdown between two male lions last year.

It had been awful and almost made her sick to her stomach, but she'd captured it and stayed out of the way.

Juni started down the path, only to have Bear block her legs, nearly knocking her down.

"Bear, I am your aunt."

The wolf let out a high whine and looked down the canyon. Then he nudged Juni back to her protected perch.

"You're not listening to me, are you?" She growled. "You let Caleb help."

But not really. Caleb was back at the jailhouse with a small army of teenaged bears and cats, guarding the captured shifters in their custody.

Juni plopped on the ground and peered into the darkness. "If only I had night vision goggles."

Bear let out a high yip and nudged the backpack Jena had brought.

Juni's eyes went wide. "Seriously?" She dug in the bag and found a pair of clunky black binoculars that weighed a ton. "Oh, no way. Jena, you *are* a complete badass."

She turned on the goggles, lifted them to her eyes, and turned toward the sound of coyotes in the distance.

chapter
twenty-nine

SEAN SLID along the dust of the canyon floor, his senses alive in the cool night air. The temperature of the desert had dropped, but the canyon walls trapped the heat, speeding his blood and making his body fast and nimble as it glided over the sandstone floor.

He could sense the serpents around him, his sister on his left side, the rest of their scaled army following, spread across the canyon floor and advancing on the distant calls of the trackers in the distance.

Rattlesnake was Sean's natural form, and sidewinding came as natural to him as breathing. He felt his body lift lightly over the ground, propelling him forward with near-silent undulation. The canyon vibrated beneath him, the rocks whispering the location of the enemy they were tracking. He could hear paws running in the distance, and the scent of human sweat reached his tongue along with the distinct scent of gunpowder, steel, and oil.

"...can't see a damn thing..."

"They got snakes?"

"*We* do, so you know they have more."

"Stupid..." The voices drifted away again. "...if it gets us the water—"

"Shh!" One of the voices dropped. "You hear that?"

Sean saw Maggie reach forward and strike first, the two men kicking off and scrambling away.

"Fuck that!"

"Did it get you?"

"Got my pant leg, but I don't know— Fuck! Where are the rattlers?"

A second strike had clearly reached skin.

"Ahh!"

Sean darted over to observe the other man running from his friend. He tripped over a log that had washed down in the last rain and fell to the ground.

Sean saw the pale band of skin exposed on the wrist along with the black semiautomatic weapon the man was clutching.

He struck out, sinking his fangs into the flesh of the man's wrist. The intruder screamed and released the gun. In a flash, Sean saw a snake to his right shift into a monitor and grab the gun in its strong jaws before it disappeared into a black crevice.

"It got my gun!" The man groaned and rolled on the ground. "My arm. It bit my arm."

The human's legs kicked out in pain, striking the side of a young sidewinder on the path near him, and Maggie shifted within a heartbeat, rearing her body up into a hooded cobra that hissed and spat at the writhing human.

Sean skidded over, smacking Maggie with his tail and knocking her over.

She hissed at him, baring her fangs, but she shifted back to a rattlesnake and went to check the other man.

He'd scooted up along the canyon wall, holding his leg, but Sean could already smell the sweat pouring off him. The man reached for the rifle on his back but fumbled, unable to take it from the holster with his body going into shock.

He stared at Sean. "We just... We wanted..." His words slurred. "...kill us all."

Sean doubted the two healthy men would die, but they wouldn't be able to shoot straight, and that's all that mattered.

He left them in the canyon and continued forward. He could smell the animals now—wolves and cats and coyotes—all with a sickly sweet smell on their breath. He could smell humans too, but they hung back, content to let the animals take the lead.

Sean scooted over to the canyon walls, sliding along to wait with the warm rock at his back.

He spotted Lobo immediately.

Among the crowd of mangy wolves, Efrén Abano was a majestic tyrant, towering over most of the foxes, coyotes, and smaller grey wolves in his pack. He was thick chested and deep black, his gold eyes peering from an intelligent face with a broad muzzle. The wolves followed him, continually watching to take their cues from the alpha who led them.

There were cats, of course, but they kept to the perimeter, nosing along the sandstone and flicking rocks from their paws.

The wolves were hungry. Sean could smell it on them. They followed Lobo in grim silence until the giant black wolf's head whipped around and he froze.

Sean knew he'd smelled the Quinns.

Though they'd been told to be silent, instinct took over and one rattle started.

Then another.

And another.

Lobo's pack was surrounded by a chorus of rattling diamond-backs, their lethal echo bouncing off the walls of the canyon, making two dozen rattles sound like a hundred.

The wolf lifted his head and let out an aggressive bark.

The chaos began a second later as wolf after wolf started snarling and barking at the ground. The snakes reared up, their muscled bodies at attention as the wolves danced in the dust, trying to run but being driven back as the snakes darted forward to strike.

"I can't shoot 'em," the two humans at the back of the pack shouted. "I can't even see 'em!"

"Should we—?"

"No! We might hit ours."

Two of the younger wolves broke away and lunged forward, but Sean smelled the threat before he saw it.

Two massive cobras waded through the pack, the animals around them falling back as they slithered forward and flanked Lobo.

"Did you see—?"

"Fuck! It bit me!"

A rattle of automatic gunfire burst in the air.

JUNI'S BREATH caught as the muzzle flash nearly blinded her through the goggles. She'd been watching the snakes approach Lobo's pack, saw the two men with guns in black tactical gear fall, and saw the army of rattlesnakes surround the larger group.

The moment the shifters had spotted the snakes, she could see them start and panic.

"You get 'em, Sean."

The majority of the group seemed to waver, milling around their large alpha and dancing away from the canyon walls, but a few of the more skittish members bolted forward. Lobo struck out, whipping his head around, and Jena knew that a snake had fallen into the canine's jaws.

"Shit." She reached for Bear, who scooted closer to her on the ledge. "Lobo got one of the snakes."

The wolf let out a sad whine.

"It may be okay." Juni was trying not to let her heart catch in her throat. "Quinns are tough as nails, buddy."

Please be okay.

SEAN SAW Maggie flying through the air, whipped from the vicious jaws of the black wolf. She hit the wall and he waited to hear her rattle, but the snake was silent.

He shifted and the ground beneath him grew hard and rough between his claws. The Komodo dragon wasn't silent, but it was massive, more than capable of deflecting the claws and teeth of the wolf. All he would need was one nick of his venomous teeth in the animal and—

A massive cat landed on his back.

The puma tried to dig its talon-like claws into Sean's back, but the dragon's skin was tough, linked bony growths that interlocked, creating an organic chain mail. The cat had never attempted to claw an animal like the dragon.

More gunfire in the distance that quickly fell silent.

Sean shook the cat off, whipping its head around and hissing with his long, forked tongue. The puma stood its ground, baring its teeth, but before it could attack again, the wolf barreled into it, shoving the animal to the side of the canyon before it leaped on the dragon and tried to tear at Sean's neck.

Useless.

The wolf's jaws were no match for the massive column of muscle covered by impenetrable skin. The only thing that the wolf had over the dragon was speed, so it leaped off the reptile and surged forward, its pack following it, yipping and howling as it ran.

JUNI KEPT her eyes trained on Sean.

At least she thought it was Sean. Maybe other Quinns could shift to a giant, venomous lizard at the drop of a hat, but Sean was the only one that Juni knew.

He stomped over to the canyon wall as the wolves, cats, and

foxes barreled past him; he nosed the ground, sniffing at something in the dirt.

Moments later, a small striped snake slithered onto the back of the giant lizard, and Sean stomped off with the serpent curled between his shoulders, heading toward the mouth of the canyon at a steady pace, his tongue tasting the air and a gang of rattlesnakes sliding and dancing around him.

"Where are the soldiers?" She looked at Bear. "I can't see the guys with the guns."

She scanned the length of the canyon and spotted two feet sticking out. They were still.

"How many did your mom say had guns?" Juni couldn't remember. Was it three? Four? More than that?

No humans were following the pack of shifters, and no more gunfire exploded in the night.

"It's fine." She dug a hand into the warm ruff of Bear's pelt. "They're going to be fine. Mariana is going to make her move."

She was nearly certain that the cat who had jumped on Sean was Mariana Cordova, but she couldn't be sure. There were two other mountain lions in the group; the one that attacked Sean had just been the biggest.

"Does that matter?" She looked at Bear, but the boy had been ordered to stay in wolf form, and he wasn't inclined to disobey his alpha. "I know that matters with wolves, but what about cats? Is the biggest the most powerful?"

SEAN SMELLED blood in the air, but as he rounded a bend in the canyon, the sight that confronted him was far from what he'd expected.

Wolves, coyotes, and foxes were on the ground, pinned by big cats, McCann wolves, and a few Campbell bears. Mountain lions and bobcats were isolated on ledges and hissing at leopards and pumas patrolling the ridges above.

Many of the Quinns had gone before him, and they were circling the two predators fighting in the middle of the canyon as the rest of the animals watched.

The mountain lion and the black wolf were both bloody from bites and rips in their flesh, but the wolf was snarling with a ferocity that made the cats on the rocks above turn and bare their teeth.

The mountain lion was going to win in the end. Sean could see it from the way she fell back and feinted, allowing the wolf to wear himself out.

The question was, would the mountain lion be too exhausted to lead her pack out of the canyon in the end?

Sean watched the honorable shifters who witnessed the combat at a distance, keeping their claws and fangs to themselves. This battle, their distance said, was between the cat and the wolf. They were battling for dominance, and it wasn't safe or smart to get in the middle of it. It wasn't right. The last one standing would be the winner.

But the dragon?

Luckily, the dragon was a cold-blooded Quinn.

Sean shrugged his sister from his shoulders, walked fearlessly into the fray, and with a burst of speed, sank his venomous, serrated teeth into the left haunch of the black wolf, flooding his system with poison.

The wolf stumbled back, letting out a confused howl, and limped away from the fight. The cat took the advantage, using her broad paws to swat the wolf into the rocks before she tackled it and sank her teeth into its throat.

The wolf lay still, blood pouring from its throat, and the cat stood over it.

Dust gathered around the two shifters, swirling and then

falling away, leaving a naked man with black hair and light eyes staring up at a woman wearing his blood on her skin.

Mariana Cordova was pitiless. "You should have listened to me, Efrén."

"C-cousin."

She shook her head. "I'm not your cousin anymore. You are nothing to me. Children dead. Lives wasted. Money poured into dirty palms and *lies*!" Her voice rose on the last word. "So many lies you told me. So much poison."

Sean shifted and stood across from them, his body shaking with the cold. "We aren't your enemy."

Efrén struggled to speak but managed a few mumbled words. "Killed... Ben. Killed..."

Mariana gritted her teeth and curled her hands into fists. Her blood-covered chest heaved with heavy breaths. "If my husband is dead" —she seemed to choke on the words— "it's because of *you*."

She started to shake, and Sean could see the red dust gathering around her feet. She was ready to shift again.

Imagine it was Juni.

The rage of a mate when its other half was injured led only to blood and pain. If Mariana's husband was dead, it could ruin everything.

"The guards?" Sean nearly shouted. "Was your husband one of the guards? We used rattlesnake venom on purpose." He shook his head. "They're not dead. We just needed to keep them from shooting. Mariana, *he's not dead*."

Shifters were starting to return to human form all around them. Young people on the ground, staring at Mariana with wide, confused eyes. Bobcats and foxes turning back to skinny teenagers, watching the chaos and bracing to run.

A massive mountain lion pawed her way through the scattered humans and animals, shifting at a safe distance from the bloody she-cat. It was Ted, who held out her hands and tried to catch the enraged woman's eye.

"Ms. Cordova, I'm Dr. Ted Vasquez and I have antivenom in my truck to treat all your people. None of them will die tonight because of a snakebite." She glanced at Sean as if to confirm.

He nodded, hoping that none of the younger Quinns had gotten scared and bitten with something more lethal.

Mariana looked confused for a moment, but she quickly lifted her chin. "Do it. Treat them. Now."

Thank God Ted understood the need for command in the moment. "I'm on it." She snapped at a wolf and another cat. "Jeremy, Lark, come help me."

Mariana kept her eyes on Efrén even as she addressed her people. "We're done with this." She looked around for a moment. "All of it. He lied to us. He lied to me, to you, to everyone he killed." Mariana looked at Sean. "These shifters are not our enemies."

Then Mariana walked over, knelt down, and twisted Efrén Abano's neck in one swift movement, killing him as he lay twitching on the ground.

Everything went silent.

She stood, looking at the remnants of the Abila clan and the outcasts they had collected. She lifted her chin and wiped the blood from her lips. "I am your alpha now."

chapter
thirty

THE OUTCAST CLAN gathered in the Cambio Springs gymnasium as Ted, Lark, and Jeremy treated the injured, and Jena and Ollie fed the kids, many of whom looked like they hadn't eaten in days.

Mariana Cordova was wrapped in a blanket and sitting next to a cot where her husband Ben was sleeping after being injected with a strong dose of antivenom. She was still covered in Lobo's blood, and her hair was a tangled mess, but she exuded authority as she watched over the young people in her care.

"I fed them, but it never seemed to be enough." Mariana lifted a cup of water from the fresh spring. Her hand trembled slightly, but her grip was firm.

Sean and Juni sat next to her, watching the quiet aftermath of the battle in the canyon.

"I'm not a shifter," Juni said. "But it could be that their health would always be compromised unless they were getting water from the spring."

"You seem in better health than the others," Sean said. "You've had the water?"

Mariana nodded. "For years, Efrén paid someone to come in

every month and take some water for his top people, but when he started to be more aggressive…"

"After the patrols increased at night." Sean watched her drink. "He couldn't sneak in any longer."

Mariana nodded, then bent to check her husband's breathing. He was a tall, dark-skinned man with closely cropped hair and a bearing that reminded Sean of the military. He wouldn't be surprised at all to learn Ben had Campbell blood.

"Is he a shifter?"

She nodded. "The only bear Efrén was ever able to find. He looked for them, you know. The lost ones, he called them. He made it sound so noble when we started. We were going to find all those who had been rejected and forgotten and give them a home and a clan."

"That's a noble goal," Juni said. "Was that in Santa Fe?"

"Yes." She took a long breath and seemed to relax a little. "We were born in Mexico City. The Abila family was not poor when they left Cambio Springs, and the ones who survived—who stayed with our great-great-grandfather—became very successful property developers in Mexico."

Sean wanted to know what had happened to the ones who *hadn't* survived, but that was a conversation for another night.

"We always had money," Mariana continued, "and somehow… we always had water too. It would be delivered once a year in large glass bottles. It wasn't much, but it was enough. We drank it once a year like communion wine. Like a sacrament."

Sean had grown up gulping water from the fresh spring when he had ridden too hard on his bike and didn't want to bother finding a faucet or a hose. He couldn't imagine sipping rationed spring water once a year.

Juni said, "Someone from the Springs must have been arranging the deliveries. There had to be family that maintained connections."

"I don't have any idea. When my great-uncle passed, he was the last one with a connection here, and Efrén told me we were on our own. That the elders here had cut us off and that we would have to survive without it." She scoffed. "Five years later, we were both desperate enough to move to the US."

"By expanding the business," Juni said. "Esencia hotels."

She nodded. "We renovated the property in Santa Fe first; then he wanted to move to Las Vegas."

"Getting closer to Cambio Springs," Sean said.

"When we first moved to Santa Fe, Efrén hired a young man who... smelled familiar. Marco was a bobcat shifter, but he didn't know anything about his family. He'd been raised in foster care. He thought he was a freak. Efrén hired Marco, taught him about shifting, gave him a job. And that's when he got the idea, I think."

Sean looked at the scattered collection of people in the gymnasium. "To find shifters who had been lost. Children we didn't know about in the Springs."

"There had to be more, right?" Mariana clenched her jaw. "After he found Marco, my cousin started... collecting people. He would travel and come home with someone—almost always a young person—and he'd find a job for them. Give them a place to stay at the hotel or at our family compound."

Sean watched the young people as they ate and took turns using the gymnasium bathrooms to shower and clean up. They were starting to get color back. Starting to look more like healthy kids and not sick addicts.

"That was a good thing," Juni said. "Some of these kids probably didn't have anyone else. You must have felt good about that."

"I did." Mariana's chin lifted proudly. "Our family wasn't big, but at first these kids... They felt like family. He acted like they were. He seemed to have a sixth sense for sniffing out lost shifters. Abilas have always been good trackers."

"When did the drug connection come in?"

Her jaw tightened. "That was Marcus Ashford. Marcus was... I don't know. Not like the others. He was older, and he was smart.

Very smart. He told Efrén that allying with the cartels was an investment opportunity, if you can believe that."

"Let me guess," Sean said. "You were just taking money for the expansion. It wasn't your problem where the money came from. And if you had to loan out some of your people for jobs now and then... That was just doing a favor for a friend."

"You sound like my cousin." Mariana shook her head. "Foolish man. I made excuses for my cousin for years, but after you killed Ashford—"

"Ashford killed himself," Sean said. "I was there. He died from his own venom."

Juni frowned. "I didn't know that was possible."

"Neither did I until I saw it." Sean surveyed the room. "So the question is, Mariana, where do we go from here? Most of your people are foxes and wolves. You have a few cats. Some birds and snakes." He looked at the sleeping man beside them. "One bear. What are they going to want to do?"

Mariana lifted her chin. "I have already told them: I am their alpha now. No more people disappearing. No more fights started for old grudges. I'm a full partner in the hotel business—I made sure of that in the paperwork—so the hotels fall to me. The investments do too." She glanced at Ted. "I am not a follower, and I am not subject to your council and definitely not the McCann alpha."

"That's fine," Sean said. "We don't expect you all to move back, bow your heads, and settle down." He remembered the sleek professional he'd seen in Las Vegas. "I hardly think that you're interested in small-town life."

"Not at all." She smirked. "Now if Alex McCann is looking for a buyer for his resort, I might make him a good offer."

Juni laughed. "I like you."

"You don't know me," Mariana said.

"Yeah, but I have a feeling about people." Juni squeezed his hand. "There's no reason you have to change your entire life, Mariana. You're clearly very good at protecting secrets."

Sean looked at the swiftly calming gymnasium. Shifters who had been attacking the Springs only hours before had bathed, fed, and were falling asleep under the watchful eye of their former enemies and the woman who would lead them into the future.

A future that finally had some hope.

"What Juni told you on the phone holds," Sean said. "No one is going to keep your people from visiting and sharing the water."

"Will your elder council approve of that?"

"Yes." Sean knew that it likely wouldn't be all smooth sailing, but the water didn't belong to them. The water was for any shifter who needed it. "Even people who are banished from the Springs have rights to come back and drink," he said. "Your people have done nothing wrong. They might even find family here if they want to look, but that's totally up to them."

Mariana nodded. "I will hold you to that, Sean Quinn."

"Remind me to introduce you to my sister Maggie in the morning," Sean said. "She's currently being a very bad patient for a very patient Scottish vet, but she'll be leading the Quinn clan once Juni and I leave."

"Oh?" Mariana lifted one eyebrow. "And where are the two of you going?"

Sean looked at Juni and smiled. "I guess we're going... wherever the hell we want."

A WEEK after the battle in the canyon, Juni and Sean were back to work, this time profiling the exclusive Desert Haven resort north of Las Vegas.

Well, Juni was working and Sean was... assisting.

"Stop." She slapped his hand as it wandered under her shirt. "I need to load these images and see if I got enough."

"Oh, I'm sure you did." He reached over and took her computer from her lap, setting it to the side. "You have to let the machine load all those images. That takes" —he kissed along the bare line of flesh at her waist— "time. You need to be patient."

Their room was a private bungalow with a view of red cliffs in the distance, immaculately planted desert landscaping, and a private plunge pool shaded by soaring canvas sails. The entire back wall of the bungalow was made of glass walls that looked over the expanse of the desert with not a single other soul in sight.

"Patient?" She sighed happily and lay back on the bed. "Says the man who can't wait for me to finish work before he distracts me?"

"Distracting?" He inched her shirt up and over her breasts. "Am I distracting?"

"You know you are."

He took his time savoring each small breast, enjoying the flavor of her skin and the satisfying tug of her fingers in his hair. He was hard as a rock, but he waited, enjoying the building pressure in his cock. Juni's sighs of pleasure and hitched breath was a delicious appetizer building up to the main course.

He peeled her satin panties off, tossing them over his shoulder as he scooted down in bed, spread her legs, and put his mouth on her sex, savoring the delicious flavor of her desire for him and building passion.

She came apart under his tongue, gripping his hair with both hands and nearly yanking him up to cover her body.

He shoved his pants down and entered her when she was still coming, the fluttering pressure of her climax caressing his cock as he slid inside.

The sensation nearly made him come, but he clamped down on the instinct to ride her and slowed his strokes to caress her and prolong her pleasure.

"Sean, Sean." She chanted his name. "Oh fuck, Sean."

He looked down and her face was flushed, her lips were red and swollen. Her eyes...

Her eyes.

Sean felt his heart nearly beating out of his chest. *I love you. I love you. You make me feel alive.* He couldn't look away. He would never look away. Every expression on her face was a new revelation. Her body was a new world.

He had the sudden epiphany that Juniper Hawkins was the greatest undiscovered country in the world, and he could spend a lifetime learning her because she was Juni, but she was also a hundred women he'd never met.

And he would love all of them.

She would be a thousand lovers, a constantly changing map of joy and sadness and curiosity and passion. She would change and so would he. What more could he ask for?

"I love you so much."

She smiled, and the sun rose in her eyes. "I love you too."

He felt tears at the corner of his eyes and wondered if she noticed. He didn't care. She could see every part of him because she would learn him just as he would learn her.

She lifted her leg to wrap around his waist, angling her hips into his body, and Sean was blind. He could think of nothing but the overwhelming pleasure of their joined bodies.

Everything, everything, everything.

Juni was everything to him.

THEY SLEPT under the stars that night in a screened porch with a glass roof and a Scandinavian modern bed decorated with bright embroidered Mexican pillows and weighted blankets. The sheets were crisp linen, and the pillows were stuffed with an environmentally friendly down alternative that cradled Sean's head and shoulders.

"I have to say, this definitely beats sleeping in the trailer."

Juni laughed. "Does it?"

He rolled over and watched her face in the moonlight. "You are stunningly beautiful."

"I'm really not." She smiled. "I'm passably cute with a good figure, many tattoos, and constantly changing hair."

"I love your hair."

"You love me, so you're biased." She put a hand on his cheek. "You, on the other hand, are sinfully gorgeous. No one should have eyes that blue."

"You're biased too." He smoothed his thumb over her jawline. "What do you think we'll look like when we're old?"

"Wrinkly and happy." She touched his upper lip. "Maybe you'll grow one of those walrus mustaches like your uncle."

"Complete with nose hair?" He snapped his teeth at her fingers, and she laughed. "You will have silver-and-black-threaded hair that sparkles in the sun." He could picture it, the delicate creases around her eyes, the laugh lines, and that shining spirit that marked her as the only woman in the world that he would ever love.

Juni's smile softened. "You're already speeding ahead. We got a long way to go before we get there."

"I'm excited." He blinked when he realized that it was true. "Juni, for the first time in my entire life, I'm excited about my future instead of dreading the past."

"Oh, Sean." Her eyes filled with tears. "I'm excited too."

"Promise you'll go everywhere with me?"

"Yes." She pressed a long kiss to his mouth, tucking a strand of hair behind his ear. "Even better? We can go anywhere we want, and then we can always come home."

chapter
thirty-one

Six years later...

"JUNIPER GILBERT, YOU GET BACK HERE!" Sean shouted from the house, and moments later a laughing two-year-old jumped into Juni's arms, wearing nothing but a bathing suit on her head.

"Juji, you have no pants!" Juni laughed as she picked up her niece and namesake. "What happened?"

She was the youngest of all the babies. She got away with everything.

The toddler babbled something about fishes and mermaids, but Juni was distracted by the sight of Sean standing in the door with a wet shirt and his three-year-old doppelgänger on his hip.

Juni squinted and smiled as she stood with her niece. "Good to know you didn't let ours get away too."

"Momma, Juji has a swimsuit on her head!" Declan put a hand over his eyes and let out a belly laugh.

Declan Quinn had been the strangest and most life-altering surprise in Juni and Sean's world. He was as unplanned as the rest of their life, conceived in Japan, born in Colombia, and as free a spirit as both his parents.

This morning the free spirit had something blue all over his face.

Juni walked over to Declan and Sean. "My dude, what do you have on your face?"

"Wha?" His eyes went wide in a practiced expression of innocence.

You learned that from your father.

"What did you eat, Dec?"

"Paw-sicle."

She looked at Sean. "Blue Popsicle right before your cousin's wedding?"

Sean shrugged. "Sure, why not? I think blue is one of the bridal colors, right?"

Declan wiggled from Sean's arms, and his father let him down. "I'll get dressed! I have my shirt."

Juni walked in the house with the wiggly two-year-old. "Why is her hair wet?"

"I was giving her a bath to help Jena out because Allie called her in a panic. Said something about flowers. Caleb and I figured we could get the younger kids ready for the wedding without her help."

"Juni!" Caleb shouted from the hallway. "Do you have the baby?"

"She's here." Juni walked back to the bedrooms and handed her niece over to her frazzled father. "Jena is at the resort already?"

"Allie and Ted needed help with the flowers or something. They're all stressing about this because Mariana paid for a bunch of stuff and..." Caleb frowned when he saw Declan zip by. "Is his face blue?"

"Don't ask."

Sean swooped down and grabbed his son, tossing him over his shoulder. "Gotcha. Fancy clothes time."

"Nooooo!"

Declan's usual wardrobe consisted of whatever he happened to pick from his suitcase most days. Sean and Juni didn't really give him any rules. Half the time he wore a superhero costume everywhere they went.

Sean reached up to tickle the little boy's belly, making him burst into laughter again.

Luckily, Kevin McCann's wife-to-be was a cheerful fox shifter from the Abila clan who had chosen blue-and-green tie-dye as one of her colors. Juni was guessing that Lola Abano was as likely to care about a three-year-old with a blue face as she was to care about the flowers not being perfect, but what did she know?

Juni and Sean weren't married. They always talked about having a ceremony in one of their favorite destinations when they could get their family and friends together in one place, but that required planning. They weren't very good at planning any further out than about three months in advance. Maybe when Declan was older, they'd figure something out.

Caleb looked at his watch. "We're running late."

"The whole town is running late," Sean said.

Juni muttered, "You know Mariana isn't."

Caleb sighed. "Okay, we better get a move on."

Juni was ready. She was already in a blue-green pantsuit and had her gear charged up.

Sean hadn't been thrilled when Allie's son asked Juni to photograph the wedding, but it had been years since she'd done one, and she happily said yes.

She and Sean were usually hopping around the world, swinging between fashion—which had become Juni's focus—and travel, which had remained Sean's favorite genre of choice. She'd taken a year off when Declan was born, but most of the time they just packed their little adventurer up and carried him along wherever they ended up.

Finland.

Ghana.

Namibia.

Brazil.

And Cambio Springs. Always Cambio Springs.

Declan might not have had a traditional childhood, and they didn't want him to, but Sean and Juni both knew their son needed a place to call home. They'd built a cottage on the hill behind the old Quinn house, and it was always kept ready for them.

They'd been in Iceland the week before, only to return to the Springs so they could watch Allie and Ollie's oldest son meet his bride at the altar. The whole town was invited, the resort had been reserved by most of Mariana's friends, and the early-spring weather meant the desert was in bloom.

Kevin and Lola were young, but that wasn't unheard of in the Springs. The fact that this was the first wedding of anyone from the Springs with the now-thriving Abila clan made it a little more nerve-racking though.

Mariana's clan had remained in Las Vegas, settling into regular visits to Cambio Springs. Some of the lone shifters had found family connections and some hadn't, but all had been made welcome.

It meant something that Ollie's stepson was the first one to marry someone from the Abilas. The Campbells would always be the protectors of the spring, which meant that accepting one of the newcomers into their own clan was a big step.

It was a step six years in the making.

As Mariana had said, trust didn't come easily for the Abilas, and it had taken months for some of them to return. Alex McCann and Mariana Cordova were wary allies, each fiercely protective of their people, but over time they had come to an understanding.

Between the two families, they'd stopped the incursion of the drug trade into the nearby desert towns. The cartels had backed off, especially after Mariana returned their money. Luckily, Lobo's reputation was enough to give them pause, especially when

Mariana let them know that she'd been the one to take her own cousin out of the picture.

No one wanted to cross her after that.

Efrén Abano was buried in a marked grave in the Cambio Springs cemetery, eternally resting in the town he claimed had rejected him. Mariana sent flowers to his grave every week, purple hyacinth surrounded by daisies. Allie delivered them because Mariana wouldn't visit.

"Juni?" Sean called from the kids' bedroom where Declan was bunking down with Juji and Becca. "Are you ready when we are?"

"Never more." She walked over and grabbed her wiggly three-year-old from his father's arms. "You look so handsome, Dec."

He looked at her with stars in his eyes. "Momma, you are bootiful."

"Thank you, baby." Could her heart take any more?

"What about me?" Sean asked.

"Daddy, you're bootiful too."

Sean grinned. "Thanks, Dec." He wiggled his eyebrows at Juni. "See? I'm beautiful too."

"And I'm bootiful the most." Declan threw his arms back and nearly fell out of Juni's arms.

"I can see that Quinn confidence did not miss a generation." Juni set him down, grabbed his hand, and started to the front door. "Caleb!"

"Coming!" He was puffing by the time he reached the door with a poised and immaculate eight-year-old Becca and two-year-old chaos agent Juniper. "Thank you, Becca."

"You're welcome." The little girl beamed. "See, Auntie Jun? Juji and I match."

"I love it." The girl's dresses were a watery, shining satin with blue and green streaks all over the skirts. "I promise I will get lots of pictures of you."

Becca beamed.

"Okay, let's do this thing." Caleb opened the door, grabbing his youngest when she bolted. "Nope."

"We'll meet you there." Sean took the keys from the entry table and leaned down to Juni. "One. One is good, right?"

"Yeah." She shrugged. "One is good. Unless…"

His eyes went wide. "Unless what?"

Juni started laughing. "Well, we didn't plan the first one, did we?"

"Sssssssss." Declan hissed as Juni buckled him into his car seat. "Imma lizard, Momma."

"That's a definite possibility someday, yes." She got him secured and straightened to find Sean still staring at her. "I'm just saying. One is good. So is three and so is five. In our life, I'm always ready for a surprise."

"Five?"

"Or one!" She grinned and got into their beat-up old Volvo. Sean joined her and started the car. "We wouldn't want to be predictable, right?"

Sean laughed ruefully. "Juniper Hawkins, with you anything is possible."

afterword

As most of you know, there were a lot of questions about whether or not this book would ever happen. Though Cambio Springs took a big break, I am delighted to share Dust Born with you at last.

Sometimes we have to put on our business hats and make decisions that our artist hearts don't approve of, but I'm so very glad that Dust Born is finally in your hands. Sean and Juni are some of my favorite characters in the series, so I'm thrilled to finally share their love story with you.

It's a story about generations and legacies, both good and bad. It's a story that reckons with the past and hopefully paints a brighter future. Whatever your past might be or whatever your family history, I wish you as bright a future as Sean and Juni created for themselves, and a family of your choosing, whether it's born or found.

While I do not have any more plans to continue the Cambio Springs series, I will never say never to short stories or novellas set in this world. Sometimes my artist heart needs the desert, so I'm happy to return to these old friends.

Thank you for taking this journey with me,
Elizabeth

acknowledgments

Endless, countless thanks to the many people who encouraged me during the writing of this book, especially the admins of my online readers' group, Hunters' Haven: Meg, Hannah, Kathryn, Tiffany, Danielle, and Anna.

And to all the members of the Haven, you are such a beautiful encouragement to me. Thank you for your love, enthusiasm, and excitement that make writing so much fun.

To my assistant, Genevieve, thank you for everything you do day to day to make life and work run smoothly.

To my girls: Chevella, Kelli, Gen, Bobbie, Wendy, and Gwyn. Your friendship keeps me on my toes and keeps me sane. Love all of you so much.

To my editor and dear friend, Amy Cissell, thank you for challenging me, encouraging me, and making me a better writer and person. Your friendship is profound and your corrections brutal. I love it.

To Anne and Linda, the wonder twins of grammar and usage. Bless you both for putting up with my addiction to comma abuse and my inability to ever remember open, closed, and hyphenated compounds.

I will never *ever* remember.

To my marvelous agent, Kimberly Brower, and to everyone at Brower Literary, thank you for your encouragement, your hard work, and for just making me feel like a fancy professional author lady.

And to Nina and everyone at Valentine PR, thank you for putting up with last minute requests, irresponsible scheduling, and my gigantic book catalogue. I honestly don't know why you put up with me, but I'm grateful.

Finally, thank you to my family. To my husband David and my son Colin—the two most wonderful men in my life—I am so grateful for you both. You teach me every day what love is in so many marvelous and surprising ways.

Words are wholly inadequate.

looking for more?

Whether you're a fan of contemporary fantasy, time travel, fantasy romance, or paranormal women's fiction, Elizabeth Hunter has a series for you.

THE ELEMENTAL UNIVERSE

Discover the series that has millions of vampire fans raving!

Immortal book dealer Giovanni Vecchio thought he'd left the bloody world of vampire politics behind when he retired as an assassin, but a chance meeting at a university pulls student librarian Beatrice De Novo into his orbit. Now temptation lurks behind every dark corner as Vecchio's growing attachment to Beatrice competes with a series of clues that could lead to a library lost in time, and a powerful secret that could reshape the immortal world.

Ebook/Audiobook/Paperback/Hardcover

THE SEBA SEGEL SERIES

looking for more?

From eleven-time USA Today Bestselling author Elizabeth Hunter, a unique world of fantasy, magic, and time travel.

Born into a powerful mage family, she's a time traveler whose life is constantly in flux. When one of the highest laws of magic is broken in the thirteenth month, Narine, her friends, and one unsuspecting professor must scour the past and set the timeline right.

Ebook/Paperback

THE IRIN CHRONICLES

Destiny brought them together; heaven will tear them apart.

Hidden at the crossroads of the world, an ancient race battles to protect humanity, even as it dies from within. A photojournalist tumbles into a world of supernatural guardians protecting humanity from the predatory sons of fallen angels, but will Ava and Malachi's attraction to each other be their salvation or their undoing?

Ebook/Audiobook/Paperback

THE CAMBIO SPRINGS MYSTERIES

Welcome to the desert town of Cambio Springs where the water is cool, the summers sizzle, and all the residents wear fur, feathers, or snakeskin on full moon nights. In a world of cookie-cutter shifter romance, discover a series that has reviewers raving. Five friends find themselves at a crossroads in life; will the tangled ties of community and shared secrets be their salvation or their end?

Ebook/Audiobook/Paperback

GLIMMER LAKE

Delightfully different paranormal women's fiction! Robin, Val, and Monica were average forty-something moms when a sudden accident leaves all three of them with psychic abilities they never could have predicted! Now all three are seeing things that belong in a fantasy novel, not their small mountain town. Ghosts, visions, omens of doom. These friends need to stick together if they're going to solve the mystery at the heart of Glimmer Lake.

Ebook/Audiobook/Paperback

And there's more! Please visit ElizabethHunter.com to sign up for the Hunter newsletter and read more about her work.

about the author

ELIZABETH HUNTER is an eleven-time *USA Today* bestselling author of romance, contemporary fantasy, and paranormal mystery. Based in Central California, she travels extensively to write fantasy fiction exploring world mythologies, history, and the universal bonds of love, friendship, and family. She has published over thirty works of fiction and sold over a million books worldwide. She is the author of the Glimmer Lake series, the Elemental Legacy series, the Irin Chronicles, the Cambio Springs Mysteries, and other works of fiction.

ElizabethHunter.com

also by elizabeth hunter

The Force of Wind

A Fall of Water

The Stars Afire

Fangs, Frost, and Folios
(December 2023)

The Elemental World

Building From Ashes

Waterlocked

Blood and Sand

The Bronze Blade

The Scarlet Deep

A Very Proper Monster

A Stone-Kissed Sea

Valley of the Shadow

The Elemental Legacy

Shadows and Gold

Imitation and Alchemy

Omens and Artifacts

Midnight Labyrinth

Blood Apprentice

The Devil and the Dancer

Night's Reckoning

Dawn Caravan

The Bone Scroll

Pearl Sky

The Elemental Covenant

Saint's Passage

Martyr's Promise

Paladin's Kiss

Bishop's Flight

Tin God

(Summer 2024)

The Irin Chronicles

The Scribe

The Singer

The Secret

The Staff and the Blade

The Silent

The Storm

The Seeker

The Seba Segel Series

The Thirteenth Month

Child of Ashes (Summer 2024)

The Gold Flower (Summer 2025)

Linx & Bogie Mysteries

A Ghost in the Glamour

A Bogie in the Boat

Contemporary Romance

The Genius and the Muse

7th and Main

Ink

Hooked

Grit

Sweet

Made in United States
Troutdale, OR
10/19/2023